Praise for *It's All in How You Fall*

"*It's All in How You Fall* is a beautiful meditation on being brave enough to start over and taking a chance on something—or someone—new. I'm not even remotely a sports person, but I was rooting for Alex and Caro's love story from the very first page. **The way Sarah Henning writes relationships will astonish you**—from friendship to romance to siblings and parents, **love is laced through every word**." —Ashley Woodfolk, *New York Times* bestselling author of *Blackout* and *Nothing Burns as Bright as You*

"Sarah Henning sticks the landing with *It's All in How You Fall*, **an unputdownable coming-of-age story** about losing one dream and finding another, perfectly balanced with a swoony romance, family feels, and deep friendships. An absolute must read!" —Jennifer Iacopelli, author of *Break the Fall* and *Finding Her Edge*

"**A sweet and delightful romance exploring self-discovery, identity, and belonging** among elite teen athletes. If you love comfort reads with happily ever afters, **this book delivers!**" —Suzanne Park, author of *Sunny Song Will Never Be Famous* and *The Perfect Escape*

"Athletes and armchair fans alike will fall head over heels for this sporty romance. Henning plunges readers into the action as injured teen gymnast Caroline Kepler spends hot summer days trying out volleyball, running, golf, and tennis while working up a slow burn with her brother's best friend. **A winning combination of heart-pounding thrills and all-star swoon!**" —Amanda Sellet, author of *By the Book*

"An honest and tender portrayal of the pressures of youth athletics and identity, Henning's characters show us how to find our balance, even once we're off the beam for good. *It's All in How You Fall* is **a must read coming-of-age story wrapped in the perfect summer romance.**" —Jennifer Dugan, author of *Hot Dog Girl* and *Melt with You*

IT'S *All*
IN HOW YOU
Fall

WITHDRAWN

IT'S All IN HOW YOU Fall

By Sarah Henning

Poppy
Little, Brown and Company
New York Boston

Poppy
Hachette Book Group
1290 Avenue of the Americas, New York, NY 10104
Visit us at LBYR.com

First Edition: May 2022

Poppy is an imprint of Little, Brown and Company. The Poppy name and logo are trademarks of Hachette Book Group, Inc.

The publisher is not responsible for websites (or their content) that are not owned by the publisher.

Library of Congress Cataloging-in-Publication Data
Names: Henning, Sarah, author.
Title: It's all in how you fall / by Sarah Henning.
Other titles: It is all in how you fall
Description: First edition. | New York ; Boston : Little, Brown and Company, 2022. | Audience: Ages 12 & up. | Summary: After an injury forces fifteen-year-old gymnast Caroline to quit competing, her older brother's best friend Alex promises to help her find a new signature sport, and, in return, she offers to set him up on a date with her former teammate.
Identifiers: LCCN 2021030875 | ISBN 9780759556676 (pbk.) | ISBN 9780759556669 (ebook)
Subjects: CYAC: Sports—Fiction. | Dating (Social customs)—Fiction. | Ambition—Fiction. | Identity—Fiction. | LCGFT: Novels.
Classification: LCC PZ7.1.H4642 It 2022 | DDC [Fic]—dc23
LC record available at https://lccn.loc.gov/2021030875

ISBNs: 978-0-7595-5667-6 (pbk.), 978-0-7595-5666-9 (ebook)

Printed in the United States of America

LSC-C

Printing 1, 2022

To those who lost a dream—
I hope you find yourself again.

Prologue

Dismount. That's all I need.

Roundoff. Layout double full. Stick. A recipe for my third Kansas state beam title—if I can just hold it together.

My mind, my back, fate: There's a lot that can fall apart and take my victory with it.

A small bell rings—I have ten seconds remaining. Olga is the perfect statue of a coach in my periphery, all crossed arms and tight jaw beside my dismount mat. My teammates are a fuzzy blur of blue and chalked skin beyond her. I set my stance, all my weight on my back leg on the very end of the beam, lead-off leg out and toes aggressively pointed.

Come on, back, we can do this. I can do this.

Without hesitation I run three steps and toss myself into a roundoff, punching the end of the beam with all my might. My lower back seizes on impact, as oblivious to the amount of ibuprofen I have running through my system as it is to how hard I've worked for this. How much I want it. The tweak of pain is enough to toss my muscle memory off autopilot, and I enter my double twist late. I know it as a sixth sense, and every minute I've spent in the gym for the last ten years adds up to what I do next to save it.

My rotation speeds up. The blue landing mat is coming faster than I like, and if I don't get all the way around, I might take a step or fall. Or worse, do both after obviously underrotating, and not get credit for the skill because I didn't complete both twists.

In less than a breath my feet drive into the cool plastic-y cushion of the mat. My eyes spot the end of the beam for orientation as my body adjusts to how I've landed. My hips aren't square, but I don't take a step, bringing my lower half in line with my shoulders with an almost imperceptible adjustment as I sit back into the stick. My arms spring over my head in salute.

A smile spreads across my face as applause rises from behind me—my coach, my team, my family in the stands, decked out in Balan's Gymnastics shirts. I swivel to face the judges for a direct salute, careful not to shuffle my feet and inadvertently draw a last-second deduction from a particularly picky judge. The movement is easier than anything I've just completed in the past ninety seconds, and yet somehow it's suddenly too much.

My back twinges, and my arms fly down in a reaction as automatic as my in-air adjustments. The smile on my face wavers as a shock of pain shoots the length of my spine, from the scoop of my lower back up to the split between my shoulder blades.

For one horrible moment, I can't move forward, can't recover my smile, can't depart the mat.

The pain teases tears into the corners of my eyes as Olga crashes the mat and draws me into a hug. Her hand cradles my head as she presses me into her body, only aware in that moment of what I've achieved, not what it cost.

"That was good, very good. Worth the cry!" Of course she's

noticed the tears. She never misses anything. "A little late on the dismount, but you're a fighter, Caroline, always my little fighter. I'm sure this is number three. Queen of the Beam yet again."

I let her direct me off the mat, squeezing me tight as we get my feet moving toward the embrace of my teammates, my back screaming the entire way.

1

"Gymnastics is a sport with plenty of fifteen-year-old retirees."

Dr. Kennedy's words tumble through my brain, bouncing off all the gray matter and viscera before landing back in the forefront of my mind every thirty seconds. It's been like that for the past hour, ever since Dad and I wordlessly left the sports medicine office and pointed his Prius to Balan's Gymnastics.

The same thing, over and over: A thoughtful lean forward from his high-backed chair. A tenting of fingers that have healed far worse cases than mine. A smile kind enough to mean bad news. Then, the hammer.

"Caroline, you've sought me out for treatment, but I want to be frank. There's no therapy or shot or surgery that can improve chronic back pain. The only way for it to heal is to stop what's causing it to be chronic."

This man—who installs new hips, who ferries ligaments from healthy body parts to damaged elbows, who kept my brother's career as the world's shortest varsity point guard intact despite a royally messed-up knee—could do nothing for me.

He can suck it. My back can suck it. Everything can suck it.

I shake him out of my head, blond ponytail brushing my ears, because it's literally the only thing I can do to try to stop the replay of the worst doctor's appointment in the history of my life.

"Anytime you're ready, Caroline."

Oh. Right. I blink at Olga's patented "coach" voice, and the world floods back in. The chalk-filled air. Lack of air-conditioning despite the sweltering afternoon—Kansas in early June. Tinny sound system blasting to eleven because for the next two hours it's the most elite of us on the gym floor at Balan's.

Okay, only one of us is *actually* elite: Sunny Chavez. She's qualified for nationals later this summer and placed thirteenth there last year, which sounds horrible but is actually super good. And now Sunny and the rest of my teammates are silently watching me from all corners of the floor mat as I hold up our pass progression warm-up.

It's something we do nearly every day—working our way up from skills we could do in our sleep to the most difficult passes in our routine, going back and forth in two groups set up on the diagonal. Olga and Dad stare from where they're perched against the tumble track, shoulder to shoulder, deep in conversation. They've been dating for a little over a year, and though I think that's weird and sort of embarrassing, I actually wish that they were whispering cringe-inducing sweet nothings instead of discussing my future without me.

"Double back," a voice breathes in my ear—my best friend, Peregrine, hinting at where we are in the routine by outright telling me what the hell I'm supposed to be doing. She's next up after me on this diagonal that we're sharing with Sunny.

I launch myself into a pass I've been successfully landing for nearly four years.

Roundoff, back handspring, back handspring, double back.

Lower back tensing, I land with just a slight hop, which is totally annoying because after beam, floor is my best event—my music is a compilation from *Hamilton*, and it is *amazing*, let me tell you—and immediately file behind Sunny so Jada can have the opposite diagonal to do the very same thing. She and Avalon are level nines, and somehow we always divide up like this: the two level tens and single elite, and the two level nines. Hierarchy, even among the best.

When I step into line behind Sunny, she turns and lifts a beautifully maintained brow, her voice low but laced with concern turned up all the way. "The appointment?"

"Yeah."

Everyone knew I was going to see Dr. Kennedy in the lunch break between our summer two-a-day workouts. My teammates, my coach—heck, probably even the delivery guy who visits every day around noon because Dad's preferred method of grocery shopping is Amazon Pantry. I really need to get Dad to the farmers' market on the Saturday mornings I have open these days.

My back has been bad news for a few years now, but nothing that a ritual of prepractice ibuprofen couldn't fix—or at least mitigate. My range of motion has been slowly worsening since I won a third state beam title in the spring, my first at level ten. I tweaked my back during that routine, but within a week it was right back to the usual dull ache of muscles worn stiff. It's chronic and annoying—a dissonant undercurrent running through my life. A constant chorus of *dun-dun-dunnnnnnn*.

When I couldn't hide it anymore and Olga and Dad began to make noise about getting my back checked out, I thought the whole procedure was going to be a cakewalk. Maybe as simple as Dr. Kennedy taking one look at my file, muttering "mmmhmmm," lining up a big ol' cortisone shot with my lumbar curve, and sending me on my way.

Though I did demand *and* receive the shot, the reality was... not that.

What Dr. Kennedy doesn't get is that gymnastics is my life. That is not me being dramatic. That's the truth.

I can't quit when I'm a breath away from not only repeating as state beam champion, but maybe winning the all-around. When I'm a blink from cracking open the last remaining level of my dreams: elite status, a college scholarship, a trip to nationals. When I'm so close I can't just metaphorically taste it, I can *see* it every day at practice with Sunny. My dreams, 3D printed on one of my oldest friends.

Said friend doesn't look at me like I'm being dramatic. Instead, her face softens and tilts, her curly bun slanting with it. She's very serious about her role as the team's big sister, and even though I still have a year with her before she heads to UCLA on a full ride, something wells up in my throat. I already miss her and she's standing right in front of my face. "You want to talk about it?"

Fresh tears spike in my eyes, sliding into the same spots still wet and red-rimmed from earlier. My lips begin to tremble, that lump growing and blocking my windpipe and any chance I have at verbally responding. I nod.

Peregrine arrives after her own double-back sequence, and for the length of Avalon's next pass, the three of us are together. The two of them exchange a glance, and Sunny announces, "I'm going to tell Olga we need five."

I vigorously shake my head. Wipe the tears that have collected with the back of my hand so as not to get chalk stuck to what's left of my mascara. Words crawl out, my voice off, hurried and hushed. "She and Dad are already talking about it. I don't want it to be a *thing*." I swallow as more tears form. Gah. This is so hideously embarrassing. "Not here."

Peregrine bites her lip and tugs on her purple-and-black braid. "Salad Bros after practice?" Peregrine asks me but looks to Sunny—the only one of us with a car.

Dinner is a possibility because we're done at five o'clock, which is part of the reason we love summer workouts. Thirty-five hours of practice per week yet we get more time to ourselves than any other time of the year. It's glorious: Friday nights, full days to do whatever we want on Saturdays and Sundays. During the school year, we're not so lucky—in the gym until nine o'clock every weekday and for hours on end each weekend for practices or meets.

I nod in agreement and Sunny whispers, "Deal," as Olga loudly clears her throat from the tumble track, coach stare going full tilt at the back of our hair-sprayed heads.

"Sorry, Coach." Sunny apologizes with a wave and then launches herself into a ridiculously perfect full-twisting double back.

2

"Done. Three tickets. We're going." Peregrine shoves her phone under my nose to prove she's acquired prime center-of-the-theater seats for the latest Marvel offering, then swivels to push it on Sunny.

We're at our team lockers filling up on midpractice snacks between floor and our final apparatus of our two-practice, seven-hour day: beam. Peregrine used this opportunity to inform us we'd be adding a side of Spider-Man & Co. to our salads. She's decisive in a way I am not and knows exactly how to short-circuit any objection from me. In this case, by blatantly announcing her intentions as she was *doing it*, which also happened to be while I had two apple slices shoved into my mouth.

Sunny closes her locker with a metallic clang and crosses her arms over her chest. "Maybe I had after-dinner plans."

Peregrine doesn't blink. "Because I love you, I won't make a dismissive joke about your elite-level life as homeschool homeroom party of one."

A mock gasp. "Being homeschooled doesn't mean I don't have friends, Peregrine Liu, *thankyouverymuch*."

Sunny exits the fake fight with a quick flip of the bird that means very little except that she'll pretend she doesn't have any cinnamon Orbit to share as the previews roll. I mean, she has like twenty times the friends as the two of us combined, as evidenced by her massive lake house birthday party literally every August. Hell, she knows more people at Northland High than we do, and she's been gone from the building as long as we've been in it. I'd like to believe that's because Peregrine and I are *so* exclusive that we only hang out with each other, but yeah, no, that would be a lie. It's more likely that my older brother, Nat, sucked up all the social butterfly genes in our family, leaving me with none; and Peregrine, for all her bluster in the gym, only says full sentences to people she knows deeply.

I will my molars to do their job on the remnants of my Honeycrisp and swallow-cough-hack for a second before downing a gulp of water. When it's just Peregrine and me and my throat is clear, all I've got is: "Well, then. Men in tights on Friday night. I feel better already."

Peregrine tosses her phone into her locker and slams it hard enough that the various clippings of The Cure taped to the door flutter in a wave of hair spray and goth/Beetlejuice glory. Last fall, Peregrine wore black lipstick to a meet and Olga flipped out, calling her Robert Smith as she literally dove at her to wipe it off before warm-ups. Neither of us knew who she was talking about, so the next day I found pictures and taped them up as a joke, but Peregrine liked them, so they stayed. "Considering the amount of time we spend in leotards, viewing dudes in spandex is good for a gymnast's soul. It's medically proven, Caro—ask your dad."

I make a face. I have enough problems as the teenage daughter of basically a single dad—my mom mostly parents via text since he gained full custody—and waxing poetic about what little

Spidey's suit leaves to the imagination is not going to get me anything other than Dad blubber about tampons in the linen closet. "Don't need to ask. Totally checks out."

Peregrine's definitely trying to distract me from everything she doesn't know yet about the appointment and from whatever *she* thinks *I* think Olga and Dad are talking about. Love her for trying, but I'm too stubborn for it to work.

While we were taking five and being bullied into watching buff actors prance around in bodysuits, Dad and Olga moved from the tumble track into her little office behind the Balan's Gymnastics front desk. And though it's impossible to see much beyond the doorframe that separates the main gym from the lobby, my eyes can't stop flitting that way as we head over to the rows of beams lined up near said doorframe.

I mean, they talked for ninety minutes and now they take it private? It can't be *that* serious if they don't include me, right? I'm not relieved when Olga sends her college-age daughter, Elena, to mind us, because that probably means they plan on being in there for a while.

I climb onto my regular beam—perpendicular to Sunny and next to Peregrine—and start in on dance skills: leaps and turns of various types. Thirty minutes in and it's time to begin working on tumbling skills. Back handsprings, whip backs, and tucks to start. And then it's on to a rotation between the low-to-the-ground baby beams and, if we're ready for it, the regulation beam with the extra padding to work the skills we've targeted to learn for the summer. For me it's a standing Arabian—a backflip with a half twist so you land facing the opposite direction. It's a blind landing, which means your feet hit before you can even see the beam.

As a level ten, it's sort of unusual to include a standing Arabian, as it's the highest value in our A-to-E skill non-elite value system. Though elite goes from A to I (aka Simone Biles territory) the idea is the same: The upper levels are all about adding together the right skills into an alphabet soup of starting value. Non-elites are still on a ten-point system, which means I don't *have* to do such a difficult skill—I could cobble together the points another way— but after three titles in a row I *want* to up my game. Which means that if my back holds up long enough next year, I'll be the only one in the state to land it in competition at level ten.

Bonus: It's super fun.

I do a half dozen on a baby beam, the balls of my feet smacking into the leather as if drawn by magnets each and every time. The adrenaline of the shitty appointment, actually freaking crying in public, and everything just feeling out of sorts has added up to me being *spot on* amid the chaos of the last few hours.

"Dude, that's *fire*. What back injury?" Peregrine's dark eyes sweep over me as she steps back into starting position for her connection of a front tuck to a wolf jump for the twelfth time next to me.

"It's all legs, no back." Okay, not *no* back, but *less* back, which is why Olga picked it—much less chance to tweak my sad lower vertebrae. Though, right now, thanks to the local anesthetic Dr. Kennedy gave me, the usual ache is slightly dulled anyway. Hopefully in a few days when the steroid kicks in, it'll feel that way for several weeks.

"Whatever," Peregrine says at my compliment dismissal— we're not exactly good at taking them, even from each other— before leaning in, her voice low. "Not even Sunny comes close to that sort of height. It's totally epic."

"Only if I land it."

Peregrine rolls her eyes. Rule number one in gymnastics: A cool skill is only cool if you can actually pull it off.

Sunny finishes her turn on the padded big beam—working an aerial to a Rulfova, which will be a gorgeous combination once she totally figures it out. And she will. A Rulfova is basically a back layout full twist, but your hands touch and your legs swing down to straddle the beam. Not easy to do on the beam with padding—her knees thunk into the mats the second she hits. Which makes my back tense every single time I witness it.

Still, the padding is definitely necessary because she hasn't gotten the rotation perfect yet, and her legs miss splitting the beam fifty percent of the time. Something about the aerial entry has her off—she can do a Rulfova just fine from standing, but add a cartwheel with no hands and it becomes a more dicey proposition.

She hops down, and the inside of her right leg is aflame with beam burn, skid marks through a light dusting of chalk. The weave of the top mat is embossed on her knees and she shakes her head. I catch her eyes—when everything comes easy to you, the things that don't are insufferable. "It looks better than you think, Sun."

Her nose wrinkles. "I'm pretty sure Jana Rulfova would roll over in her grave if she saw it in its current state."

"You'll just have to perfect it before she rises from the dead specifically to judge you," I deadpan. That earns me a tight-lipped smile as she fixes the curls that have escaped her bun and turns for the baby beams.

I've got one foot up on the pillowy blue mat when "*Caroline*" rings across the gym. Olga is standing in the threshold between the gym and the lobby, Dad at her back. Neither of them looks pleased—not angry or sad but, like, exhausted. All the warmth and distraction I got from time with my besties evaporates as a cool thread of dread pulls over my skin. "A moment."

They want to discuss Dr. Kennedy's recommendation.

No. That's wrong: They want me to take it.

They'll say they know what's best. That I have my whole life ahead of me. That I'll have my body forever, and I should take care of it.

And taking care of it means quitting.

Dad basically confirms that, looking down and away. Olga's braver, her dark eyes not wavering under bangs that have gotten thicker and blonder over the course of the past decade. Yet still, her neck is flush, discomfort riding her expression.

Time stands still everywhere but inside my churning mind. The other girls freeze too, just as they did on the floor earlier, watching the train wreck that is this showdown for when my career will end. When my life as I know it is over.

My hopes and dreams line up in my heart, piling and piling until the lump in my throat is back. The moment never seems to end as I blink at the two people who probably love me the most—apologies to Nat and Mom but it's true—their eyes full of pity and heartbreak over the fact that my back, and by extension *I*, just *can't* anymore.

But don't they know what I *can* do?

I'm *this close* to mastering a standing Arabian on beam—a move not many *elites* do.

I've got both a Gienger and a Tkachev in my back pocket to make a run at the state bars title.

My full-twisting Yurchenko is finally getting some good height to go with a stick.

I've mastered three tumbling sequences with a double back and have plans to perform them all together in the same clap-along-worthy routine.

And yet it's written all over their faces, their body language, the charge in the humid air, that they want me to call it quits. End it. Finish.

It's silly, but a line from *Hamilton* sticks in my brain. Though my floor music has no words, I can still hear George Washington's voice loud and clear: *Not yet.*

I'm not ready.

Olga and Dad need to see what I can do. What they're asking me to step away from. "Just one more," I say with a stubborn smile as I haul myself up from the mat to the familiar chalked leather of the beam. It's not a request—it's a statement. That cool dread has burnt off and all I feel is heat—frustration, urgency, anger.

When I was a little kid, Nat's best friend, Alex, nicknamed me "Flip" because I'd constantly yell "Watch this!" and toss myself into a new trick that always involved going ass over eyebrows. But now I don't need to command attention, because their eyes are already on me. And I'm ready to show off. To prove I can do it.

I set my stance. I don't need to check my spot. I don't need to peek behind me. I just need to do it. While they're watching. Because they're watching.

Watch this.

It takes less than a second to execute a standing Arabian.

Up. Backflip. Half twist at the crest. Feet hit blind.

I'm up, flipping and twisting, riding on confidence as the world spins in a washing machine rotation—the blue of the mats, stippled beige insulation of the ceiling, and pinpricks of other human beings surrounding me blurring together into a familiar kaleidoscope.

But then something's off.

My hips aren't square as I rotate toward the beam.

Or maybe I didn't get enough height.

Or I got too much.

In that fraction of a second all I can do is try to save it. My back tenses before the rest of me. My feet reach for the beam, but I can't see anything except the ceiling.

One foot finds the edge of the apparatus, the ball of my foot splitting the curve from the top of the beam to the side. My other foot, though, is completely off and into the dead air over the mat. All of that is the least of my worries, because I've over-rotated the flip part, which means the upper half of my body is too far forward and I'm falling face-first toward the beam, the mat, and the unprotected space where the mat isn't quite long enough to be flush with the metal leg supports.

My hands are out, but there's only so much my reflexes can do in the edge of a second. My knee hits first, jarring my back before my stomach can belly flop against the rigid body of the apparatus. My sternum hits the opposite edge, banging, sending more nasty reverberations up my torso as my hands scrabble for purchase against the beam. The side of my face skids with a burn across the chalked leather from jawline to temple.

And then it's over.

I'm lying there in a heap, with everything aflame—my face, my knees, my back.

Oh, my back.

The usual cranky ache has been ripped open—no longer dull,

everything sharp and shooting from the scoop of my back outward. It's streaming over my skin, heavy enough that my lungs struggle under the weight of it.

If my lungs expand, so does the pain.

Dark spots float through my vision and there's blood in my mouth, my jaw snapping shut on impact and taking some of my inner cheek with it.

Everyone is in motion.

Sunny, the closest, lunging.

Peregrine hot-footing over and under obstacles from the baby beam side, a purple-tinged blur.

Avalon and Jada barreling in from the water fountains.

Olga. Dad.

So much of gymnastics is in the landing, which means so much of gymnastics is in falling. But why did I have to fall like this here and now? I literally face-planted on my chance to prove them wrong and that hurts more than, well, my entire body right now.

Sunny arrives at my side first, narrowly beating Peregrine. They both help me roll with a muffled flop onto the big mat, which takes some of the pressure off my back as the mat's inner foam contours to my body. Peregrine squeezes my hand as I try to blink my vision clear of those swarming purple spots, and the ceiling, the lazy industrial fan, and my teammates' faces come into view.

"You were right, Peregrine, my Arabian *is* fire. It just burned me hard."

"It's still epic," Peregrine insists.

"What hurts?" Sunny asks, cutting to the chase, never one to give my self-deprecation the time of day.

This makes me cough out a laugh and I regret it. "Everything?"

Sunny's fingers hover near the side of my face and the strip of skin that's raw enough I know without looking I've left a layer or two of epidermis on the beam. "Hang tight, that's going to need some ice."

She vanishes, and in her place Olga and Dad appear. Olga's pulled taut by crossed arms and a stiff jaw as if she's braced for the worst. All color has drained from anywhere north of Dad's collarbones. He deals with medical catastrophes literally almost every day as an emergency room doctor, and yet, he looks as if he's the type to pass out at the sight of blood. And I'm not even visibly bleeding.

It's no surprise that Olga's the one of them who speaks. "How's your back?"

"If I say 'just fine' would you believe me?"

Olga doesn't dignify that with a response.

I force myself to sit up, Peregrine pulling my hand to help. I work harder than I'd like to admit at keeping my face plain as my lumbar curve quivers and seizes through the range of motion. This isn't the everyday ache—that initial searing scream at the base of my lower back widens into a banshee wail. Warm and pulsing and alive as the rest of my body turns to ice, my fingers quivering.

I shake my head and drop Peregrine's hand, falling back into the embrace of the pillowy mat. My breathing is shallow and a struggle. Tears immediately re-form. I squeeze my eyes shut because I can't look at anyone while I admit this day has just gotten much, much worse.

"It's not fine. Most definitely not fine."

3

Instead of Salad Bros and movie magic, my Friday night ends up being Dad, Olga, and I in the emergency room where Dad works, waiting for the results of my MRI.

As if my embarrassment about literally landing on my face while trying to prove a point could get any worse, the never-ending stream of well-wishers/nurses/EMTs/janitors/rent-a-cops who stop by my room makes me want to just die on the table.

I've been here before, of course. My gymnastics career and general recklessness have garnered me three broken bones—right arm (twice) and left pinky toe—plus damaged tendons in my right foot and left wrist. Oh, and one concussion too. Even Mom freaked out about that one from her hotel in Dubai when it happened. I suppose I'm lucky I didn't get another concussion with the way I smacked my head against the beam this time, but they already checked me for that and said I'm good to go—my back took the worst of it.

Anyway, it's actually such a common occurrence that my brother isn't even here yet. He told Dad he still had an hour of drills left with his varsity basketball buds before he'd head over. Dad tried to push him into cutting it short, but I told him Nat just

16

owes me a snack instead because I am physically and emotionally running on empty. Still, I wish Nat would waltz in with all his confidence and noise and distract them for like two seconds while I mow down a protein bar, because the tone at Kanza Basin Medical Center has never been quite this performatively sympathetic. Maybe Dad's coworkers just want to get a visual on Olga, who I don't think many of them have seen in person before.

I grab my phone and text Peregrine and Sunny: Can Spidey swing by ER room 12 and save me from Dad's coworkers? Peregrine immediately responds with a gif of Spider-Man giving an in-suit thumbs-up.

Sunny isn't playing along, though: Need us to come by?

Me: Nah.

Because that would just make it more embarrassing, honestly. I just want the hell out of here.

And if I could so much as breathe without tremendous pain, I would get up and walk the two miles home while Dad and Olga field their admirers. Therefore, it's an actual, honest-to-God relief when the ER doc on duty, Dad's poker buddy Edgar, waltzes in with images from my MRI scan. He's technically Dr. Holt here, but he won't let me call him that. I've known him since I was in diapers, and he's been a steady figure since Mom left, just one of a stable of guys who show up on shared off days because their medical brotherhood doesn't flinch outside these hyper-sanitized walls. Plus, he's been through the divorce rodeo three times and was quite the expert as Dad waded through that mess with Mom.

I stow my phone as Edgar's arrival sends Sue the fourth-floor receptionist packing and the glass door blessedly and privately slides shut.

"How we doing, Caroline?" he asks as he extends his knuckles in an overly aggressive fist bump. I have no idea why he's asking—

he knows way more about how I'm doing than I do because of the scan results in his other hand. I bump his knuckles gently, careful of anything that might jar my aching back. The local anesthesia from my shot at Dr. Kennedy's that made my workout ibuprofen-free for the first time in forever has worn off. "Same, Edgar."

He putters around the side of the bed, headed for the light board. It clicks on with a low-grade buzz. I try to shift to see it better and fail, my lower back screaming at me. "Pain still a five? Not an eight or ten?"

"Nope. Five."

He cocks a brow, and his eyes swing to Dad and Olga for confirmation. "Are you sure?"

"Her pain threshold is part of the problem," Olga answers tightly. She's tired enough that her nearly perfect American accent fails her, her mother-tongue Romanian shearing sharp sides to her syllables. People think she's Russian because of her first name, but yeah, nope. You might lose an eye if you verbally assume such, by the way.

"Her five is someone else's ten," Dad explains.

"Well, that's no surprise." Edgar puts four scans of my torso up for display. Clip, clip, clip, clip. Two are straight on: front and back; two are from the side: left and right profiles. He speaks to the one that's from the back. "Caroline, I am well aware that you have chronic back pain that would be at least a five for most people, who would right now be screaming 'ten!' in answer and begging for pain relievers."

It's a compliment and I sort of smile, but Olga's right—it's part of my issue to begin with. Chronic happens with overuse, and if you address things early, you can't overuse them.

Edgar continues, pulling out some sort of doctor-official

dry-erase marker. "What we have on top of your usual chronic inflammation is a severe lumbar strain. That means you've damaged tendons and tissues enough to cause acute inflammation." He circles an area on the blue-black-and-white image, highlighting my left side. "Here and here."

Yeah, that would make sense. I swallow. "What's the treatment? Time off? Until it heals?"

"Actually, they don't want you on bed rest. Activity is good for something like this, as long as you're gentle and not doing a... what was the skill you fell on?"

"An Arabian."

"Yes, that." He gestures and sort of does a weird ski squat like he's demonstrating a skill...that looks nothing like a standing Arabian. The effect is very Mr. Bean, which he must realize at the last second as he straightens and pats down his white coat. "The cortisone shot you got should kick in and help with this too. So, good on you for preemptive care. Are you psychic?"

"If I were psychic I wouldn't have done that particular Arabian."

"Oh. Yeah. Sure. Of course." He laughs a little too hard. When the seal bark of it dies, Edgar resets in a way that is...unsettling. Gone is his smile and playful demeanor. All of his bedside manner falls away, revealing the truth of what his bad jokes and over-the-top personality were hiding. He looks like he's got a bomb to drop but isn't sure where to set it down so it won't make a mess. The dry-erase marker wavers in his hand but he doesn't cap it. Instead, he glances to my dad and Olga.

Dad knows this man well enough to feel the change in his demeanor harder than the rest of us. His back straightens in the guest chair as he blinks at his old friend, lines gone slack around his brown eyes. "Edgar? Is there more?"

19

The doctor looks at the marker in his hands. "Yes, Jimmy."

Edgar smooths his coat yet again, the marker still awkwardly held in his hand. He glances at me for a brief moment before returning to the safety of speaking in Dad's general direction. "I'm curious—you saw the sports medicine doctor today, correct?"

All three of us nod.

"Did he happen to perform an MRI as well?"

Dad and I shake our heads.

"No CT scan? Or an X-ray?"

Again, we shake our heads. Dad explains, "It was an initial consult with Graham Kennedy at Sports Solutions—questionnaire, physical exam, etcetera."

"I see," Edgar says before dropping his chin to his chest. When he draws a deep breath before continuing, my own lungs stall. "I'm not as well versed in this area as Dr. Kennedy, and perhaps he needs to examine these scans, but..."

At the pause he's no longer Edgar, this man who never fails to show up to poker night with Corn Nuts (ew) and margarita mix, but an honest-to-God authoritative doctor figure from any medical drama. This is how my dad must look to people who don't know him, who are relying and hanging on his every word.

The *doctor* turns to the profile image of my body facing to the left and circles a spot about an inch wide at the deepest curve of my lower back. "In looking at these images I noticed something more...*permanent*. Spinal stenosis."

Dad shoots to his feet. In two lunging steps he's nose deep into examining the image, blocking it from both Olga and me. "What?" Olga asks, though it doesn't seem to be as much of a question as a curse. She ends up standing too, hitting her tippy-toes to look over Dad's shoulder at the light board. Meanwhile, I'm left on the bed with this bombshell that I totally don't understand and only the backs of three heads to read.

Dad leans into a more normal posture, arms crossed, and answers both Olga's verbal curse-question and my nonverbal one. "Narrowing of the spine."

That... does not sound good.

"It's either congenital or, probably in this case, caused by degeneration through heavy use." Dad sighs. "Basically, there's so much inflammation, it's left little room for the spinal cord and there's a pinch point."

Suddenly, the quiet is screaming in my ears, the fluorescents above flick into stage lights, and a wave of nausea floods over me as all I can smell is the tang of Purell and bleach. "A pinch point... in my spine."

"This is likely the source of your chronic pain." Edgar is the type of guy to quote Adam Savage from *MythBusters* and loudly proclaim, "Well, there's your problem!" And he's not doing that right now. He's actually super reserved and... quietly respectful? It's confusing but I appreciate the fact that he doesn't do the Dr. Kennedy smile when he meets my slack-jawed expression. "I would call on your sports medicine doctor for his confirmation, but this is something that, while manageable, could require surgery if you incur any further damage."

Surgery on my spine. The thing that allows me to walk and jump and flip.

I'm going to be sick. Half-digested Honeycrisp apple on hot-wash-abused sheets.

That's more of a gymnastics death sentence than the not-so-gentle suggestion of a dumb-ass sports medicine doctor who didn't even do an MRI and knew I was toast without investigating the cause.

I was already pissed with Dr. Kennedy, but now I'm extra mad that he suggested I quit without even driving this particular nail in the coffin first.

Dad looks as mad and shocked as I do. Instead of the pale-faced terror he exhibited beam-side after my fall, color rises on his cheeks. He rakes a hand through his light brown hair. His medical brain must be running a mile a minute. Dad understands the seriousness of that MRI just as plainly as Edgar.

All three of them pull away from the light board, and from my place on the bed, I squint at left-facing me. My vision is twenty-twenty, and though I'm ten feet away, I can make out the narrowing in blue-black-and-white relief. It's just a little dip between my L4 and L5 vertebrae maybe the width of a fingernail.

Something terribly small that means something so crazy big.

Maybe Dr. Kennedy knew without looking and was trying to spare me the news that my chronic pain was actually a *spinal injury*. Somehow, just the switch of terminology is terrifying. Like the difference between a skirmish and a battle. I feel like I've just lost the war.

"Gymnastics is a sport with plenty of fifteen-year-old retirees."

"Edgar, will you excuse us?" Dad asks.

"Yes, yes." As he leaves, the doctor looks to me. Now he smiles, and it's in a way that breaks off a piece of my heart. An apology, not mitigation, coming from my dad's buddy with the Corn Nut addiction and three ex-wives, not some authority figure with a medical degree. "I'm sorry, Caroline. I wish I had better news."

Edgar exits into the hum of the ER, and when the glass door is tightly shut again, Dad pulls his chair bedside. Olga paces along the other side of the bed, her flip-flops smacking decisively with each angry step. The smack-and-muffle is almost a thread of conversation itself, Olga's inner thoughts as my longtime coach floating into the charged room. Dad, though, is the first one to speak.

"We can send it over to Dr. Kennedy for his opinion, but—"

"Dad, we know his stupid opinion already." My voice shakes and my heart has morphed into a fireball in my throat. I feel like I've swallowed bees. "Like this information is going to change it. All it does is give my chronic back pain a fancier name. It's the same—"

"This is *not* the same." Olga stops pacing and whirls around on me. There's not an inch of wiggle room for argument in her expression. But I'm stubborn and so I try anyway.

"It is. Get past the lumbar strain and it's the same as it was this morning, just named. I'll just keep going—"

"You cannot keep going."

"Yes. I. Can." My fingernails dig into the skin on either arm. I'm tense, rigid—poured in, hardened, never moving. Though I'm aware this is far less impressive when exhibited from a hospital bed.

"If you keep going, it may become worse and stay worse" is what Olga says.

"Or it *won't*." My voice is high and my vision swings, and Dad and Olga blur on either side of the bed as something hot rises in my chest.

"But worse is the more likely scenario," Dad interjects.

"Maybe," I snap. "Everything about this situation is a maybe."

"Spinal stenosis is *not* a maybe, Caroline." Dad wrenches his chair around, lunges at the board, yanks the MRI scan off the clip, and tosses it into my lap, his voice rising to an honest-to-God yell. "It's permanent. It's caused by degeneration. Which you make worse *daily* in the gym."

My dad is not a loud man. This explosion sits among the three of us like the sudden eruption of Vesuvius. He's breathing hard, cheeks pinking over graying stubble.

His eyes slide to Olga's across the foot of my hospital bed. Something passes between them and...*wait.*

"You *want* me to quit." My eyes swing between them. And everything I worried about before that final Arabian busts into the open, the truth, rather than just my anxiety. "You *both* want me to quit."

For a moment after the words are out of my mouth, it's completely silent. Olga sits gently on the bed, obviously searching for a retort that isn't a total lie. She won't lie to me. She's never lied to me.

Olga puts up a small hand, calluses from long-ago bar rips pink on her palm, still evident half a lifetime in the future. She places the hand on my ankle, warm over the thin hospital blanket. "Caroline, I don't ever want to lose a gymnast. Especially not the best beam worker in the state of Kansas." I'm so angry that I can't even enjoy the fact that she's right. I *am* the best, three years running. "But this is more than gymnastics. This is your future."

"My future. My choice."

At my words, they don't react. No immediate nods. Compromises. Sparks of a plan to beat this.

Nothing.

I try to swallow the urge to fall apart but completely fail. I hug my arms across my chest. Trying to find stability. My center. Something. Anything.

I meet Olga's eyes. My lips tremble. "Please..."

It's all I have left to say.

"Please, what?" My coach's quiet voice is sharp enough to

draw blood. "Watch you lie to me about the pain? What good is in that? For you or for me?"

The tears finally start, pressure building since the doctor's office, a blink from release. "Please don't make me quit. I can't. This is my life. It's your gym but it's my life."

"I know."

It's a single answer to all of it. I believe her.

Olga scoots up the length of the bed toward where I'm propped up on pillows and grabs my hand in hers—warm, comforting, strong. "Caroline, you will always have a place with me at Balan's. Once you're sixteen, I'll hire you to coach mini-gym, work the front desk—I can pay you more than Nat makes at that stupid country club." The offer would be funny if it weren't so screwed up: old enough to retire, too young to be a paid employee. "You know I'd love to nurture a career in coaching—you would be fantastic. *Fantastic.*" A big fat tear leaps my lower lashes and plows down my cheek. Olga wipes it away with her free hand. "I want you in my gym. *Always.* But no, I will not watch you self-destruct."

With each deep breath to find the words, my back cries out in pain until my lungs give up. And so do I. When I speak, my voice is barely above a whisper. "I'm not self-destructing. *I'm living.*"

Olga's mouth falls open and then closes. She squeezes my hand and stands, pushing her bangs out of her eyes. They glisten in the unforgiving light as she exchanges something wordless with Dad. Olga is crying. I've known her for ten years and have never seen her cry except out of absolute happiness—for the team, for her gymnasts, when all the hard work finally pays off.

Not when all the hard work costs us something great.

There's a banging outside the glass and Nat appears, sunglasses sliding down his nose. He balances a protein shake, fabric grocery bag, and basketball over a sweat-stained tank and shorts. "They were out of cookie dough Quest bars, so I got you s'mores and cookies & cream. Hope your taste buds can lower their standards, Caro."

He tosses the grocery bag in my general direction. My back hurts too much to catch it, though, and it sort of bounces off my stomach and onto the bed, protein bar wrappers crinkling against each other. Nat takes a sip of his shake, finally cataloging our faces—my trembling lips, Dad's flushed cheeks, Olga's glistening eyes. "What?"

Olga stands and snags the ball straight out of Nat's hands. "Hi. Outside now, yes?"

It's phrased as a question but it's not. Nat's usually one to argue but blessedly doesn't, allowing Olga to escort him into the hum of the rest of the ER. The door slides closed with a soft pneumatic click. That whisper of dread I felt in the gym is now wailing louder than my back. That fat tear has become a flood, the lump in my windpipe wrenched open by a sob I can't smother. My shoulders shake, which makes my back seize up. But I can't stop it.

Dad leans in, cradling an arm around my neck, an awkward balance of providing comfort while not applying pressure because it'll make everything that much worse. The flash of anger from earlier is gone, his overarching calm resolute.

"It *is* your body, Caroline, you're right, and it should be your decision. And after Dr. Kennedy's recommendation today, I was ready to make it your choice. Olga and I talked through the options—a short sabbatical, maybe a handshake decision that this would be your last season, or just playing wait and see after the cortisone shot took effect." He shakes his head and gestures to the scans. "But this—this is something else entirely."

26

Even though his voice is level, there's a sadness within it that nearly matches what's swelling within me. "Further damage will affect more than your season and your gymnastics career—it'll affect the rest of your life."

"Dad..."

"You accomplished so much, and I am so very proud of you for what you've achieved and all the hard work you put toward being the best for ten years. But I can't watch this. I can't pay for this. I can't drive you to the gym five days a week knowing you'll harm yourself in a way that even surgery might not fix."

"Dad, please."

He stands. Hands on hips. Red in the face, trying to sniff away the fact that his own tears have begun.

"There will be other sports, other passions, Caroline. But no more gymnastics."

4

My life is over. Not literally, but it might as well be.

Dad tells me not to mope. Mom texts a "thumbs-up" in "support" from Beijing. Nat offers to help me get a spot at the country club where he's working as a groundskeeper, pretending that he'd be happy to have his baby sister around a job he does with a half dozen other guys from the Northland High basketball team. Which is...nice. If a little misguided because I'm probably too young to be employed there. And I don't need money. I need *me* back.

The me I am at the gym *is* the normal me.

Still, because I always at least *try*, I go through the motions of what I think summer might look like to a normal teen.

I sleep later than I ever have (hello, eight o'clock hour!).

I walk to Starbucks and order my cold brew just the way I like it in all its super-caffeinated, growth-stunting glory.

I blaze through all the suggested summer reading for sophomores at Northland (*Lord of the Flies*, *The Call of the Wild*, and a bunch of other work by dead white guys).

I fry my shoulders and the tops of my feet in an attempt at lying out—this me and previous me have the same iridescent pale skin tone, so that was an idiot move no matter how grumpy I am.

28

And honestly, the pool's too loud and lonely and swimsuits are too much like leotards.

I hit the movie theater with Peregrine and Sunny every Sunday afternoon. It started with a showing of that Marvel offering the weekend of my fall and subsequent quitter's intervention by Dad and Olga, and has spiraled into a way we're staying connected. It's like dipping a toe into my old life, if only for a millisecond. What's weird is that I barely talk to Peregrine and Sunny during the week. Somehow, if we interact Monday through Friday, it just reminds me of where they are without me.

By the last week in June, our movie showing is literally the only thing I'm looking forward to. Otherwise, I'm struggling to find anything to fill my time that also fits my attitude.

I must look rough, because Nat tried to convince me to play basketball with him and his buds at the park an hour ago. But that would've required me looking like an idiot around older boys, so, um, no, never. My brother's not big on rejection, so he didn't ask twice and just left, the ball echoing into nothing as he walked to the court. While I used to fill my time with the same sport every active hour, Nat is like a shark—he can't stop moving, and he doesn't care what he does to pass the time. He even joined the cheer squad as a freshman when they needed dudes to lift up the smaller girls. He *claims* he sticks with it because he enjoys it, not because it requires him to stare up girls' skirts.

Meanwhile, though I'm not supposed to *do* gymnastics, I can do other stuff. Sort of. My lumbar strain has healed and my regular doctor—I refuse to go back to Dr. Kennedy—says I don't need surgery at the moment for the stenosis. I just need to be "kind" to myself, whatever the hell that means. I'm trying to take it seriously, though, so I spend hours on end stretching.

Yeah, I know. But to me it's relaxing and feels good, and it's something I actually enjoy.

And so not even three weeks after my life ended, I sit, rolled forward in a full middle split, head in hands, watching two perfectly tanned tennis players grunt through a pretaped set as rows of smartly dressed British people clap politely.

"Ah, the moping continues and has moved into the living room." Dad comes out of his office dressed in his on-call outfit: khakis and a button-up with the sleeves rolled up. He'll do whatever he can get away with before he has to shrug into his official on-duty doctor coat.

"I'm not moping."

"You can't fool me. My other doctorate is in moping." This is true. Dad's still not done moping over breaking up with Mom, and it's been five years. Though Olga has helped.

I wrinkle my nose. "Both of those doctorates should point to the fact that I can't help the fact that I'm moping."

"And now you're an admitted moper. I win." He smiles, but his eyes aren't in it.

Ugh, yeah, I confirmed he was right. "It's not like I have anything to *do*." It's almost four o'clock—right now I should be in the thick of the afternoon session, finishing up on beam as the lower levels march in. Then conditioning and stretching and home.

"You can *do*. You're cleared to do anything but gymnastics. Try something new!" He totally catches me rolling my eyes and starts excitedly tossing out potential activities before he loses me all together. "Soccer would be fun. Or what about volleyball? Or basketball?"

"Dad, it's been weeks and I'm still four ten." It's not uncommon for gymnasts to shoot up after quitting but, um, apparently I'm not in that group. "Plus, if I miraculously grow five inches, I'm still only five three, which is, like, a no-go in every single sport you mentioned."

"Your brother is living proof that's not true."

"Yeah, because he's played basketball for *twelve* years. Seriously, stop selling this. I'm perfectly fine filling my days with moping and stretching."

He doesn't stop selling it.

"Maybe we're looking at this all wrong." Dad begins pacing. Jesus. "What about nonathletic activities? Band, choir, mathletics? I'm sure there's got to be a camp—" Dad's phone chimes with the tone he keeps for hospital business. He hesitates and almost doesn't check it. But then duty gets the best of him and he holds up a *wait* finger, eyes flashing down before a frown glances across his features. When he looks up, I know he has to leave—on-call is *on-call*—which is a relief to the pressure behind my eyes.

"It might be a late night. And I know I'm behind on ordering groceries. You're in charge of dinner—Nat *does* get a say, unless that say is trying to convince you to do Happy Cow as a meal, yes?" He digs into his back pocket for his wallet. Out comes a pair of twenties, which he dangles in front of my face.

"So ice cream as sustenance doesn't count as trying something new?"

"Not when I'm paying for it. Bruno's or Burger Fu or grocery sushi." Dad pockets his wallet. "Save a dollar or two and bribe him to eat a vegetable, will ya? He raided the chocolate stash and I'm fairly certain he'll forget he's fifty percent Snickers when he's done with his pickup game."

I glance down because *I'm* the Snickers glutton and he'll never guess it in a million years... I haven't touched a Snickers publicly since age twelve. My moping comes with a side of chocolate. "Got it."

Dad takes a step toward the garage door, fishing out his keys. He turns back, a tight smile on his lips. "I'll check the community center for camps tomorrow."

I know he's trying. But if this conversation is a sign that Dad is *still* feeling guilty about forcing me to say goodbye to my hopes and dreams? I'm totally fine with that. I might be slightly bitter, but if I have to live with this nonphysical pain, so does he.

5

When I'm hungry enough, I slip on my flip-flops and head to the park—a half-mile shot straight up from our cul-de-sac. It's hot, the afternoon lifting in a sizzle off the pavement, and the neighborhood already smells of nice-night barbecue. Hedgerows bound the park, basketball and four-square in the middle, a slight hill leading to both a little duck pond and a ribbon of parking spaces. The ducks themselves are on break, snuggled together in a little huddle on the lawn, their white feathers winking in sunlight dappled by the trees.

As I approach, squinting because I totally forgot my sunglasses, there's a lone figure on the far half of the basketball court working a lazy layup.

I'm about to call his name, but then the sun shifts, and that's when I realize the shadow is way too long to be my brother, who's been left in the dust vertically by all his friends. It's not Nat—it's Alex Zavala, aka Nat's BFF since diapers. They've played basketball together nearly as long, and of course they're doing the Northfield Country Club groundskeeper gig together. They're basically inseparable most of the time, and it's almost kind of cute.

My flip-flopping does not allow for a quiet approach, and

Alex's eyes drift my way as he rebounds a miss. "If it isn't Caroline Kepler. What's up?"

Alex's got on a tank top with a Nike swoosh across the front and orange basketball shorts. He's sweaty from playing, rivulets running from under a KU ball cap, but he's the type of guy who never looks schlubby, even after hours in ninety-degree heat.

"Hey, Alex, where's Nat?" I make a point to glance around. Two Nalgene knockoff water bottles with "Northland Basketball" printed on them sit on the nearest bench.

He coughs out a laugh, dimples winking. "Um, I'm surprised you missed him." Alex lifts his chin, and I follow the line of it across the park, past the playground equipment.

Even with Alex's stage direction it takes me a moment to see him, because he's literally past everything, including the perimeter of the park, standing on the sidewalk, another basketball in his hand as he gestures his way through a conversation with a dark-haired boy and girl. Though I can't see their feet, they were definitely on a run, handheld water bottles in their grips, rubbing perspiration out of their eyes as he continues to talk. And talk. And talk...and, oh God...

"Is he *shirtless*?"

Alex shrugs. "Shirts versus skins. He insisted. Despite the fact that there are two of us, which makes the team breakdown pretty easy. Very worried about a farmer's tan from the Northfield uniform, that one."

Have I mentioned that my brother is five feet four inches of vain? He also doesn't burn like me, thanks to inheriting Mom's olive complexion. "What's he doing?"

"Filibuster flirting. He's supposedly inviting Ryan Rodinsky to our stadium stairs session tomorrow, but what he's actually doing is hoping that his crush on Liv Rodinsky might pan out if he talks her ear off long enough…"

"While shirtless." Confidence can only get you so far before it veers into arrogance. "Her boyfriend's graduated, not dead. Nat doesn't have a shot."

Alex laughs. "Grey Worthington is totally going to roll up any second now in all his toothpaste commercial glory. And Nat's only going to fall over himself to try harder."

"Ugh, you're right. I can't watch."

"Me either." Alex holds up the ball as an invitation. "Horse? I'll let you go first."

He flicks the ball my way and I get my hands in front of me just soon enough that it doesn't rebound off my collarbone. The ball thuds to the court and sort of meanders back toward Alex. "You don't want me to play."

"Yes I do."

I squint at him. "Did my dad put you up to this?"

He squints back. "Up to what? Beating you at horse?"

"How do you know you'll beat me?"

"The way you didn't catch that ball is a good indication, I think."

"Shut up."

He tosses the ball to me again. This time I catch it. My back tenses on impact, but so does the rest of me. And it doesn't hurt.

Alex nods a go-ahead. "Put up, Flip."

I hesitate for a moment at the use of my nickname—nearly as old as his friendship with Nat itself. I don't know what Nat has or hasn't said to his friends about the end of my life via my stupid awful back, but I doubt Alex would ever try to intentionally burn me. Finally, because he's smiling at me and his tall form blocks Nat's one-man show, I say, "Ugh, fine."

I set my feet and line up my shot, imitating what I've seen Nat do on the court a bazillion times. When the ball leaves my hands, my attempt at imitation fails me—the shot is hard and flat, its arc nonexistent before it smacks off the rim with an audible crack.

Alex rebounds and makes an easy floating basket. My shot looked like a cannon blast, and his just hangs there like it has wings.

"Okay, so what, now I shoot from where you are?"

Alex arches an incredulous brow. "Caroline, have you never played horse before?"

"It's been a while."

"Yeah, you shoot it from here." He palms my shoulder and sweeps me into the spot on the pitted concrete where his Jordans just were. Not a single whiff of anything unpleasant as he moves, despite how sweaty he is. If I hadn't known him the majority of my life, I'd say this confirms that Alex Zavala is basically too perfect to be human.

I set my feet, bend my knees, and zero in on the rim, line up my shot...and completely miss. Again. The ball clangs off the backboard and boomerangs right back to me. I raise my hand just fast enough to avoid being smacked in the face, my wrist awkwardly knocking the ball away.

Three minutes later and the game is over, Alex sprinting his way to HORS before I finally get a letter on the board with a fluke bank shot from the corner of the three-point line. The final score, if you can call it that, is HORSE to H.

Of course, when the E drops in, Alex doesn't gloat—Nat would totally gloat and squeeze in a flex—rather, he simply tucks the ball to his hip and holds out a fist for me to bump. "Good game."

"Game? I have no game." I tap his fist anyway, but that wasn't a game so much as it was a massacre. Dad may think I can trade one sport for another, but hand-and-eye coordination for gymnastics is completely different from anything with throwing or catching. Exhibit A: that massacre from literally five seconds ago.

My skills do not compute.

Still, Alex is nice about it. "You have more game than your brother."

We both check, and yep, Nat's still there, gesturing wildly. At least it looks like Liv is laughing.

When I glance back, Alex is smirking at me. "That wasn't a pity compliment."

I cock an eyebrow at him. "Mmmhmmm."

The smirk morphs into a full-on grin with a side of dimples. "Okay, it was more a knock on Nat than a pat on the back for you, but that three of yours had some major juice on it."

"Whatever."

He tosses the ball at me, and I catch it—mostly with my boobs, but my hands secure the thing. "Play again?"

"Are you trying to see how many times you can dust my ass at horse before the Rodinskys extract themselves?"

"Maybe."

"Based on our last game, we might hit ten rounds before they can physically move down the street."

Alex thinks for a millisecond. "Or we could play actual basketball. Tank top versus tank top—don't worry, I know which team you're on."

That makes me smile but I hesitate, narrowing my eyes against the sun's glare to stare at him, seriously searching for any clue that Dad put him up to this. But Dad's not nimble enough for this conversation to be more than a coincidence. Basketball was something he rattled off like he wasn't aware I don't reach the five-feet mark unless I'm in heels. "And *I* know you're more than a foot taller than me. I've lost before I've begun."

"I've seen you tumble. Just flip over me." Alex's hands are on his hips and he's waiting patiently.

I bounce pass the ball back to him. "Alex, I don't do ball sports."

His dark eyes sweep away and he sort of cough-laughs. "I really think there might be a better way of phrasing that."

Oh God, okay, *yes.*

I totally didn't think of how that would sound until it was already out of my mouth. And I'm talking to someone who has, you know—not that I'm thinking about his...God. Ugh. "Gymnastics is not...," I clarify, my words strangled and my cheeks a solar flare, "*this.*"

"Of course not. This is the stuff of mortals—my granddad is seventy and plays every Sunday after church with his buddies." That's actually really impressive—I want to see Alex aged fifty-plus years hitting that floating shot. "There's no such thing as casual, pickup gymnastics."

This hits me in the gut in all the wrong ways—how I wish gymnastics were a sport I could do into my seventies. That feeling passes; while my double back won't stay with me over the decades, other pieces of the sport will. The stretching, the child's play. Which gives me an idea. "Actually, there is." I stab him in the sternum. "Alex Zavala, I challenge you to a handstand contest."

Suddenly, he's verbally backpedaling worse than I did at the balls comment, but props to him for not physically backing away from my finger. "Let us not forget that as you pointed out, I'm what you might call *tall*—my center of gravity is like a foot and a half above yours and you have a decade of practice on me."

"Right, like how your height and twelve years of organized basketball didn't just help you toast me in horse."

He shakes his head, smiling, and I needle him some more.

"What are you? Scared to lose?" If knowing Alex Zavala for the majority of my life is good for one thing, it's knowing that questioning his fear of losing is always a bluff worth calling.

"No, I'm scared I'll win and you'll punch me. Tiny fists hurt." He's had a lifetime on the other end—his older half sister, Lily Jane, and I could totally swap closets without getting a tailor involved. Genes are weird.

I smile up at him. "There's no way you're winning, giant."

He smirks, eyes shooting for a second to Nat, who is literally miming a dramatic elbow-to-the-face foul with Ryan as Liv drink-laugh-coughs into her handheld bottle. Yeah, we have the time. "What are the rules?"

I toss him the same look he had when I inquired about the specifics of horse. "I count to three, we kick up, and the person who stays up longest wins." A moment of hesitation crosses the planes of his face, and then he bounce passes the ball into the grass by the water bottle bench. I take that as a go-ahead. "One, two, three."

On three, Alex's hesitation is back. I'm in the handstand for a few seconds before his feet go up, his legs bent and loosey-goosey as he puts too much juice on it and is past vertical immediately. He spins out of it, tank top peeling down in a flash of golden belly in my periphery as he crashes split-legged to the court—Jordans and booty smacking one, two, three.

Meanwhile, I don't waver, fingers flexing to grip the warm sand-blown concrete. Balance extends from the ends of my fingers through my locked arms, my elbows tucked to my ears, belly button pulled to my spine, tensed legs, toes pointing against the soles of my flip-flops.

Like riding a bike. And damn, it feels good.

Alex immediately gathers himself and kicks back up like his fall never happened, but his attempt is too soft and he fails. His third try hits vertical for a full second before his shirt flops into his jutted chin, his back arches, and he's down. Again. "Oh my God, how do you do that? Can you do that all day? Take phone calls? Drink a milkshake?"

I don't laugh, because I'll totally fall over, but I'm not so rusty I can't have a conversation. Well, sort of. "Triple yep."

"Jesus Christ, you're not human."

Okay, that makes me laugh enough to wobble. Still, I make a controlled dismount and flip my hair up to standing, my face probably pink.

"I was present at her birth. She's human." Nat's back. "Also, for future reference—I know for a fact you think gymnasts are cute and all, but my sister is off-limits."

My brother chest passes his ball at my chin, as if to prove my humanness because he knows I'll whiff it, but Alex's hand shoots out, cutting it off with a thud. I would thank him for saving my face, but I'm completely flabbergasted that Nat would think there was anything romantic about me doing a handstand. With *Alex*. Who is mostly the polar opposite of my brother, so he's actually not even dignifying that weird overprotective aside with a response. Instead, he gathers the water bottles and tosses one at Nat, and with the same razor-sharp precision he slices apart the other half of that statement. "Dude, you weren't even two. Long-term memory doesn't start until three."

Nat takes the bait and doubles down. "Human birth is something you don't forget. It isn't remembered—it's seared into my brain. I mean, have you ever seen your mother's—"

"Stop talking right the hell now or I'm going to vomit and you're not going to lay a finger on the dinner money Dad gave me because my stomach cannot trust you."

"Wait, dinner?" Nat's whole posture changes. *Squirrel.* "Did Dad get called in?"

"Yep. And if you want to eat more than whatever ramen is in the back of the pantry, you better not throw any more balls at my face or start talking about Mom's body parts."

Nat smirks into his water bottle lid as he goes in for a drink. "Technically, I was talking about Alex's mom's body parts."

"That's most definitely not better, Nat."

My brother swallows a huge gulp of water, wipes his mouth, and looks his best friend straight in the face before he says, "Have you seen your mom? She's hot."

My eyes shoot to Alex. "Why do you hang out with him?"

He doesn't hesitate. "Habit."

Nat just laughs and gestures to the parking lot beyond the duck pond. "Alex, dinner's on us if you drive."

6

Alex indeed joins us for dinner, gracefully offering us towel-covered seats in his ten-year-old Dodge Challenger. Well, the towels are for the two boys—I'm not sweaty enough to leave salty stains on his beloved upholstery.

Because of Alex's presence (and generosity), Nat nixes my grocery store sushi altogether for a trip to Burger Fu. We snag a patio spot, because even if by the grace of modern deodorant technology the boys don't stink, they look sweaty and could do some major damage to the leather booth seats inside.

The second we're seated with two sets of Bunny Fu Fu burgers and fries plus my caprese-arugula salad special, Nat starts giving me shit like it's supposed to be dinner and a show. He hasn't even swallowed his first bite, and he's leveled his eyes on me, lips cocked to the side as he chews. "Why the heck did you order salad, Caro?"

"Uh, because I like salad."

"But you don't *need* to eat salad." He tosses a fry at me. "Live a little. Enjoy a trans fat. Consider it reentry into the world of normal people."

I flick it off my plate. "No thanks."

Confusion crosses Alex's face as he takes a bite of his own burger, but he doesn't ask. He doesn't need to, though, because I can feel Nat revving up. Maybe he's high off talking with his soon-to-be-senior crush, or maybe he's just hit his breaking point on both niceness and silence, having spent weeks holding back on giving me shit for my world-class moping. I'm not surprised when he says, "Come on, Caro, we can't keep ignoring the elephant."

"What elephant?" I pointedly shove a forkful of baby arugula, heirloom tomato, basil, and little balls of buffalo mozzarella into my mouth and chew.

Of course, I can ignore the elephant, but Nat can't and won't. My answer registers—*barely*—before my brother plows forward. He does look before he leaps, but most of the time he doesn't care what he sees and just does it anyway. He says to Alex, almost as if I'm not there, "Caroline's back is shit and Dad made her quit gymnastics."

I don't see Alex's reaction as he immediately says, "I'm sorry, Caroline." I can't look at either of them. I can only zone in on a single tiny piece of arugula in front of me.

Nat has basically been my personal devil's advocate since I was born. Always arguing. Always pushing. Always, always, always. I love him more than my left arm, but I also often wish he'd take his half-shitty knees and spend a couple of months climbing Everest.

Nat keeps going. "It's been *weeks* and yet she's still stretching for two hours a day like her life depends on it."

"There's nothing wrong with staying flexible," I sniff.

"I didn't say anything was wrong with it." Nat's wound up now, animated, big and loud. "But look, handstands in the park, splits for hours at a time, salads at the best burger place in town? All proof that you can't let that shit go."

I suddenly wish I'd just kept the forty dollars to myself and watched Nat overcook his ramen. "I think you need to mind your own business."

"I'm your big brother. Your business is my business." He points a charred fry at me. "It's my job to help you move on."

I'd kept my tone pretty light for the amount of bullshit piled upon me over the course of the last few minutes, but that's over now, my snark out in full force. "I'm going to need to speak to your manager if you think a couple of weeks is enough time to move on from who I was for ten years."

Nat's about to respond with some comment that will inevitably up the ante and probably lead us into an actual fight. And because we both know how that will play out, Alex cuts him off with a question aimed at me. "Caro, is there anything we can do to help?"

I shake my head. "I'll be fine." My eyes snap to Nat's. "I just need *time*."

"No, you need something *to do* with that time. Like a new sport."

"Ugh, is that why you asked me to play basketball today?"

"No, I asked you because you looked like you were trying to sink forever into the carpet."

I squint at him. "So it was just a coincidence that you and Alex both asked me to play basketball today? It had nothing to do with Dad pushing the same argument on me right after you left for the park?"

Nat swirls the charred pointer fry in a copious amount of ketchup—my anti-vegetable brother getting in two servings in the worst way. He's like eight percent body fat, but it's going to be a cold splash of water when he realizes his metabolism can't save his arteries from that shit. "He may have texted me, but that was about cheerleading, not basketball."

"Cheerleading? Ew, no."

"What about—" Alex starts, but Nat isn't through and cuts him off, eyes blazing at me.

"I dare you to say that again and see if your fancy Greek yogurts don't taste like soy sauce for the next week," my big brother says, and ugh, he would. Passive-aggressive pranks that make my life harder are exactly his style. "It fits all your talents and I know people. You do too—Kashvi would totally vouch for you. The squad could use someone who could tumble as well as her."

Kashvi was two levels below me when she quit Balan's, so I technically can tumble *way better* than her. But it doesn't matter—I push back. "Nat, you'd hate having me on the team."

"No I wouldn't."

"Yes you would, so no."

"I'm proud of what you can do . . . I mean, I give you shit but it's cool. And the squad would think it's sweet, even if you have to dial it down a bit to play it safe. Why are you fighting this suggestion so much? It's perfect for you." Nat glances to Alex for backup and gets a little shrug. "You've got the skills, plus it's low rep, so your back won't be angry."

Nat's watching me—he knows it's a good idea, a natural one. He's right. But. No. My head is shaking like there's no off switch. Again he asks, "Why?"

I stuff a wad of salad in my mouth, swallowing it down as sadness balls up in my throat. Maybe I could get clearance to tumble like we all know I can. Maybe I could perform some cool skills. Maybe I could pretend that is enough.

But it's not.

When the weight of their double stares and the silence becomes too much, I squeeze my eyes shut and answer into my arugula. "It's too similar, okay?" I spit the words out, ugly and loud and raw. It's as if they've been ripped straight from my gut and thrust out into the summer night, as palpable as the call of the cicadas, the smothering humidity, the hot-tar asphalt smell so thick it's almost a taste.

Nat stares at me as if I have two heads. "But isn't that a good thing?"

"You're the token boy. It's not the same. The girls...I can join but I won't be one of them, Nat."

And that's the truth of it.

I know I could make the squad without Nat or Kashvi breathing a word. Cheerleading is competitive enough that if I provide value, I'm on the team. No one will give a crap who I am as long as I can make them look good across the football field or basketball court from some other school.

But they will never be my people. My people are in the gym, and I'm no longer there.

"Are you looking for an after-school activity or rushing a sorority?"

Nat says it like a joke, but it hits all wrong, the sharp edges of sarcasm in the question hooking in and drawing blood. Suddenly I'm actually pissed more than I'm sad. That's been happening a lot these days. Maybe it's easier.

"You know, I don't need this." I push away from what's left of my dinner and stand—I need to get away from here. From this argument. From my brother. From the truths that lurk between the lines. "I'm done with this shitty dinner date. I'm walking home. See ya, Alex."

7

I make it across four lanes of traffic and back into our neighborhood alone.

The barbecue smell in the air has only grown, and fireflies wink in the shadows, out too early to put on a real show against the stately colonial-style houses that line the park. But I'm too pissed to enjoy any of it, walking fast enough I might as well be running. I think about yanking off my sandals and sprinting across the grass in the easement along the sidewalk.

Home is a mile from here, past the park and straight through to our cul-de-sac. Dad won't be there to serve as a buffer from Nat, which sucks, but I have nowhere else to go. Mom is in Beijing still (I think). Peregrine's house is less than a mile from mine, but it's across both the highway and railroad tracks and involves going back the way I came. Sunny lives four miles in the opposite direction. And honestly, seeing either of them right now, all healthy, their untraitorous bodies freshly showered after practice, will probably just make me cry.

I have the park basketball court in my sights when a rumble hits my ears. A warning growl. A blue Dodge Challenger sweeps to a crawl beside me. Alex is nice and all but he could've taken the long way around. The passenger window comes down and my dumb-ass brother hangs his face out like a human Welsh corgi.

"You know I'm just on you about this because I love you. Stop overreacting."

I don't respond, eyes pinned straight ahead. The car follows as I race-walk at five miles an hour despite my flip-flops.

Nat tries again. "Caroline, please get in the car." He repeats himself three times. A minivan slows and swerves around Alex with a honk.

"No. Bye. See ya."

"Caro, come on. I know you're touchy about the gymnastics stuff. I'm sorry, I shouldn't have pushed you. I just didn't think—"

"That's your problem, Nat. You never think." I whirl on him, my face immediately flaming. I want to rip out my hair and I totally would if I hadn't conned Dad into buttery highlights at the beginning of summer. "If it isn't about you, it isn't anything at all. Go away."

"Caro—"

"*Go away.*"

My brother begins to respond because he always wants the last word, but he's cut off by an engine roar. Alex catapults them back up to speed and they shoot up the hill to the cul-de-sac and our house.

At least someone is listening to me.

A few minutes later Alex's car is back. He passes with a wave, but then the rumbling stops, brake lights shining. He reverses until he lines up the open driver's side window with me. The look on his face is one of genuine concern, brows pulled together, one white incisor biting down on his bottom lip. "Caroline, I'm sorry about your back."

"Thanks." My voice is tight and so much more tired than just five minutes ago, all the adrenaline trickling out of me. It's then that I realize he called me Caroline, not Flip. He did that at dinner too. The second he found out I quit.

"I'm sorry about the handstands. I wouldn't have even brought up gymnastics if I'd known you were . . ." He starts gesturing. *"Here."*

Here: forced retirement at fifteen. A place where I don't know who I am or what to do because my identity was completely wrapped up in leotards and chalk and hair spray for so long I literally do not remember another way to live.

"I suggested the handstands," I say, because he shouldn't feel bad. Alex didn't know what he was doing—Nat did. "Nat's right that I can't let go. But I don't want to."

The way my sentence ends—high and with the promise of a sob—it's clear I'm teetering on the edge of dumping on him. Still, Alex doesn't run away and he doesn't push me to get the word vomit over with. Instead, he simply turns on his hazards and watches me as I find the words. Somehow cars are nicer about passing him now even though he's facing the wrong direction.

Maybe it's not him—maybe it's me. Maybe I look so distraught I'm guilting people into not honking. Anyway, I appreciate that Alex waits for me, because I never get that sort of pause from my own brother.

"What do you think will happen if you let go?" He's watching me like he can read the barcode on my soul.

I can't look at him. I stare at my feet instead. "That I won't . . . I won't be me. Not anymore." It's something similar to what I admitted at dinner and yet it feels so much worse without the heat of anger behind it. I will myself not to cry as my identity crisis slides into full view, but that's where we're headed on this runaway train.

Alex gets out of the car. Steps his big-ass Jordans toe to toe with my Old Navy flip-flops and turquoise polish.

"Caroline, look at me."

And I do.

"You are still *you* without gymnastics. Part of life is moving on. We're not the same as we were when we were little kids, and we're not the same now as we will be when we're adults."

Gah, he's right. I know he's right. But still.

"I am *nothing* without..." My voice goes up an octave as my throat begins to close. I'm gesturing again because I can't say the word, even if it's all I've thought about for weeks.

Alex's brows meet in concern just as a tear slides out of the corner of my eye. Oh God. I swipe at it, but like with everything that's not gymnastics, I'm too slow, and Alex sees that I'm crying before I can hide it.

"Caro..."

"I *was* what I do." I bat at my face. God this is embarrassing. "Level ten, winning awards, on the path to a college scholarship and possibly elite status. That's who I was. And everything was tied in—my friends, my passion, my talent. I was and then I was not. And face it, the rest of high school is going to suck. I'm wallpaper, window dressing, a doormat. A girl without a country. *Nothing.*"

Amazingly, he doesn't bail. Doesn't get back in his muscle car and gun it away from his best friend's hot mess of a sister. Nope. He actually inches closer and puts a big hand on my shoulder. His mom's a therapist and I sort of wonder if some of it has rubbed off on him. "You are something—*someone*—without gymnastics. You'd feel better if you do something. Anything."

I *have* been doing things. Ignoring my friends except on Sundays. Moping my way through a severe sunburn. Eating all the chocolate I haven't had in the past three years in one gluttonous swoop.

I take a hot shaky breath.

"I don't know how to do anything else."

I stomp my foot a little on the sidewalk because I'm stubborn, and it's stupid because I strike the concrete just right to send a tensing jolt up my jerkwad lower spine. "I've spent ten years doing one thing. At the expense of literally everything else. I mean, good lord, the most consistent thing I've done out of the gym is watch you two play basketball, and I could barely get on the board playing horse."

"Okay, so maybe hoops isn't your thing—"

"That's an understatement." I rub my eyes with my forearm. The sun is barely hanging on and I wish it would go down completely and leave my tears to fall in the dark of a Kansas night. "*Nothing* is my thing." God, maybe my stubbornness really has slid into stupidity. Did I really fall from the top of my game to being relegated to doing *nothing* for the rest of my life?

Another big Alex hand finds my other shoulder and both squeeze with an idea. I can almost feel it zip out of his brain before it falls from his lips.

"How about this?" he asks, but he doesn't wait for me to actually answer his question. He probably knows it would just be a snot-filled slurp anyway. "How about I coach you?"

I gape at him. Bat at the wetness on my cheeks again. "What?"

Alex smiles, and suddenly he looks like the boy I've known forever and a day and also not like himself at all. Like a total adult. The wheels are turning behind his dark eyes, and it's completely baffling because the hamster in my head has gone for an extended water break. "Consider it an education. I coach you in the sports of the mortals. One sport a week for the rest of the summer."

Gym class.

Alex Zavala is going to give me my own personal gym class. Somehow that sounds less weird despite me being the only participant than saying something like "private lessons." Which, you know, might give the wrong impression.

"It won't fill the hole you're feeling, but it'll at least help you adjust to this life AG."

"AG?"

"After gymnastics."

I sob-cough and read his eyes, finding my voice. "Really?"

"Really. You say you don't know how to do anything else? You will when I'm finished with you. Whether it's just for fun or whether you want to actually go out for a team, you'll know how to do something a mere mortal can do."

I should just nod and be grateful but instead I say, "Why?" He blinks and I clarify. "Why would you want to do this?"

He doesn't hesitate. "Because I can and it's the least I can do." He doesn't backpedal or try to explain further. He just watches me as the opportunity he's set between us hangs in the balance.

The heat has suddenly hit me. I wet my lips. "Okay."

Though I haven't moved, I feel as if I've finally taken a step. Alex must feel it too because he flashes a grin. "I'll pick you up tomorrow afternoon. Say, three?"

Nat usually gets home from work at two, so that seems a bit of a crunch. Plus, my big brother's excuse to talk with the Rodinsky siblings pops into my brain. "But don't you have stadium stairs?"

"Nice try. We're doing them after dinner."

"Oh." No matter how he plays it, I have this sinking feeling that

I'm intruding on his summer, even though he suggested this whole thing. "I can just meet you—" I start because, yeah, I don't have a car yet but I am very capable of walking pretty much everywhere. As he's seen already today.

"Nope, I'm picking you up. Not letting you chicken out."

"I'm no chicken."

"I know," he says, backing away. "Later, Caro."

The car rumbles to life and my brain kicks back into gear. "Wait! What sport are we doing? And don't say basketball because we both know how that's going to go."

"Just leave it to me. And wear actual shoes."

I glance down at my flip-flops and give him a thumbs-up.

He waves, clicks off the hazards, and disappears into the last fingers of daylight.

8

It's closing in on three in the afternoon when I hear the distinct growl of Alex's muscle car approaching the house. Nat's off doing Nat things, Dad's at the hospital, and I've tried on every pair of non-gymnastics athletics shorts I own three times. Not because I'm worried about what Alex will think, but more because I'm literally not used to doing sports that don't require spandex. Everything feels too loose, and I have no idea what's actually appropriate. Other than, you know, not a leotard.

I settle on running shorts, a sports bra, and a tank Olga got the team for the holidays with a fadeout of Nadia Comaneci's famed 1976 floor routine pose—knee cocked out, toes curled under, wrist flip. Honey-blond ponytail and mascara because my eyelashes don't exist without it, and I'm as ready as I'll ever be. Oh, and sunscreen, because I don't tan. I broil, as my still-pink shoulders will tell you.

Before Alex can get out or honk, I jog down the front steps. He's got the windows rolled down—the Challenger's big metal frame is hot to the touch. I wrench open the door and pop my head in. "Why does your car sound like a shark? The *Jaws* music plays in my head every time you approach and that's just way too dark for you."

Alex laughs. "A shark? Lily Jane always says it sounds like a lion."

I slide in, shut the door, and situate my seat belt. "If you're a lion, you're Simba. The baby one. Not mini-Mustafa."

"Is that a compliment, or...?"

"You're a *lion*. Yes, it's a compliment."

He simply puts the car in reverse and taps the gas. "This just got weird."

I cough out a laugh. "Welcome, I've been waiting for you."

Because I have. Everything's weird outside the safety of who I am in the gym and at school. Also weird: hanging out with Alex without Nat. But if he didn't peace out after the Simba comparison, I think we're probably good.

Alex heads around the park and out to the main road. Left is Northland High and the gym; right is Northfield Country Club; straight is the community rec center and pool. Alex turns right.

My first thought: Interesting.

My second thought: Thank God Nat's not still at work. There's something that sort of feels like embarrassment sitting in the pit of my stomach because Alex is helping me, and that feeling will be magnified 300 percent if and when Nat finds out. So I breathe a sigh of relief that we're likely headed to Northfield when I know for a fact Nat's at the community pool working on his tan (Alex was dead-on about Nat's farmer's tan concern). Nat actually invited me to come along to the pool, but I turned him down on the pretense of moping.

I also know for a fact Alex hasn't told Nat what we're doing or I would've heard about it 0.00023879 seconds later. I vaguely wonder how Alex managed to skirt their typical inseparability without spilling the beans. And I wonder why he hasn't told him—Nat *did* say I was off-limits, but it's not like this is a date. But I'm not going to be the one to tell Nat. So, yeah.

We pull around to a parking lot tastefully marked STAFF, and Alex rolls up the windows and kills the engine. We get out and I follow him to a little building that looks somewhat like an elf house, if said elf paid fifty thousand dollars per year to belong to this country club. Alex swipes his employee card, gains entry, and disappears for two seconds before returning with...a volleyball.

Sport number one is definitely not what I was expecting. At four foot ten and change, I don't exactly scream *volleyball player* while walking down the street.

And though I'm wearing actual shoes, as promised, Alex doesn't head for the bowels of the enormous hillside clubhouse—where I imagine one could hide not only a volleyball court but also the Goonies' treasure and possibly a sliver of Nat's ridiculous confidence—but for the cabana area...and the sand volleyball court. "Wait, I wore shoes and now you want me to take them off?"

"Yes. You need to be ready for anything."

My lips twist. "Including sand volleyball, a sport that isn't played competitively in high school in Kansas?"

"The basics of volleyball are the same no matter the court— and the sand will be better for your back."

He taps the ball toward me and this time I catch it easily. I'm sort of proud of myself until I realize this isn't a sport where you're actually supposed to catch the ball while in play. So maybe I will be good at it once I get past my idiot instincts.

"And speaking of eligible sports, come here, Caroline." He frowns slightly as he yanks a nearly severed stick off some sort of dwarf tree that's one in a line that separates the beach volleyball setup from the golf course. Alex doesn't say anything, but it's clear he thinks someone should've caught this busted branch before he did. Possibly another grounds worker above his own pay grade. Still, he uses the stick's demise to his advantage, pointing to the sand.

"If you're going to date a new sport, it's got to be worthwhile. We don't want you dating a loser and hitting a dead end."

"Okay, Dad."

That buys me a flash of white teeth. Sarcasm is something on which we've always agreed.

"First things first, even if this is just for fun, I want you to have the tools to be competitive if that's something you want to do." Alex uses one end of the stick to write an *F* in the sand, a line underscoring it. Below it, he draws letters:

V. XC. T. G. G.

The last *G* he marks with a circle and a strike-through—like on a no-smoking sign.

Next, he creates a new column topped with a *W* and strikes another line before writing a couple more letters: *B, S&D.*

The last line is predictable because I think I've got it now— the crossed-out *G* was a dead giveaway. An underlined *S* leads the way on the final list, followed by the letters *T&F, S, S.*

"Caroline Kepler, meet all the sports that exist for girls according to KSHSAA governance."

Fall: volleyball, cross-country, tennis, golf, gymnastics (marked out, sigh).

Winter: basketball, swimming and diving.

Spring: track and field, soccer, softball.

My choices written in sandy relief.

"You forgot football," I chide him because Nat's crush Liv is basically famous for being the starting quarterback on Northland's football team.

"I wouldn't recommend that one, short stuff, but you're right, there's nothing stopping you from doing any of the boys' sports."

To that end, he adds an *F* to fall and a *W* to winter: wrestling.

I read the list again, lingering on the sad, crossed-out *G*. The irony is that last fall I turned down the school's gymnastics coach—Ms. Clarke—because my team schedule was so bananas there was no way I could compete for her too. Plus, with my back already a mess at the beginning of my freshman year, there's no way in hell Olga would've let me spend any time in a gym that wasn't under her watchful eye. "You did a lot of research for this."

It somehow embarrasses me that he thought about more than just the mechanics of picking me up and getting me here.

Alex literally shrugs it off. "I just organized my thoughts. If I'm going to teach you something, I want it to be useful."

"Okay." God, he's too nice.

"I figure we'll work for an hour today and you can train those skills the rest of the week before we move on to another sport. If at any time you find a sport you love and think is the one, we'll focus specifically on it for as long as you want."

That makes sense. "And we're starting with volleyball? Why?"

"Because if your back can handle it, I think you'd make an awesome libero and, if you want to compete, the tryouts are in early August." I'm about to ask if all the fall sports have tryouts at the same time when he gives a self-effacing grin. "Also, I knew there was an open window of court time for me to snag between three and four today."

"Way to use your resources, Zavala."

"I'm not a dumb jock and you know it."

This makes me laugh not only because no one would ever accuse him of that—he's on Northland's championship mathletics team, after all. Alex also happens to be a letterman in sports that aren't stereotyped as being full of a bunch of meatheads: soccer, basketball, and tennis. Much like Sunny, he'd literally be the most annoying human being ever if he weren't so nice.

He grins and points me and the ball in my hands over to the court. "Let's get started."

Off go my athletically appropriate shoes and socks. I suddenly feel a hundred percent more at home, even as my heels sink into carted-in sand instead of a fluffy blue mat.

We line up on the same side of the net, oriented so that neither of us gets a full to-the-face look into the steaming afternoon sun. I smack the ball to him—just like in our basketball game last night, it's got too much velocity and there's exactly zero arc.

Somehow Alex turns a line drive to his chest into something workable, bumping the ball off both wrists before catching it, easy as pie. "The key with volleyball is timing and contact." Alex tosses up the ball and pops it my way.

I bang my wrists together and try to tap it back to him, but I swing instead of bump and the ball goes sailing straight up toward the blinding sun. It plummets back down, and on instinct, I toss myself toward it, trying to correct my mistake. I get one fist under the ball as my knees hit the sand, popping it up with such force it thunks Alex in the shoulder as he unsuccessfully dodges. Still, he's at least fast enough to avoid a volleyball-to-cheekbone collision.

The ball drops with a thud to the sand and I stare at it, this poor thing that's in for a wild ride whenever it comes my way. It's going to be a long hour for you, little volleyball.

Alex scoops it up and meets my eyes, face blank. "You don't know it, but that whole sequence was actually not too shabby."

I squint at him and rise to my feet. I don't bother to dust off the sand—there's going to be a whole lot more where that came from. Screen print Nadia's just going to have to live with some manual exfoliation. "Are you going to be the type of coach who blows smoke up my ass? Because believe me, that won't work. I've been nitpicked to death since I was five. Something can always improve and we both know what I did just now was shit."

Alex pops up the ball and catches it, a little smile on his face to go with a shake of his head. His hair is so perfectly gelled into place it doesn't move. He plows forward. "Not if you're a libero. You bumped the ball and kept it in play. Plus, you dove—body sacrifice is crucial to the position. How's the back?"

"Uh, fine?" And it actually is. I don't know if the cortisone shot is masking the pain or if nearly a month's rest has paid off or what, but I'm going to roll with it. Still, I'm stuck back on the words "body sacrifice."

"So what exactly is a libero? You've said that word twice like you think I know anything at all about sports other than gymnastics. I can give you the lowdown on the specifics of an Amanar, including a biography of the gymnast it was named after, but if you go deeper into another sport other than what I may have seen in a movie, I'm going to have no idea what you're talking about."

There's a flash of sun-bright teeth and Alex smooshes both palms against the ball, biceps tensing for a hot second as he clasps the poor thing in a vice grip. "A libero is a special position—do you know what a designated hitter is?"

"The name makes it pretty obvious."

"Well, it's like that. Sort of. In baseball the DH is very specific to the league and its offense, but the idea's the same—a specialist who comes in to do one thing and is allowed to do that thing only."

Great. He wants me to be a specialist in a sport I've never played. His confidence in me is completely misplaced.

"A libero in volleyball is a player designated specifically for the back row. The position can't move forward, block, or serve—it's designed for defense, plain and simple." He cocks a brow. "You do know the difference between defense and offense, right?"

I hold up my pointer finger and then peel it down and pop up my middle finger. "You do know the difference between this finger and the first one, don't you?"

Predictably, he just laughs. "Learned that part from the movies, eh?"

"Or from one of the approximately eleven bazillion basketball games I've attended since Nat—and you—started playing."

"Touché, Caroline. Anyway, like I was saying, a libero is pure defense. The player doesn't have to be tall like the ones closer to the net. And actually, your low center of gravity and mega body awareness are huge positives."

"Okay, so what do I have to do?"

"Keep the ball in play. Don't let it hit the sand, don't let it go out."

A little raised white line marks the in-play sand from the out-of-bounds sand. "Okay. Now what?"

"Back up."

I do, and without warning Alex smashes the ball on a down-ward trajectory straight for the sand two feet in front of me. I dive, both hands out and facing the sky. I get a fingertip on it but the ball taps the sand, pops up a few inches, and then rolls in Alex's direction. He scoops it up. "Again, but dig with your fists—like you did the first time."

The ball is my responsibility before I even get completely vertical again. I hit the sand, this time on my side, fists out. The left one catches the ball and it sails high enough Alex catches it. "Good. Next time you do that, reset, because the ball is coming right back to you."

The moment I'm to my feet, the ball comes again. And again. And again.

The hour flies by and before I know it, we have to leave because some sort of four-on-four pairing of teams has arrived to play. Ever the rule follower, Alex is off the court before the stroke of four—he's spent as much of his life on court rotation for tennis as he has for anything else and moves like clockwork.

"Want to cool off at the cabana? My treat."

"Heck no." I produce a ten-dollar bill from the little hideaway pocket in the front waistband of my running shorts.

"Your money's no good here, Caroline." Alex shrugs me off and keeps walking, my hard-earned allowance flapping in the half-dead Kansas breeze.

"Oh come on." I sprint ahead of him and start walking back-ward as we pass the pools (yeah, plural) and hot tub, tennis players and golfers shuffling by with massive bags. "I owe you something. You did all that work."

"I offered. And I did that work because I'm not just Nat's friend—I'm your friend. This is what friends do."

Maybe. But still. I mean, he already has a job and three sports to train for. Plus, you know, a family. And friends. This is too much. "Please, for my sanity." We hit the steps of the cabana and I flail-gesture at the rosebushes that line the railing. "If I'm so pitiful that you'd take the time to do this and get nothing in return, I might as well just crawl into those rosebushes and suspend myself in the thorns until the end of time."

"Your sense of debt is wildly overdeveloped."

I ignore him. "Brownies? I make a mean brownie." They have black beans in them but no one can tell. If Nat hasn't figured out that they're healthy, Alex won't. "You've earned at least two pans today."

"Not necessary." Two frozen lemonades materialize in his hands. Between this and my Snickers meltdown, I've probably had more sugar this week than I have at any one time in the past five years. Still, I yank the wooden spoon off the lid, ready to go to town—it's freaking nuclear out here.

We hop on bar stools to eat as people in bright tennis whites saunter by, tan arms already glistening in the heat. The lemonade is sweet and tart and frozen solid, my wooden spoon working hard at first to collect more than just sugary frost.

And it is *delicious.*

I toss my money at Alex again because I shouldn't be gumming up his employee tab, but he bats it back without a single comment. Which only makes me more desperate to find out how I can repay him for his kindness. Let's be honest, he actually really thought about this and put way more effort into helping me than I did into helping myself.

I try again.

"You're doing something nice for me. I want to do something nice for you."

I fail.

"I'm doing something nice because I want to. I'm not your brother—there's no end game."

Okay, maybe my being Nat's little sister has something to do with wanting to even up with Alex. With Nat, everything is a bargain, everything has a price.

Still, I squint at Alex—his neat hair, orthodontically perfect smile, the beloved car he bought with his own savings fuzzy in the distant staff lot behind him. What on earth do I have that this boy wants? Despite his Sunny-like perfection, there has to be something. I just can't see it.

But I'm going to find out and I'm going to pay him back.

9

As we head back to Alex's car, his sand-written list of sports is swirling in my brain, warring with my certain guilt over owing him something for his attention.

I'm sort of curious about how Alex coaches a sport he actually plays. He didn't really teach me basketball the other night, but considering that everything he plays is on the list, he could try with something else. "How about tennis for the next sport?"

Of his three sports, tennis is probably Alex's best. I mean, he's a literal tennis star, winning state last year, and he's been to national tournaments and stuff, so his tips will likely be excellent. Plus, my size won't matter nearly as much as with everything else. I mean, I think. Maybe. They don't *look* big on TV. And the people who just wandered by weren't giants or anything—and bonus, they were older than Dad, which means the sport might not be hell on my back.

Alex smirks as he unlocks the car. "Tennis is harder than it looks."

"It's on the list." I slide in next to him. The seats are hot as hell.

"After today, I'm not completely convinced I should arm you

with a racket. If you actually get a piece of the ball, I want to keep my head."

A protective towel lands in my lap and I contort myself to spread it out on the upholstery without opening the door. The backs of my thighs and shoulders are immediately thankful. "I'll take that as a compliment. But for real, it's a fall sport. You don't have to be super tall, and agility and flexibility are bonuses."

Alex's face goes deadpan. "You've been watching Wimbledon, haven't you?"

"It's on seven hours a day, and if you'll recall, I'm not at the gym for those hours, sooooo..."

"You're watching the best in the world—they make it look easy."

The Challenger roars to life, and I know he's trying to drown out my retort. Nice try but it won't work. "Prove it. It's the next sport."

Alex's face breaks into a little smile and I know I've got him. He rolls down the windows, letting the hot air escape the car before we wind through the lot. "Fine."

"Free next Thursday?" I ask, mostly because it's exactly a week from today.

Alex's schedule is a whole lot more complicated than mine—we're still parked, so he whips out his phone and checks the calendar. His lips kick up. "Thursday's good for me."

"Excellent, gives me time to do my homework with Wimbledon."

Alex taps the gas. "Watching Rafa Nadal flex after winning an eighteen-shot rally isn't going to make you a natural at tennis."

"No, but it couldn't hurt. You know, for science."

After a few minutes, we hit a red light and a natural pause in the conversation. I'm about to ask Alex if he wouldn't mind dropping me by the grocery store so I can get the ingredients for my sad-sack brownie offering and walk home when he surprises me by asking, "So, what are the specifics of an Amanar? And who was she—he?"

It takes me a moment to realize he actually cataloged some of the information I blathered about out on the court. "It's a vault named after a Romanian gymnast—Simona Amanar. Yurchenko entry, two and a half off." His eyes sort of glaze over and I realize I'm not speaking normal teenager English. "I can show you some-time, if you want."

He sucks in a breath. "Are you cleared to do an Amanar?"

"Um, well, probably not. And I've never landed one anyway." I mean, only 0.00000589 percent of the gymnastics population can land one, but it's still somewhat embarrassing to admit that despite all my training there's something I can't do properly. "I meant I could show you a video."

Alex can probably YouTube as well as any other sixteen-year-old boy. Lord knows Nat spends most of his nonmoving hours watching videos of people daring each other to eat pig feces and scale buildings. But instead he says immediately, "That'd be cool."

And the student becomes the teacher.

The light turns green and I'm surprised when Alex shoots another question my way. "Can the girl on your shirt land one?"

"Oh, no—this is Nadia Comaneci. She's Romanian too, but her career ended long before Amanar even started. Something as difficult as that vault wasn't even a pipe dream then." I pull out my phone and page through my videos for the last meet of my season—regionals. The Amanar is something Sunny started per-forming last year. When we hit a red light, I shove the queued-up screen under his nose. "Here, look, watch."

The competition floor is raised, and the video is taken from the athletes' area, which is nearly four feet below that, but I think I still managed to get a decent angle of Sunny performing the vault. The video is less than twenty seconds long.

Sunny waiting to salute, rubbing chalk on her hands as her eyes zone out in visualization.

Saluting and checking her mark.

Sprinting down the runway, arms pumping and legs flexing under the weight of each step, her competition bun the only thing immobile.

Then the skill: a round-off onto the board, back handspring entry to the vault table, and then two and a half twists while flipping through the air.

Like my Arabian, the landing is front-facing and therefore blind. Sunny's feet hit the mat before she spots it. She takes a big step forward—a good three-tenths off—but considering the difficulty, it's solid.

"Damn."

I'll admit—I'm quite pleased with Alex's reaction. "Right?"

The light changes and the car growls into motion. I can't help it; I start paging through the pictures from that same meet. Selfies with the team in a never-ending rotation of pairs, triples, and the whole team. I even got a few of Olga, all serious eyebrows and pinched lips as she gave advice to Peregrine before a bar routine that won her yet another medal.

This. This is what I'm missing. I've opened Pandora's box and now I can't wrench myself away. My heart clenches as I page through my old life one smile, laugh, mid-motion conversation at a time.

I've basically lost touch with the current time and place when Alex's voice cuts through the void. "Um, so is that Sunny Chavez?"

There's something in his tone that demands I catch a glimpse of his face. He's watching the road a little more intently than before, his posture pin straight and no longer relaxed. He's golden brown from spending so much time outside, but I swear his cheeks flush with color rising into his neat hairline.

"The one and only." I can't help but grin a little as I watch Alex seem to shed his perfectness before my eyes and display real, messy, human emotions. "Do you know her?"

"Used to." Yes, he's red. Definitely red. "Freshman year mathletics."

Of course. Sunny was at Northland before I got there, but decided to go the homeschool route after becoming elite. She would've been a sophomore when Alex and Nat were freshmen.

Something Nat said during his weird overprotective rant pings through my brain. *I know for a fact you think gymnasts are cute and all, but my sister is off-limits.*

Oh.

That uptick on my lips widens into a full-on grin. "Alex Zavala, do you have a crush on Sunny Chavez?"

His nose crinkles and his eyes stay pinned to the white lines. "Did."

"*Did?* I'd say you *do*. Look at you—you're sweating."

"I'm not."

"You are." I pointedly press the back of my hand to his forehead. He perspired less kicking my ass with volleyball drills in ninety-five-degree heat.

Oh my God.

I nearly start cackling with glee because suddenly, surprisingly, I have a way to pay back Alex Zavala. I click my phone to life and check the time. Four fifty-three. Perfect. "Drop me at the gym?"

"The *gym* gym?"

"*Yes*. I figured out how to repay you. You *like* Sunny but have no access to her. I do." I press both hands into his forearm as his wrist hooks casually over the wheel. "*Please*, let me do this for you."

He rubs the back of his neck with his free hand. "What are you going to do?"

"Reintroduce you. And if that goes well and you want to, maybe more. I promise I won't embarrass you or force anything. I just want to help." Alex's face softens and I can see I've wormed my way in. For good measure, I toss his words right back at him. "I'm doing something nice because *I want to*."

That does it. He sucks in a breath. "What do I need to do?"

I nearly cheer. "I just need you and your car at Balan's Gymnastics at five." When practice ends. "That's in seven minutes. Get a move on."

"We're really doing this now?" His voice is sort of strangled.

"You're not doing anything except dropping me off and looking handsome." I pat the blushing cheek nearest to me, getting all up in his business. "I'll do the rest."

To my delight, he hangs a right, pointing the Challenger toward Balan's. I shoot off a text to the group thread between Sunny, Peregrine, and me saying I want to do dinner tonight if they're free.

Peregrine must be at her locker collecting her things, because she texts me back immediately.

Sure! Sunny and I were just talking about craving bibimbap. Okay if we do that?

Yes, perfect. Meet you at the gym in five.

Alex drives in silence, jaw working in my periphery. As we turn into the business park housing Balan's I think I get it—he's overanalyzing what's about to happen. Working it through his brain like he would a drawn play on the soccer field or basketball court. Or working three shots ahead on the tennis court. Nat goes bouncing off the walls when he's nervous, but Alex, it appears, folds in on himself like a dying star.

Which means he truly does have real, live, messy feelings. He's not just this perfectly formed big brother figure but someone whose insides can go all squishy too. I figured his confidence and consistency spared him the roller coaster of human emotion.

This turn of events is incredible.

As the gym comes into view, I spot the upper-level squad moving outside to head home. I yank off my seat belt as he hugs the curb to the sidewalk. "Keep these windows down and stay here," I tell him. Then I pop open the door as I see Sunny's ghostly form behind the shaded entry glass, curly pony bouncing as she waves goodbye to Elena, who's usually stationed behind the front desk. "In the wise yet fictional words of Angelica Schuyler, I'm about to change your life."

It's a total dork thing to say and I fear I've confused him more with my *Hamilton* reference, but then I hear him through the open windows over the clang of the door as I slam it.

"Then by all means, lead the way."

10

I'M not as smooth as fictional Angelica Schuyler or probably fictional anybody, but I step onto the sidewalk leading to Balan's front door with a huge grin on my face.

I greet my friends that way, and though they both are smiling when they push out onto the same sidewalk, their faces host a flicker of something else—something serious? Tentative? Unsure?—as they flip-flop my way.

I've all but halted my forward progress, cocking out a knee and sticking close to the parking lot, Alex's rolled-down window strategically about eight feet behind and beside my right side. There's no hiding him, and I won't have to yell across the space between us to include him.

They've changed out of their gym gear and into street clothes. Sunny's in a tie-halter sundress the color of chopped watermelon, and Peregrine's in a gray athleisure skort and...the same Nadia wrist-flip tank top as me. "Well, *bună ziua* to you too, Peregrine," I say, dusting off the Romanian greeting Olga taught us in kindergarten. I tug at the edges of my tank top until recognition slides across her features and she one-ups me because she can.

"Nu ne-am văzut demult."

Whatever the heck that is pole-vaults my comprehension level, a decade with Olga or not.

Peregrine catches my confusion. "Long time no see."

Oh.

Sunny laughs and it's bright and airy. Her head is tossed back, thick eyelashes curling toward the summer blue sky. "Wait, seriously? I thought you were trolling us with Klingon."

"Mom insisted I actually use our Duolingo account for something besides High Valyrian." Peregrine shrugs and tightens her ponytail. "And, anyway, if we're talking *Star Trek*, I'm more of a Vulcan kind of gal."

"What is there other than *'Live long and prosper'*?" Sunny asks, holding up the Vulcan *V* symbol. "Which they don't say in anything other than English?"

I'm about to rein it in once I can figure out how the hell to integrate Alex into the inadvertent nerd spiral I started, but then the boy goes and just does it himself. "Peace and long life."

All three heads whip his way, and Alex has his own Vulcan *V* hanging out of the car. With all of our faces pointed at him, he grins. "That's how they answer *'Live long and prosper'*—*'Peace and long life.'*"

Somehow this is a surprise despite his very recent echoing of *Hamilton* lyrics. Of course he's an expert in pop culture, just like he's a star athlete and nice and hot and, yeah.

"Sunny, Peregrine, this is my ride, Alex Zavala."

Now Peregrine is the confused one. Because they've crossed paths, well, a lot. "Uh, I know Alex. Hey."

He closes the *V* in his fingers for a quick wave.

"Okay, yeah, you do, but Sunny doesn't," I say, and hold my breath. It's been almost two years, and if there's one thing I know about crushing on someone it's that you remember way more about your crush than your crush remembers about you.

Sunny shades her eyes and takes a step in his direction. The sun is at her back, casting a shadow toward his car, but he's lit up like the Olympic torch.

Square jaw. Dark eyes. Neat hair. Golden-brown skin that gleams with the perspiration he accrued on the way over here. Then he smiles, and the way the sun catches his teeth is blinding in wattage.

I hold my breath, trying *very hard* not to facilitate.

"Wait, no, I *do* know you." Sunny lights up when she figures it out. "Mathletics! You're the skinny kid who sat with Topps." She sweeps her arms high above her head because Topps is Tobias Topperman, a champion mathlete, Lily Jane's boyfriend, and basically a brick wall with a beard and a driver's license that claims he's only seventeen. He's a football lineman, which sort of explains it. "I mean, not that you're small."

A blush crawls across her face because it's a pretty observant comment, considering that all but his smiling face, broad shoulders, and a single long arm are blocked by the Challenger's driver's-side door. Her cheeks pinking harder, Sunny flails a sweeping gesture toward her own body, which makes it to five feet with shoes on. "Everyone looks giant to me, though."

"To be fair, Alex is on the varsity basketball team, so he's an *actual* giant. No matter your perspective," I say. While this is cute, it's also hella awkward. Plus, what I've just said isn't totally accurate because no one over the age of five would call my brother tall and he's on the same team. "Okay, so dinner, yes?"

"Thank God," Peregrine answers, and she starts toward Sunny's SUV, which is parked in the far corner of Balan's lot, under one of the very limited number of trees.

"Thanks for the ride, Alex!" I say cheerfully, complete with a wave, and grab Sunny's hand because Peregrine is already yards ahead of us—she's about as food motivated as Nat, and that's saying something.

But Sunny hesitates. "Alex, do you want to come?"

The glee I felt ten minutes ago at the realization of Alex's crush on my surrogate older sister is nothing compared to Sunny inviting my surrogate older brother to our dinner unprompted. *Nothing.* Let's be real, *glee* has not been my thing for almost a month now, so I chomp down hard on my cheek and stare at him from over Sunny's shoulder. *Yes, say yes. Do it. You guys would be so cute.*

"Thanks, but I've got stadium stairs calling my name."

I nearly form the words *but you're meeting Nat after dinner* before the Challenger's engine lets off a new lion's growl.

And with a wave and the opening lines of "My Shot" thrumming through the open window, Alex is gone.

We pile into Sunny's hand-me-down Hyundai Santa Fe, which brims with sunflower adornments—hanging from the rearview mirror, standing sentry in a front-facing vanity plate, and in more than one bumper sticker on the back—and weave through Thursday night traffic to Eomma, a Korean restaurant across the street from Northland. The school's old brick bell tower casts a shadow across the on-street parking as Sunny snags a spot.

Before exiting the vehicle, Peregrine paints on lavender lipstick, swiping at the corner of her mouth with a pinky as she checks her work in the passenger seat's visor mirror. "There, now no one will think we're too matchy-matchy," she deadpans, and finally unbuckles her seat belt.

"One thousand percent less embarrassing now, Per," I say with a laugh. This girl and her lipsticks—they say everything so she doesn't have to.

"Who do you have to be embarrassed in front of?" Sunny asks, a mischievous upsweep to her question as she locks the car. A perfect brow arches toward the baby hairs she likely slicked down with some water after changing. *Alex Zavala?*

"Noooooooo." I'm so horrified that my answer is automatic and high-pitched. I make a beeline for the door and pull it open for my friends. They don't move to enter, even while standing in the full brunt of a July sun—they just glue themselves into a human wall of two and stare at me.

"So, uh, why were you with Alex?" Sunny asks.

I can't explain why, but the whole private lessons truth sits funny on my tongue—like I'm cheating on my friends instead of facing the reality that I had to quit the thing we had in common. Both of them are watching me and I suddenly realize that the longer I delay, the more they won't believe anything I say.

Peregrine folds her arms across her chest. "Are you and Alex a thing?"

"Huh, what? No!"

Her eyes narrow. "So you just happened to be riding around in his muscle car, without Nat, like that's a normal thing you do on a random Thursday night."

"Nat pawned me off," I fib, and escape into the confines of the restaurant.

Peregrine is at my back before the hostess can extract herself from a far table and just-arrived guests to seat us. "Pawned you off from where?"

"The country club," I sputter. I don't explain why I was there. Instead I just say, "I've got to do something with my time."

Peregrine halts her interrogation at the sudden void created by what I'm not saying. *"My time," now that I'm not with you at the gym.*

Sunny, ever the mom, helps me out. "And so you spend it with your brother and his friends?"

Well, no. "Well, yeah."

Sunny grins and Peregrine's purple lips purse into a hard line. "Well, we're glad you texted. Movies are great, but I'm excited to actually talk to you." She greets the hostess. "Three, please."

The restaurant is already half full though it's not even five thirty. The hostess steers us to the back, where there's a little round bistro table tucked between two windows. She grabs another chair and placemat from an adjacent four-top, shimmying everything around. Sunny jumps in to help before snagging the chair that backs up to the wall.

Less than ten efficient seconds later our waitress arrives, armed with a grin, our menus, and a tray lined in delicate saucers. "Kimchi?" It's not really a question as much as it's an introduction from our waitress, a bottle blond about our age. She slides the dishes, full of fermented cabbage, radish, and cucumber, onto the placemat with staccato efficiency. She has two of the radish one and makes a point to set one of them directly in front of Sunny. When she does, my friend's eyes light up, and the waitress answers with a smile of her own. "That way you don't have to ask for more."

"Is asking for seconds that rare?" Sunny asks, cheeks pinking.

The waitress grins. "No." Then she catches eyes with Peregrine. "Water, no ice?"

"Yes, please. Ice for these jokers."

The girl nods. "Like your lipstick."

"Thanks, Bridgette."

I'm getting the sense that Bridgette is used to seeing Peregrine and Sunny. Which is weird because we haven't been here since last summer, when we liberally abused the fact that Sunny had a car and our allowances wouldn't spend themselves on vegetarian bibimbap. I would ask what's up but I suddenly don't want to know how many dinners I've missed at this place over the last month.

Sunny focuses on her metal chopsticks, squeezing a couple of little radish cubes for liftoff straight into her mouth. "We were surprised to see you, Caro."

"I texted," I answer, diving for my chopsticks for something to hide my reaction because a water glass won't do it. Why am I being weird? I successfully reintroduced Alex to Sunny—so successfully, I might add, that *she* asked *him* to dinner. I'm past the hard part, so why is my heart kissing my tonsils?

Peregrine plucks a chunk of spicy cabbage with her chopsticks and meets my eyes. Her face is grave—even her violet lips seem to darken. "You haven't been to the gym since *you know*."

Oh.

Yes.

I'd been so distracted by Alex and Sunny and evening the score that it didn't even occur to me that I hadn't acted like they expected me to when I showed up to Balan's as a non-gymnast for the first time. I—I just completely missed the heaviness of the moment.

And...that's okay? I mean, my heart seizes at the weight of it all. I'd been wrapped in bubble wrap and didn't even know it.

The power of distraction. Or doing a good deed. Or Alex Zavala.

"And then you were there"—Sunny arches a brow—"rolling out the Romanian and wearing your Nadia tank like it was nothing."

"Chauffeured by Nat's best friend, *like that was normal,*" Peregrine adds over a mouthful of cabbage. "I mean, it still would've been a surprise because you were randomly texting and then *there in the flesh,* but I didn't have literally any of this on my Bingo card for the last week of June."

Sunny sets down her chopsticks atop her personal bowl of fermented radish. "What we mean is—is everything okay?"

"Yes."

Sunny goes into full incredulous-gym-mom mode. "Yes, really yes?"

"Yes, really." I swallow a particularly spicy bit of cucumber and cough, waving my hand in front of my face.

Peregrine's not buying it either. "You're silent all week until Sundays. And so it's *weird* not only to hear from you on a Thursday but to see you five minutes later."

I press my napkin to my lips, tears in my eyes and not from the spice. "I know. I'm sorry. It's just difficult...with things being different." I swallow again. "I guess I needed to rip the Band-Aid off. I'm glad I asked, I'm glad you answered, I'm glad Alex could drop me off, and I'm glad we're here."

Sunny smiles, eyes sliding to Peregrine's. "Maybe we should make this a weekly thing."

"Definitely," I agree, trying not to feel as if these two already have a weekly thing and I'm being tacked on.

The waitress appears with water—two with ice, one without—

and we resoundingly order three vegetarian bibimbap. Some things never change.

When Bridgette leaves and silence descends, I'm extremely eager to get any attention off me. I take a sip of my water, set it back down firmly in front of me, and drill my forever BFF with the same unrelenting gaze I give the middle distance before a tumbling pass. "So, Per, speaking of Northland soccer players with whom *I do not have a thing*, I saw Ryan Rodinsky the other day."

Peregrine stills, kimchi frozen halfway between the little dish and her lips. "You mean the Ryan Rodinsky who can't pull the fucking trigger?"

Sunny's face scrunches with a social math equation. "Wait. Is this the science partner? The one whose sister is the Northland quarterback?"

"The one and only, who spent all last year flirting with Peregrine in biology."

Peregrine shoves the kimchi into the side of her mouth. "I'm not sure I completely understand the definition or point of flirting, because if that's what it was, it didn't work because he's had my number *since March*."

"Oh shit." Sunny's eyes are wide as saucers. "You're telling me you *saw him* nearly every day after giving him your number for, what, three more months? And didn't call him on his bullshit? Or text him yourself?"

Peregrine shrugs but her features go cat-like. "If he wants to call me, he knows where to find me. Until then, he can just keep on rotating through Northland's entire cheer squad while trying to ignore the fact that I'm the one he'll be smiling at throughout all of AP chem next year."

"Wait," I say, brows lurching together and a halting palm

thrown in the air, "did you just miss a chance at a chemistry in chemistry joke, Peregrine?"

"Oh my God, I think I did," Peregrine admits with a laugh as she presses the back of a hand to her mouth to keep in her recently deposited kimchi.

Sunny lifts a brow. "You must really like him."

"Or have low blood sugar."

And just like that our food arrives, steaming and glorious. Piling the remainder of the kimchi into our steaming stone bowls, we dig in.

11

The weekend is a blur of the farmers' market and Sunday movie day—a special matinee of *Forrest Gump*—and then suddenly it's Thursday.

Aka tennis day.

Somehow, between my engagements, I found time to stretch and watch a few more hours of Wimbledon. And though Alex is probably right—the best in the world sure do make it look easy—I'm actually super stoked to try another ball sport.

Though I won't put it that way. I've learned my lesson.

The rumble of the Challenger's engine hits our cul-de-sac just before three, and I'm out the door before he's all the way in the driveway. Sunglasses, sneakers, skort, and yet another gymnastics-themed tank top. This one is black and has the names of all the winners of the World all-around title from the United States up through 2021 listed in lowercase white lettering. (Individual all-around doesn't happen during Olympic years for some reason.)

Kim + Shannon + Chellsie + Shawn + Bridget + Jordyn + Simone + Morgan.

As I open the car door, I can tell Alex is trying to read the names and put it all together, but when I slide onto the pre-towel-covered seat, he doesn't ask. Instead, he simply moves a used protein powder shaker bottle out of the way and gestures that I fill the cup holder with my water bottle.

"Such a gentleman—picking me up, covering the hot seats, harboring my drinks."

"It pays to have a sister," he says, teeth flashing.

Funny, but somehow I don't think Nat would answer the same about me. He won't give me credit for anything, and Alex doles it out to Lily Jane like it's nothing.

Alex smells of soap and deodorant, and the air is blasting, swirling it all around. I feel like I'm being aired out among pine trees and I love it. It's currently ninety-five degrees and I'm going to need all the Swiss Alps bliss I can get.

We get to the *T* in the road and rather than turn right toward the club, Alex turns left. Toward our high school.

"Not Northfield?"

"Spend all my time there. Thought Northland would be better."

Alex just finished his spring season, making the all-district and all-state teams (duh), but his non-KSHSAA tennis stuff happens at Northfield with his longtime instructor, Coach Bev. That's how he and Nat and the other basketball dudes got their jobs at the country club in the first place—Alex's connection.

Northland High looms before us a few minutes later. It's ancient redbrick that's been added onto eight bazillion times— being the oldest school in the district will do that to a floor plan. The actual boundary too, which isn't so much a square as it is a particularly creative puzzle piece. Alex loops into the circle drive where drop-off occurs during the year and parks under a shady maple that's probably as old as the building's cornerstone. He gets out and retrieves a fancy Babolat tennis bag from the trunk, plus an unopened can of coconut water.

Both courts are empty and Alex picks the one on the right, winding through the fence and setting his stuff on the bench. He unzips his bag and hands me a silver-and-blue racket with pink tape on the handle.

It's lighter than I thought it would be. I take a swing, but Alex stops me on the backhand and examines the way my fingers cup the grip. I suddenly wish I'd taken the time to remove the polish I picked off when Forrest was comparing life to a box of chocolates.

He spins the racket so it's totally up and down and leans in over my fingers. Alex nods to himself in the way the dentist does right before he tells you to floss more.

"What?"

"It's a little big but it'll do—I guess LJ's hands are larger than yours."

I'll take his word for it. It feels fine.

He doesn't move away. "Put your other hand on the racket."

"How?"

"However. I just want to see what you'll do naturally."

I immediately place my left hand on the racket.

"Good, now take it off."

My hand flings away as if it's on fire.

Alex nods again and digs through his bag for his own racket plus a can of balls. He stuffs a ball in each pocket and lets the third one bounce, dribbling it with his racket as he walks to the sunny end of the court.

I chase him. "Wait. What was that? Do I have some fatal tennis flaw?"

"No. You have a natural semiwestern grip. It's interesting."

I gape at him.

"It's what most pros use these days. It's fine." I've been Amanar-ed. He grins. "Get on the other side. We'll warm up with some simple volleys."

I step into the shady side, grip the racket with both hands, and sink into a squat—just like I saw on repeat over and over on TV. My thighs lock into place because they know how to do this.

And, just like when we were on the volleyball court, Alex doesn't spare me with his first shot. It's not a serve; it's a volley as promised, but there's juice behind it. And distance.

I'm standing in front of the baseline and the ball hits so close to my toes I have to shuffle back to get swing time. My racket goes back in my right hand and rockets forward. I make contact and almost cheer...before it line drives right into the net.

"I hit it! Into the net, but I hit it!"

Alex laughs at my excitement but doesn't let me revel too long. "You did. Your turn to volley it back."

I retrieve the ball and line myself up in basically the same position he's in on the other side of the court—we're noon and six on a sundial. Like he did, I bounce the ball a few times, getting a feel, and then when it's at waist height, swing it his way. It makes contact, but is again super flat, just missing the white tape at the top of the net. Alex easily returns it with a backhand, guiding it right back at me, and I'm surprised.

So surprised, in fact, that I completely whiff it. I gesture toward the other end of the court. "I thought you were going to hit it over there."

Alex examines the strings of his racket. "You did? I don't see you over there."

Oh right. "Well, I anticipated you were going to hit it over there and I froze when you hit it straight to me."

"The point of volleying in warm-up is to get a feel for the ball. I *want* you to hit it. You'll know when it's time for you to move around the court." He nods, ball cap dipping low enough to shade his eyes. "Retrieve it and let's do it again."

And we do.

Over and over and over again.

He's right, of course. When he wants me to move, I move. Pretty soon, we're actually volleying without me stopping and starting and dumping the ball into the net. One drink break later and we move to only serving. Well, Alex is serving. I'm still retrieving.

"Can't I serve?"

"That's a whole different lesson."

"We said a sport a week, right? I mean, you don't have time to teach me this and something else."

"No, but we did say if you like something enough, we'd just stick with it. Remember?"

"Right." Well, yeah. And I do like tennis, it just seems premature to say this is what I like without *a*, knowing what else is out there, and *b*, knowing how my back is going to feel in the morning after the twist-and-hit motion I've done repeatedly for the past hour.

Which means we need to talk about the payment I cooked up.

I don't knock him over the head with a review of my week-old interaction until I've nearly hit him five times running with serve returns he deflects at the last minute with the tip of his racket. Might as well smack him with another line drive. "Soooo, what did you think of Sunny?"

In response, he swipes at some phantom perspiration as color pops into his tan cheeks.

When he doesn't actually say anything, I add, "She remembered you!"

He glances away. "She remembered *Topps*. He's extremely memorable."

Yeah, LJ's boyfriend, Topps, who might be the hypothetical Kevin Bacon connector of Northland High (varsity football, award-winning mathletics, and senior status combined with a full beard will do that for a guy). "Only because he smells like a reboot of *21 Jump Street*."

Alex smirks. "He does have a cop vibe." Suddenly he realizes what we're talking about and his eyebrows crash together. "Wait, what do you know about *21 Jump Street* anyway?"

"Don't deflect. Or pretend Nat hasn't watched his fair share of eighties TV shows."

"He has, but you—"

I smack a ball at him and, to my satisfaction, he has to jump out of the way to avoid taking it straight to the shinbone. "I said don't deflect."

Alex snags the ball with the toe of his sneaker as it rebounds off the wall of fence surrounding the court and whips it into his waiting hand with the ease of the tennis/basketball/soccer player he is. As he walks off court, angling toward his coconut water, I follow and pointedly stare at him as I gulp down my own refreshment.

After a full minute, Alex sighs and I know I've worn him down. It pays to use Nat's tactics.

"It was fine?" He's turning redder by the second. "What... do you want me to say?"

Actually... I. Uh. Don't. Know.

In terms of our deal: That it was successful. That he still thinks she's cute. That he thought about his interaction with Sunny all week, like I did. But what comes out of my mouth is a garbled mess of sudden empathetic embarrassment (I think). "Well...um. Did you...were you happy about it?"

Alex's face shades with a question that he drowns in coconut water.

"What?" I tap him on the hand and squint at his profile as my sunglasses slide down my nose. I should've gone his route and worn a ball cap. Or, more accurately, stolen one from Nat.

Lashes lowered, Alex again rubs at some phantom sweat, hauling the collar of his tank up to dab at his chin. It obscures his mouth and muffles what he says next. "So, um, did you talk about the, uh, *it* afterward? At dinner?"

I can't help it—my face splits into a grin I can't hide. He wants to know. He really wants to know. But the first thing to hit my mind involving him and our conversation is the girls asking if *I* had a thing for him. My smile falters—I cover by attempting to look sly; my voice tilts up an octave. "Maybe."

It works, because suddenly Alex looks like he's about to toss that coconut water and whatever he had for lunch. "Caro—"

"Not really." My eyes skip past him and across the street, toward Eomma. "I mean, they asked why I was hanging out with you."

He arches a brow. "Did you say *ball sports?*"

"Gah. No."

I don't elaborate but Alex lets it be and crosses back to his side of the court. I follow suit but I'm not done. I stand there, racket dangling at the baseline. "So, you're up for seeing her again, yes?"

In response he serves and oh my God, it's not a softball first-day serve, it's a real, hundred-mile-an-hour bomb.

It's all I can do to get my racket out in front of my body so I don't have an ice-cream-scoop-sized welt over my appendix. But, to my credit, the ball actually does make contact with my racket, and not only that, sails back over the net in what resembles the fancy drop shots I saw during my Wimbledon stretch sessions.

Alex seems surprised—I mean, I am too—and scrambles toward the ball. He dips his racket arm so low it scrapes the court as he just gets the webbing of his racket under the ball. The ball pops nearly straight up, catches the top of the net and, after teetering for a dry second, falls unceremoniously to my side. I'm still at the baseline and never would've gotten it anyway.

Alex picks himself up off the court, logrolling to his knees. I don't wait for him to be truly vertical. "Alex, this is another sport. Another sport should equal another interaction. I *owe* you. An interaction per sport. One a week. That's not too much. Just enough to move you up in her mind's eye."

He's silent.

"Come on, if she were still at Northland, you'd probably see her every day." For emphasis, I cock my thumb over my shoulder toward the school, home to nearly a century's worth of awkward, hormone-filled meet-cutes. "What's once a week? Answer: just enough to make an impression."

Again, he's silent.

"I saw the way you blushed and then heard *with my very own ears* you ask if we'd discussed you during dinner." The mention of blush begets more blush on his end. "You can't deny that you wouldn't mind if you got another chance to talk with Sunny."

I stare at Alex again. Silent. Arms crossed as much as they can be with my racket in hand.

It takes less time than it did at the bench to get a response. "Okay." He pauses. "But..."

I toss up placating hands and his words die out. "I won't be awkward about it. I promise."

"You're not awkward." His dimples flash. "Heavy-handed, maybe."

I arch an eyebrow. "Did you not say literally about a week ago that I had, and I quote, *game*?"

"That was in relationship to Nat. Next to him, we're all Oscar Isaac."

"Oscar Isaac is always a compliment, no matter how you look at it."

"I'm making my point terribly."

I place both hands on my hips and lean in. "That's what liking a *cute* gymnast can do to a guy, I bet."

Alex is blushing again and seriously can't look at me. Gah, I will never get over the fact that he likes Sunny. Not ever. I like this version of Alex Zavala. The imperfection of feelings actually seems to make him more perfect.

Maybe he is Oscar Isaac lite.

"How about this?" I offer. "If I make a fall sport and you two haven't connected, I'll invite you to Sunny's end-of-summer birthday bash. It's at a lake and it's fun and Nat comes, so it's not weird that you'd be there with the two of us."

He doesn't say yes, he doesn't say no. Instead, an alarm rings from both his watch and his phone. He glances at it. "Time to go home, Caro."

I don't have a watch on and my phone is too far away to see, so I just squint at him. "You trying to get rid of me?"

"Nah, I'm supposed to play hoops with Nat at five. It's a quarter till."

Wow. Two hours, gone like that. I haven't felt that way about time in a while. I hand him Lily Jane's racket and grab my water before dutifully heading to the car.

Something makes me hope Nat's already at the park when we pull up to the house. I... don't really want to have to explain *this*. Especially with my ever-expanding offer rolling out between the two of us.

Again, we're quiet on the drive. We pass the park, and yep, there's a vertically challenged shirtless idiot warming up solo on the court.

Phew.

"So, what's the next sport and when?"

A little devilish grin snaps Alex's dimples into action. "Based on today's performance, I have some ideas. But I'm going to have to get back to you with the timing. Are you cool with playing it by ear? Got plans? A hot date?"

Only with you is on the tip of my tongue but for some reason I don't say it, even though it's a joke. Alex parks in our driveway and I hop out. "Whatever and whenever, I'm up for it as long as you are, Zavala."

He squints at me through the rolled-down window as I slam the door. "That sounds more like a threat than an affirmative answer."

I shrug and lift a brow. "I guess we'll see. Night, Alex."

12

It *was* a threat.

I've seen every version of *Emma*, including *Clueless*, and so therefore I know that when matchmaking goes bad, it can go terribly, but now that I know how to make Alex Zavala blush on command, I cannot help myself. I need the jolt that comes with his cheeks going flush, gaze averted, body language flustered. The banter and embarrassment. The flutter in my stomach at his tentative tone in asking point-blank if he'd come up in conversation.

Yes, I need it.

So I have to get Alex and Sunny to cross paths again.

Plus, we did another sport. Which, in my mind, means another run-in with Sunny needs to happen. It was all I could think about during our second girls' Eomma dinner right after my tennis trial. And though I am loath to share Alex's heart with the world, I know there's no way I can get away with my promised interaction quota smoothly without a coconspirator.

Friday afternoon I text Peregrine. I need your help. Time to talk?

She types back almost immediately. Okay.

I'm about to suggest a place when the little typing bubbles reappear. Sunny just dropped me at home.

Perfect. I text her back: I'm walking over ASAP.

Nat's playing hoops with Alex, of course. I text him, and Dad, who's at work. And then as soon as I steal one of Nat's hats (I learned my lesson from Alex) I'm out of the house and booking it toward Peregrine's.

I'd told her I was walking, but I end up running. Past the sweaty pack of boys at the park courts, my hat pulled low so that hopefully Alex won't see me. Under the highway. Over the railroad tracks. Alongside rush-hour traffic.

I make it in eight minutes flat, even with several stoplights, and tag Peregrine's doorbell with a sweaty palm. The doorway seal gives way as a lock is turned, and there's Peregrine on the other side of the storm door barefoot and in a romper I recognize as one of her favorite gym-to-real-world tricks.

I'm wearing a tank with Laurie Hernandez's smiling face and famous phrase, *I got this*. Peregrine opens the storm door and blinks at my clothes, now drenched. "Did you . . . run?"

Suddenly I realize my mouth is super parched, so I just nod.

She nods back. "Pool," she says by way of direction. "I'll get you some water."

I don't argue.

In the kitchen, Mrs. Liu is straining curds in cheesecloth, and Mr. Liu is fussing over dough. Pizza night. The Lius take cooking very seriously. Homemade mozzarella and handmade dough to go with sauce made from tomatoes put up last summer.

"Caroline!" Mr. Liu spins his dough into a ball before returning it to an oiled bowl. "Are you here for dinner?"

Peregrine swings toward the cupboard with the pool-appropriate glassware. From stage left, Peregrine's older sister, Artemis, slides in to save me. "She might not want to wait *two hours*, Dad."

"I should've made the cheese last night. I know. Sue me," Mrs. Liu says, bent over the prepubescent mozzarella. "Good things are worth the wait!"

Artemis arches an eyebrow and rescues a bag of baby carrots from the fridge. "Or a trip to the store."

"Once you've made your own cheese you'll never go back."

At the tap, Peregrine tops off my water glass and rolls her eyes. "You say that like you aren't lactose intolerant, Mom."

"My stomach does much better with homemade," her mom sniffs. "Caroline, if you'd like to stay, we have plenty."

"Thanks, Mrs. Liu."

Peregrine tugs my arm and we slide through the French doors and into the Lius' amazing backyard. I follow her to the pool, which is off the deck and down a shale-stone path. The Lius' back-yard is basically a palatial summer oasis. Her house is much newer than mine, but the work is all Mr. Liu, a zoologist who also happens to be *really* handy. He did most of this himself over the course of our childhood. Landscaping, the deck, an in-ground pool (he had help with that part), a fire pit.

There's a corner of the pool sitting in a sliver of shade. We park ourselves there and slide our bare feet into the water. It feels glorious.

"Okay, so what's..." She waves a hand toward my damp and disheveled form, concern creasing her eyes. "Going on here?"

Deep breath. "Here's the deal—I *made* a deal. With Alex. He offered to help me learn other sports to help me take my mind off gymnastics and to fill my empty days. I wanted to repay him and came up with a half-baked plan to try to set him up with Sunny. Turns out he's had a crush on her since his freshman year."

Peregrine double blinks. "He *what*? Sunny? Really?"

"Yes. And I just *had* to help because—"

"They'd be perfect."

"Yes. That. Exactly," I say, watching Peregrine's mind moving a mile a minute, telegraphed through body language I know well—scrunched brows, bit lower lip, intense focus. Her shins swirl a pattern through the water as she thinks. "It was sort of a snap deal that turned into a real thing when you guys said you could do dinner."

She nods a little. "That was suspiciously strange but it makes sense now."

"Yeah. Not my smoothest moment but I'm new at this. So here's the thing: I want to get him one interaction for every sport he teaches me. Two down, a summer's worth to go. Sort of. Anyway, it works out to one interaction a week. They can't all be the same. And they can't be weird. And she can't think what you thought—that I have a thing for him. Because I don't."

"Too late, she already thinks that."

Crap. "I thought I cleared that up pretty well at dinner."

"No, you denied it too hard. Like, so hard you were turning red."

Oh God. Was I? My body needs to get with the program. "Well, now you know I don't have a thing for him. And I want to help connect them. I mean, you should've seen the way he looked at me when I figured out about his crush. Dying star. Like he was just going to disappear into the ether."

Peregrine shakes her head. "Who would've thought? I mean, seriously. Why on earth would he be embarrassed about someone knowing that? It's not like he's got no shot in hell. Ninety percent of the population would rate him hot—tall, dark, handsome, cool car, plus he's both a jock *and* a mathlete, for heaven's sake. He's got two of the biggest high school social classes covered without breaking a sweat." My stomach flips as she drives it home. "Oh my God, he's basically the boy version of Sunny."

"Yes. *See?* It's written in the stars. The earth might stop spinning if they never find each other." That's a little dramatic. But still. "Which is why I'm hoping you'll help me make it happen."

Peregrine snags my wrist with hands dry from chalk and rough from bar work. The purple ends of her ponytail split across one shoulder as she nods. "I can absolutely help. Let's go for it."

Oh thank goodness. "Do you think Sunny will notice?"

"Probably. She's not an idiot. But at least if we both try to maneuver her, you won't come off all weird like you have the past week."

"I'd like to avoid weirdness on all fronts."

I bite my lip. "Should we tell her?" That would be a total violation of Alex's trust, even more so than pulling in Peregrine, but it also would make things less weird and more likely successful. Maybe.

Peregrine shakes her head. "No. If she asks, yes. But until then? I think we're best going undercover."

I nod. Sunny is as much of a control freak as the two of us. Gymnast trait, yada yada. But that's exactly why it's *extra delightful* when something *unexpectedly delightful* happens to a control freak. Otherworldly magical. At least from my point of view. Peregrine's too, apparently.

Peregrine drops my hand, her features hardening into the same look she gives the vault as she sprints toward it. Oh, I've missed her. This version of her. Not the drive-by one I get with each passing Sunday. "Okay, so what was your next setup?"

"I—uh." I suddenly realize I was so focused with getting her on board that I have exactly no plan. "Honestly, I hadn't thought about it."

After a beat, her perfectly shaped brows push together. "What's your next sport? Maybe we can combine the two?"

Hmm. The sweat I've worked up gives me an idea. "We'd talked vaguely about running—you know, cross-country is a fall sport and it doesn't take a lot of specialized skill. And won't be hell on my back."

"Okay, well, we're not going to get Sunny to a track without her knowing something is up."

"Or even on a planned route."

"Yeah, it would be quite suspect to invite her over to my house so we can sit on the front lawn and wait for you to jog by."

Uh, yeah, no. Not Emma Woodhouse–esque at all. I glance into the sparkling waters of the pool and dig for a little courage. "Um...do you guys ever hang out on Saturday morning?"

"Sunny and I?"

My nose automatically scrunches. "Yes. And please tell the truth. I can take it."

Peregrine studies her hands. "You noticed we'd been out to dinner together before, didn't you?"

"The extra kimchi and waitress name drop made it sort of obvious."

It takes Peregrine a moment to answer. I wait, stuffing my hands under my thighs and putting all my weight on them until the hard rub of concrete gives me something to focus on besides my heart tossing shattered pieces into the abyss of my pre-dinner gut.

"We decided to go there the night you got hurt...and then we kept going."

Then I realize I got hurt on a Friday. "Why not tonight?"

"Because we had dinner there yesterday." Oh. Right. Maybe we should move our girls' dinners to Friday nights. She pats my leg and focuses hard on the deep cerulean of the middle of the pool. "We need a destination for Saturday morning."

I bite my lip. "Farmers' market?"

I've gone by myself and have been trying to get Dad to go, and even if he hasn't taken me up on that offer, it doesn't mean it's not something other people normally do on a summer Saturday morning.

Peregrine nods. "Oh yeah, that has legs. My parents go every week. Wouldn't be weird to invite her along. Could be *perfect*." Her voice has a conspiratorial tilt.

"So, how about I text Alex and see if he's still up for a run? It's not too far and we can take a water break in the middle at the market—there and back."

Peregrine nods it out. "If we time it right it won't be weird at all and will seem perfectly spontaneous." She blinks at me. "A literal thirst trap."

"Because water and Sunny and meet-cute—I get it."

Out come our phones. We type our messages in tandem. Backup plans forming, depending on the answers.

Hey, run tomorrow morning? Farmers' market and back before Coach Bev tortures you?

There are no immediate typing dots. By my clock, it's 6:03, which likely means Alex has just completed his game with Nat and the boys and is probably being convinced to catch dinner somewhere.

"You aren't telling him this is a *meeting*?" Peregrine asks, peeking over my shoulder.

"I'm already taking his time. I want to do something nice in return."

Peregrine squints toward the middle of the pool. "Wait. Why not just let him do something nice?"

Why does no one get this?

My best friend makes it even more clear that she doesn't understand. "Aren't you sort of cheapening his generosity by forcibly repaying him?"

"Eye for an eye, Peregrine."

"That's literally not what that means, weirdo. Are you sure you don't have the slightest, tiniest, maybe-so-deep-you-don't-recognize-it crush on Alex?"

"I—" My phone vibrates with a text.

Sure thing. Seven okay?

Peregrine reads over my shoulder as I do the math in my head. "That'll put you there before seven thirty. On a weekend. Yikes." Does Sunny like to sleep in? I seriously have no idea even though I've known her for ten years. Ugh. "Alex has tennis lessons later in the morning. Probably needs to get back and fuel up beforehand. Plus we have to build in flirting time."

Peregrine's phone buzzes. Watermelon? Sunny sends an immediate follow-up with five watermelon emojis to emphasize how much she indeed likes the melon.

I snag the phone from Peregrine and start typing. Mom says they have some but it's not really in season yet, so they're only available early. Go when they open and grab coffee too?

Sunny's answer is immediate. Let's do it.

Peregrine and I exchange a small high five. "Let's indeed."

13

Alex appears in my driveway at seven. He's got a fancy handheld water bottle slung snuggly between his knuckles and palm, and yet another version of a KC Royals hat shading his face. His running shoes are actually that—blue Nikes that correspond with his hat. Of course he can make even jogging look effortless.

I shut the door quietly—both Nat and Dad are blessedly still asleep—and skip down the steps. "Someday I'll have to pick *you* up."

He shrugs. "You can drop me off. We'll take a different route back."

Considering that this will leave me with fewer questions from Dad or Nat, should they wake up, I'll take it. I don't know why I want to keep this whole Alex coaching adventure a secret from them. But I do. I just feel icky about it. Exposed somehow. Even telling Peregrine was difficult, and in less than an hour Sunny'll know too. But...I just want to keep it as close to the vest as possible, you know?

I take a running step toward the mouth of our cul-de-sac, but Alex doesn't move, and I realize I've caught him in yet another staring contest with my endless number of gymnastics tank tops.

I present the shirt, stretching it out long. It's one of those holographic prints where the image changes with movement. I make sure to wiggle it around (appropriately) to catch sun. The image flips and twists, and I can't help it—I'm thoroughly enjoying his expression of intense concentration, as much as I can see it with the hat shading his features.

Stumping him with my clothing is probably my actual new favorite sport.

Alex lifts the bill of his hat up a little and squints. "Simone Biles?"

I rock the print from side to side in verification: Simone completing her groundbreaking triple-twisting double back on floor. "You, sir, are correct!"

Dimples flash. "What do I win?"

I drop the shirt and turn to begin to jog. It's already 7:03. Gotta get moving—it's two miles there and I honestly don't know if I'll need a walk break. "The answer is nothing because if Simone's entered, she's already won. There's absolutely no way to beat her so don't even try."

Alex just laughs. Nat would play hurt and claim it's not fair—Alex isn't going to touch that argument with a ten-foot pole. Simone is *the* GOAT. There is literally nothing to disagree about or "well, actually" when it comes to her greatness. This boy is smart enough to realize that.

We fall into a rhythm that's two strides of mine to his one. That's going to be a problem that only my pride can mitigate. And even that might not be enough.

Two miles there. Sunny. Two miles back.

I've got this.

Maybe.

We pass the park a half mile in, and I realize that even though it's much cooler than any other time I've attempted running this summer, I'm sweating bullets because Alex's "slow" jogging pace is well above my natural cadence, stride length or no.

Luckily he's really trying to distract me from the fact that I'm breathing way harder than him by delineating all the merits of running. "In most sports, running is considered punishment, but I love it. It's meditative, calming, the path from novice to advanced is uncomplicated, and it makes you better at any other sport you do," he says. "Basically, the benefit-to-effort ratio is high."

He's right. I know he's right. Practice is all it takes. And this is my third time jogging this week.

"Plus," he says as we hang a right on the main drag toward both the farmers' market and the country club, "running should be pretty gentle exercise when it comes to your particular type of back injury."

I swallow a gulp of air and try very hard to sound just as conversational as he is. "So you're saying running is my backup sport." Another breath. "In case I don't make another type of team," I clarify, mostly so that me sucking wind at this increased pace will sound like a natural pause.

"Don't think of it as a backup—think of it as *background* work." He smiles and I'm starting to wonder if he baked up our entire conversation on the way over. "Makes you stronger, clears your mind."

I smirk as best I can while out of breath. "You've really downed the Kool-Aid, my friend."

"Who needs Kool-Aid when a runner's high is available?" Alex glances over his shoulder. "Come on, pick it up—I can see you've got more speed than that."

"Speed I have. It's the sustained part that's difficult."

"Ah, but that's the easiest thing to change. Get a good base and I'll take you to the track."

I swallow back another gulp of summer-heavy air. "Yep. Okay."

I zero in on all the things he said he likes about running.

Meditative.

Calming.

Going to get easier every time I do it.

Suddenly I can see Northfield Country Club ahead and to the right. Northfield sits on a hill like some high-and-mighty mansion for a modern recluse, given the fancy-yet-medieval iron fence that encircles the property to keep it private but visible in all its glory. The green lawns Alex and Nat help maintain are even and lush despite the drought Dad claims we're in. Sixth-driest summer on record? Not according to Northfield Country Club.

The club takes up an entire city block. Maybe two. It's hard to tell with the curve of the road and all the gated entrances.

And with Northfield blocking our view, we can hear the farmers' market before we can see it. An accordion player who shows up to literally every outdoor festival in town is parked right by the closest entrance. It's as easy to spy his customary top hat as it is to hear his rich notes over the light Saturday morning traffic.

We're almost there.

And I'm happy to report I can actually breathe now. My body has gone from gasping to keep up with Alex's stride to some benevolent form of autopilot, where movement, breath, and sweat are all coordinated. My steps are smooth and strong, and Alex is right: My back doesn't hurt at all.

Maybe it's just that Alex seems to make everything look easy and proximity is one hell of a drug, but I feel like I could do this all day. Or at least all the way home.

Alex slows as we hit the market boundary. I expect him to take a drink, but instead, he grabs a dollar from his pocket and drops it in the accordion player's *secondary* top hat, which is used for change. I imagine the guy wearing both hats like a layer cake and walking home in full jingle.

"See ya this year at Northfield, George?"

The man lights up but doesn't miss a note. "You better believe it, champ!" Of course Alex knows the accordion dude—er, George—who is now motioning to me like he's going to share a juicy secret. "Don't let him fool you, he likes when I call him champ."

Alex laughs. "He's right. It's an honor."

"It is." George winks at me. "The boy's whole goal in defending that tennis title is to make sure he gets to keep the title *I* bestowed for the next year."

"True. Totally true."

A family comes over to request a song, and we both wave at George and enter the market. I take a few steps on my tippy-toes to whisper-ask Alex, "Sooo, does he just follow you around playing 'One Shining Moment' the whole tournament or . . . ?"

Alex sucks down a gulp of water over a bubble of laughter. "That would be something, but no. They put him right next to the champagne tent. Goes over better than you'd imagine."

Nat's sardonic voice pops into my head: Hot night, rich people, free booze—an accordion can only add to the ambience.

We enter the massive parking lot that transforms into the farmers' market every Saturday from April to November. It's all tents and pickup trucks, with wares ranging from goat's milk soap, honey, dried and fresh flowers to tables and tables of gleaming early summer produce, of course.

Tomorrow is the Fourth of July and the vendors are *ready*.

Fat early tomatoes stand in neat rows. The first of summer's sweet corn ears are piled high, tips exposed in a display of perfect worm-free kernels. Zucchini is, well, everywhere, because zucchini. Meanwhile melons are just starting to come in, being doled out one at a time so that customers think they hit a jackpot. All of it mingles with charcoal cook fires of breakfast being made at arm's length.

My stomach growls approvingly.

Alex points his chin to the right, around the serpentine *U*. "I think the fountains are over here."

They are. I know they are. But I still pretend to hunt for them while actually looking for any sign of Peregrine and Sunny. Trying to find two girls shorter than five feet in the heavy early-bird crowd while similarly vertically challenged is not ideal.

Alex and I manage to stay side by side. We're sweaty enough that people give us some space. We end up slow-walking behind a family of five—two coffee-clinging parents with a double stroller and a stubborn preschooler leading the procession.

This is totally fine because it gives me more time to search.

"Are you sure you don't want some of my water?" Alex holds out the fancy running bottle. "I only had a quarter. Not sick either. Promise."

"Antsy to get home?"

"No. Just. It's hot."

I mean, it is. My shorts are sticking to my thighs—the quads I trained for a decade already filled out the fabric pretty well before sweat added to the cling.

A minute later, one of the stroller kids spikes a bag of Cheerios onto the pavement in a fit. The parents are completely overwhelmed, and Alex snaps up the bag before either of them can react. As he hands it to the dad, who is profusely apologizing, I shoot off a quick text to Peregrine.

Here. Headed to the fountains.

We're back to our march-crawl, and Alex is again tipping his bottle my way. He's taken the top off so that in theory I could just pour water straight down my parched throat.

He wiggles it in front of my face. It does look enticing and I realize I probably seem super stubborn, but the fountains are literally at the end of this row. Somewhere over coffee dad's head. "Thank you, but really I need the goal."

Alex shrugs and caps the bottle. "Or the breather."

This makes me crack a smile—and I elbow him.

He squirms away on contact, years of soccer and basketball threaded through the automatic reaction. He pointedly rubs a sturdy oblique. "I'm pretty sure you tagged my kidney."

I laugh but then he fist-bumps my shoulder. "Maybe we need to give soccer a try next. Throwing elbows is crucial to success at any level."

"It's a spring sport," I remind him.

"So? More time to hone your skills before tryouts. You could even join a fall rec league."

True. "I'll think about it. I want to try all the fall sports first, though. Just for sequence's sake."

And to buy me more chances to make the perfection that is Sunny and Alex happen.

As oncoming traffic steps around us, it's hard to miss the fact that more than one woman has tossed us a little smile. A wave or cheerful eyebrows at the children ahead, then a pause and a smile directly at me. Me, not Alex. Smile, eyes glinting up to our faces, then down to our hands, which are not touching, by the way. But the watchers expected them to be.

They think we're on a date.

Somehow, two teenagers simply walking side by side implies first love.

All at once I'm embarrassed, annoyed, and kind of impressed that anyone would think Alex Zavala is walking around with me out of anything else than the kindness of his heart—well, and a relationship forced by a lifetime of parallel lives.

I'm suddenly aware that I've stopped moving forward and shuffle-jog to catch up to Alex when I'm slapped with another realization.

What if Sunny thinks this too? She clearly did during the first interaction. She literally told Peregrine that. How am I going to cover this—

"Caro!"

Crap. Well, I'm about to find out.

14

The family ahead of us peels off at the sight of honey sticks, and there, only ten feet away, are Sunny and Peregrine. Sunny squeals my name, and her arms yawn open for a full-body hug despite my obvious perspiration and the fact that she's balancing both an iced coffee and a droopingly full reusable bag over one shoulder.

"I'm sweaty," I apologize preemptively, but it means nothing because she's already wrapping her arms around me.

"So am I. So is everybody—it's July!" Sunny says as I return her embrace. She smells of vanilla body wash and her half-finished coffee, and she isn't sweaty as much as she's warm—like a cinnamon roll, not a slice of pizza.

"No, like she's *really* sweaty," Peregrine deadpans over Sunny's shoulder before pointedly asking, "Did you guys run here or what?" She slips her phone in the back pocket of her jean shorts while everyone but me is somewhat distracted—I bet if I had my phone out and available at this very moment, it would've shown her responding to me.

That's when Sunny seems to notice Alex. I mean how can you miss him? Maybe this'll take more work than Peregrine or I think.

"Oh, hey," Sunny says by way of greeting. She takes a step

back, her thick lashes flicking as she takes in my shoes, shorts, tank top. "Yeah, did you guys really run?" She plucks the bottom of my shirt. "Love that tank on you."

I nod in answer to her running question and curtsy. "Aw, thanks, Sun. Simone makes everyone look good."

"True that," Sunny confirms. "Alex, is this your handiwork?" She gestures to my general aura of perspiration. "I didn't think anyone could get Caroline to run other than Olga on a tear. You must be talented."

"Or a masochist because running is terrible," Peregrine supplies.

"This was actually *my* idea and Alex was *nice* enough to come with me." I emphasize *nice* in hopes that Peregrine might actually help me here instead of insinuate that our leading man conned me into some sort of early-morning Ironman.

"That *is* nice," Sunny says, and she shields her eyes for a second to really look at Alex. "And so now you run back?"

"Um, yep, it's an out-and-back route. Two miles, water, two miles." He shakes his water bottle. "We're here for the fountains."

"Oh, why didn't you say so? They're this way," Sunny directs helpfully, turning on a dime. She glances back at Alex, working her way down from his face to his exposed biceps to the water bottle in his grip. "But don't you have water in that thing? I swear I hear it sloshing."

Oh no, we can't have her thinking Alex is rude. "Let it be known Alex gallantly offered me water, like the gentleman he is, but I declined."

Peregrine's mouth twitches. "And you didn't bring your own because you just wanted to make your morning run experience more terrible without water?"

I scoff. "It wasn't terrible. It's *meditative* and stuff," I insist, using

Alex's promotional materials. "Or it will be, once I'm used to it. I'm just *new*. I needed a goal. The water fountains are my goal." I pointedly jog the last few steps there like I'm Rocky chugging up the stairs in Philly or whatever.

As I'm gulping down several sips of water, Alex gamely attempts small talk. "So what's in the bag?" he asks Sunny.

"Baby watermelon!" Sunny scoops it out and presents it in all its rare early-summer glory. "Snagged the last one from the guy over by the breakfast burritos."

"Score," Alex says politely, though we both totally saw other melons as we made our way through the market. "Worth coming early for something like that."

"It was Peregrine's idea. I totally wanted to invite you, Caro, but Peregrine said you had plans. I had no idea *running* was said plan." There's a hint of sorrow in Sunny's voice. "Since when are you running?"

I wipe water from my mouth. "This is my third time."

"Were you here last Saturday? Wait, will you be here next Saturday?" Sunny's voice goes high with possibility. "We could actually *purposely* meet up next time. I'd wait on my coffee if you wanted to meet us and get some after, Caro." She turns to Alex. "And you're invited too, of course, Alex. For melons and coffee and general girl stuff. We won't exclude you. We're not like that."

I try not to sear an answer onto Alex's cheekbone because *yes* we're doing this next weekend.

"Or," Peregrine offers, tipping her iced-coffee-hold-the-ice straw at him, "if you want to run away screaming, at least you already have the shoes for it."

Peregrine, WTF? We don't want to give him wiggle room to run away from time with Sunny.

Alex laughs. "I would love to do all of that, but Saturdays are practice days for me. Nine to two." He gestures to his watch. "I've got to run home and grab my gear."

Because I can't resist a good pun, I school my face and tap my temple. *"Run home. I see what you did there."*

Alex finger-guns me. We all laugh but I'm suddenly feeling guilty about Alex shoehorning in a run with me before *hours* of practice. Gah, why couldn't I have figured out another way to do this—

Sunny cuts off my spiraling train of thought with a cuff to the wrist and squeeze. "Hey, wait, how about the lake house tomorrow instead of our usual movie?" I can tell that she's trying to atone for not inviting me to the farmers' market, even though it wasn't a problem at all. She and I could probably just run overcompensating guilt circles around each other forever. "Fun before fireworks. Paddle boarding and this little watermelon?" As she taps her bottomed-out shoulder bag, Sunny's eyes flick to Alex. "I mean, unless you have plans?"

I nearly leap at her. "I'd love to!"

Peregrine breaks into a genuine smile that points to the fact that she did not plant this field trip in Sunny's brain. "Yeah, awesome idea."

Sunny smooths a nonexistent flyaway off her face. "Alex, you could come too, if you want. The same nonexclusionary terms apply. We're all friends here."

I glance pointedly at Alex and this amazing second chance that's even better than the first Sunny suggestion. Like my family, his usually watches the city fireworks from the lawn in the park, but maybe he doesn't have plans beforehand. I know I don't—Dad has a scheduled shift treating people making unsafe decisions with their fireworks stashes before dark.

But then he glances down and putzes with the lip of his water bottle before meeting her face-to-face. "That's super nice of you, Sunny, but I've got a family thing."

Gahhhh. I don't think he's lying.

Sunny repositions the bag on her shoulder. "Of course." Her attention flicks to me and Peregrine. "But you two are sure you're good?"

I nod and Peregrine follows suit. I'm about to make a joke about how Nat will probably invite himself—a last-ditch effort to get Alex to change his mind—when Alex playfully slugs my shoulder. "You know, I've got to go so Coach Bev doesn't roast me alive, but Caro, stay with your friends. Don't let my schedule keep you from hanging out."

Sunny waves him off, the melon bag slapping her hip. "Nonsense, we can share Caro. We'll see her tomorrow." She glances between us. Before I can protest or engage Peregrine somehow to keep this going, Sunny has hooked her arm in Peregrine's and is dragging her in the direction of the dude who makes goat's milk soap. "She's all yours, Alex."

It takes about a mile for Alex to say something. We make the curve onto the street that leads to our neighborhood. The same one where he stopped me on the sidewalk and pitched the idea of coaching.

"You totally planned that, didn't you?"

Aw, shit. "Was it that obvious?"

Alex does me a favor and doesn't double over in laughter mid-stride, but it's hard to miss his dimple flash as he bites it down. "So much so, I'm pretty sure Peregrine knows."

Double shit. I really, really don't want Alex to know that Peregrine knows. I just stare at the sidewalk in front of me. "She's smart."

"So is Sunny."

"Yes she is. But she also isn't nearly as naturally suspicious as Peregrine."

The rosebushes that separate our little pocket park from the street loom ahead. Though it's not even eight in the morning, the squeals of children already echo from the playground on the far side from the basketball court.

Alex takes a sip of water from his bottle and then holds it out for me, the little slip of fabric already off his knuckles, the bottle free and unattached and waiting just for me.

God, it's tempting.

"Don't be a martyr. You've just confirmed you lied the first time about why you wouldn't take any."

I roll my eyes as a joke, but then accept the bottle. I pull off the top, slow my stride to a shuffle-step, and manage to tip water in my mouth without dousing my whole face. One gulp and I'm a whole new girl. "Thanks."

Alex nods as I hand it back to him. He takes another sip of his own, then clears his throat. "You could've told me that's why you wanted to stop at the market."

"I owe you."

Alex completely stops running. "Caro."

I slow to a walk and turn around. Alex is standing there, hands on his hips—well, one hand, and one hand full of water bottle. He looks . . . put out?

"I just knew they might be at the market. One simple interaction. As promised." His expression doesn't budge, so I add, a little more forcefully than necessary, "Why didn't you accept either invite? I didn't plan that! That was all Sunny. I had nothing to do with that."

"Caro," he repeats, advancing. We're nearly toe to toe, and even though I've been here before and recently, I'm struck by his size—the solidity of him, yet the warmth both in demeanor and in actuality. It's like standing next to a marble statue you know is stuffed with cinnamon rolls. "I would've had a great time this morning with or without a meeting."

"Okay...why do I feel a 'but' headed out of the gate?"

"*But* I want you to tell me if your intent is a run-in with Sunny."

Ugh, Peregrine's concern from last night reverberates through my mind. *You aren't telling him this is a meeting?* My voice is strange in my ears. "I wanted to surprise you...or not let you down." I add the last part even though he's already announced that letdowns are not possible.

"Caro." He takes a deep breath and I realize Alex is searching for words. Maybe the heat's gotten to him more than me. On closer inspection he's actually red and sweating. "I came on this run because I wanted to spend time with you, not because I thought I'd get a chance meeting with Sunny."

That didn't exactly cross my mind. I mean. "Oh."

"I appreciate your efforts," he continues, batting at a runaway tear of sweat sliding down his cheek. He doesn't break eye contact. "But...I don't want you to think I'm only hanging out with you so you'll work your..."

"Magic?" I grin.

"I...uh, yeah, but no."

"Okay, maybe that last meeting wasn't *magic* because Sunny

sent us off like we were a *thing*, but I promise I can make it up to you."

He squeezes his eyes shut and his head drops back so far his hat nearly falls off. "Caro."

"Seriously. I'll be better than Emma Woodhouse." *Emma* is probably not his cup of tea, book, or movie. And well, she's actually terrible at setting people up except that one time. "Okay, wait, no. I'll be as good as Angelica Schuyler with Eliza and Hamilton." I *know* he gets that reference. And her setup was successful. "I'll—"

"Caroline."

I stop. I wait.

He seems relieved. "I appreciate what you're trying to do. But I also want to know that *you* want to hang out with *me*, not for a setup."

"But—but..." I'm stammering and my mouth is dry and I try to will my tongue to move in a useful way. "But we're running because you're coaching me."

Alex punches out an exasperated sigh. "Yes, but I offered to coach you because I *like* hanging out with you and helping you find a new sport to love, not because I thought I'd get something out of it." *Oh.* "It's different."

He seems so desperate for me to understand. I suppose those real human feelings I saw last week run deep and are more complicated than I thought. God, I'm dense—or maybe I've just had a lifetime of forcing difficult things into perfection. Hearts and people are quite a bit different from bending gravity and timing.

I stick my hands out front to assure him I mean no harm. "I'll tell you next time. I'm so sorry."

Alex adjusts his ball cap and tugs his sweat-drenched tank

away from where it was outlining his abs. Not that I noticed. "Thank you."

I nod and Alex starts walking again, long strides pointed past the park and toward my house. Even though I was supposed to drop him off—but I don't point that out. Now's not the time.

The sidewalk is just big enough for both of us, and there's a cross-breeze going this direction that I didn't notice earlier. It makes eighty-two degrees feel like maybe seventy-nine. Glorious in comparison.

"So did you like it?" He nods toward the path ahead. "Running?"

With you, yes. But I can't say that because it'll come out all wrong and I can't deal with another misunderstanding. What I mean is, I think I like running with people more than alone—it makes the time fly. But I don't know if that's true, or if it really is that Alex makes this fun in a way I can't replicate with anyone else.

So instead, I tighten my sagging ponytail and choose my words carefully. "I can see how it can be all the things you say it is with practice."

"But?"

"Not going to lie, I'm super happy to be almost done."

Alex palms my shoulder. "All right, let's finish it off."

He launches into a jog, and I chase after him.

15

Sunny's lake house Fourth of July invite ends up being a logistics problem.

Peregrine and I are still months away from our drivers' licenses, and Sunny, who would typically cart us the hour to Lake Dabinawa, will already be there. Turns out her parents had plans for a lake weekend well before Peregrine and I invented our farmers' market shenanigans. Of course, Sunny offered to drive in to get us and drive back, but there's no way we're putting nearly four hours of windshield time on her across the whole day. So Sunny extends her non-exclusionary hangout policy beyond Alex to Nat and Artemis.

Immediately thereafter, Peregrine shot a smirking emoji to our group thread. We'll make Artemis and Nat arm wrestle for the chance to take us.

I added a cry-laugh emoji. I mean, we know who'll win that one.

Yeah, Nat. Because Artemis isn't playing. She'll demand gas money and Nat will actually want to go to work on his tan.

In truth, we were both wrong.

Our siblings each wanted to get in on the lake day action, and Nat offered to drive all of us in his Jeep. "All" as in all four of us.

"Are you sure you want to do this?" I ask him as my hand hovers over the door handle, waiting for him to unlock it.

"Why wouldn't I?"

Nat has been to Sunny's lake house birthday the last couple of summers, but I always assumed it was for the food, because Sunny's dad can grill like no other. Today's gathering will be much simpler—and likely vegetarian because that's how the Chavez family rolls when not entertaining a horde. And so, well, yeah. "Uh, because you have places to be. Things to do. Layups to master."

"First of all, my layup is technically perfect and therefore your uninformed eye can shove it," Nat says as the doors unlock and we slide in on the steaming upholstery. "And second, do you see a lake around here where I can lie out and enjoy the watery breezes?"

I squint at him as I lock in my seat belt. It's possible he enjoyed said breezes as much as the food, but still. I wonder if Alex has told him about our deal and if he's planning to eavesdrop. But I don't want to give Alex away, so my angle becomes his overt kindness in driving us. "This is suspect."

"No, it's *suspect* that Artemis wants to come too. She has a pool in her own backyard."

"Okay, but a pool is not a lake...?"

"Close enough that there's no reason she'd need to come to a lake where she'd have to spend hours with her little sister and her friends." He waggles his eyebrows and I suddenly know where this is going. "*Unless* she has an ulterior motive, like *seeing me*."

My eyes roll so hard I think they might fall out of my head. "I hope she brings a pint of rotten tomatoes to toss at you."

"She's the type who would."

Artemis might actually live up to her violent namesake if he pulls the same shit with her that he does with Liv Rodinsky. I mean, she's majoring in business and accounting, and if she didn't suffer fools before, she definitely won't after a year of studying for a career defeating corporate bro-schmoes. I wouldn't put anything past her.

We arrive at the Lius' place, and Nat taps three cheery times on the horn. Peregrine and Artemis emerge with twin waves.

"In the back with you, Caro."

"Huh, what?"

"In the back. You and Peregrine. I want to quiz Artemis on college life."

Um. What? "You could do that at the lake."

"Just get in the back."

I would fight him but the girls are fast approaching. Instead, I exit and hold the door open. "Nat says college girls in the front, high school girls in the back."

Nat puts on his best grin from the driver's seat.

To my surprise, Artemis doesn't hesitate. "Okay."

Peregrine's upper lip curls and her eyes narrow. "Okay? He just made you sound like some sort of 1960s stereotype." She makes her best Beatle-mania face. "*College girl.*"

Okay, I'm the one who made her sound like a stereotype, but I'm still not going to save him.

Artemis shrugs and slides in. She answers her sister but is looking at Nat. "It gets curvy as we approach the lake, and I bet Nat takes curves like he's on the autobahn. I'm less likely to get motion sickness in the front, and if I do, he'll be the one who pays."

And we're off to the races.

119

Sunny's family lake house is on Lake Dabinawa, about an hour west of the city. I've been to it several times, but always for her end-of-summer birthday bash. Never just as a one-off, hey, let's soak and sunbathe and gossip all day.

It's an honest-to-God log cabin (it's been in her family a long time) surrounded now by properties that could eat it for lunch and use the remaining splinters to clean its teeth. But the thing is, no one would let that happen because, like Sunny herself, this little house literally makes everything brighter. Red geraniums call out an invitation from window boxes, and twinkle lights stand at the ready for nighttime along the roofline and in the trees.

Sunny greets us and we wave hello to her parents, who are inside, making what will most likely be a delicious lunch.

"Sunny, can we take the canoe?" Nat asks, gesturing to Artemis as we hike around the side of the house. Behind the cabin there's a rambling deck with stairs to the lake and dock, and between the two winds a dirt path that dead-ends in a patchwork garden Sunny's mom maintains with seemingly just her fairy spirit and a supremely green thumb. It's a smorgasbord of sun-loving plants too wild and varied for someone like me to name. I only know the obvious—in this case, the giant green stalks of soon-to-be sunflowers. They ladder toward the sky, ready to open in a few weeks. Some are already taller than all of us but Nat.

I'm sure he'd be proud of this if he noticed the flower stalks at all, but he's having too good a time giving Artemis shit.

And she's taking it. Like, legitimately laughing and giving it right back in a way I haven't witnessed anyone else do with my brother. She doesn't balk at the canoe idea and it's all just bizarre.

"Sure. I thought we could do some yoga on the paddle boards anyway."

"Sweet." The pair of them angle off toward where the canoe is tethered and Peregrine and I stop walking almost at the exact same time.

"Something smells questionable," I whisper, pointedly looking the other direction in case either of them turns around.

"That's for sure," Peregrine agrees. She isn't even pretending not to watch. The look on her face would split my brother's skull in two if he weren't the most hard-headed individual in the universe. "They have literally said like two words to each other the last four years, despite all the gymnastics meets. And now they're boarding that tiny canoe like they do this every Sunday."

Okay, but there is the matter of their participation on the Northland cheer squad ruining that particular sisterly hyperbole from Peregrine, but still…it's not normal behavior from them. She's right. But it's to our advantage. Artemis might dunk him in the lake, but at least Nat'll be distracted enough not to crash any conversation Peregrine and I can start about Alex.

I grab Peregrine's hand and we jog to catch up with Sunny, who is hauling the stand-up paddle boards out from their careful storage under the cabin's deck.

"I mean," I say, "he has a history of liking brunettes and she *is* laughing at his jokes."

Peregrine tugs on her purple-tinged black ponytail and then dabs the same hand on Sunny's raven curlicue bun. "Hear that, Sun? If we laugh in Nat's vicinity, we're screwed."

I drop my face into my hands. "Can we not use the word *screwed* in reference to my brother, even if it's in the negative sense?"

"Not a problem," Sunny says, and I unpeel my hands to look at her. She thrusts a board and paddle at me. "Because we shouldn't be talking about Nat—we should be talking about *you* and Alex Zavala."

I would run but even as strong as I am, I'm too short to properly haul the board at a hasty pace. So I turn toward the dock as if walking away from this conversation. Because I am. Until I eradicate this line of thought from Sunny's adorable head, there's no way she's going to let the Angelica Schuyler vibes work. "Ugh. Can we not?" I scramble for a way to turn this into discussing *her* potential with Alex without outing his interest in her, and I stomp down the hill because it seems easier to navigate than the extremely steep stairs while I carry the board.

Sunny is used to hauling the paddle boards and speeds up effortlessly to be right in my sight line with a perfectly arched brow. "You brought this on yourself when you got caught."

Caught? Oh. Ohhhh.

"I wouldn't be asking *again* about Alex Zavala at all if you hadn't decided to get all sweaty with him on a Saturday morning." Sunny's eyes twinkle as we hit the wood planks of the dock. "You did say the running was your idea, did you not? Like you'd just casually go running for no reason at all. The boy is proof of your ulterior motive in sweat-wicking fabric and Nikes."

I secure my ankle leash, check my life vest, and push my board into the water, giving Peregrine time to jump in and help me here. Instead, my wait-and-hope strategy for my bestie dies on the vine as Sunny glides into the water and drags her into the conversation as a witness for the prosecution. "Per, help me out here. Have you ever seen Caroline around a boy so frequently in her life? Purposefully—and not Nat or because she's with Nat."

Peregrine's eyes flick to mine as she steadies herself on her board. I really hope she helps me out way more than she did at the farmers' market. "Er, no."

Come on, P.

"But," she says, squinting at Sunny, who is now somehow in front of us, leading us toward a current that will work in our favor and keep us away from where motorboats are allowed. Safety first. "We do have to factor in the fact that we want our girl Caroline out there, spreading her wings and doing new things, since she can't be with us."

There we go. I mean, it sucks but it's true. "I have a lot of time on my hands to try new things," I add. More truth.

Sunny executes a turn on her board and the two of us copy her as best as we can. There's a cove a little ways down and I'm pretty sure that's our destination. The wind picks up, which means that to continue our conversation, Sunny has to half yell across the water. "Are you doing any other *new* things with your new six-foot-five BFF?"

Oh. God. Seriously, this cannot keep trending this way.

"No," I say, more measured than I feel. A pointed attack might be the only way to actually get her to believe me. Or at least dig me out of this conversation. "Why are you suspicious anyway, Sunny? That's Peregrine's job. You're the mom."

That's her role—in the gym originally, but outside of it too with the two of us.

"Moms *are* suspicious."

"Not my mom," I squeak.

"Moms who don't parent over text from a boardroom in another country *are* suspicious," Sunny clarifies, waving things off. "And so is Peregrine. She made that clear when you rolled up to practice with him...though now..." Sunny turns around and looks between us. I find myself very interested in the angle of my paddle. Peregrine messes with her ponytail again. Sunny isn't buying either one of us. "What's going on here, girls?"

For a beat we're both silent. Still looking away. Making it worse. Sunny stops paddling and stares us down like Olga does when the team's ready to move on to something new but someone is still mid-conversation and oblivious.

Peregrine is the first to break it up. "Caroline is learning to be something other than a gymnast."

A smirk pulls at the corners of Sunny's mouth. "A girlfriend?"

"No!" I insist. "An athlete! I'm learning to put my athletic talents to good use elsewhere."

As my cheeks flame, Peregrine lays it out with punctuated precision. "Sun, she needs something to do. Alex offered to coach her in other sports."

I hold my breath.

"Why didn't you say so?" Sunny reads my puffed-out cheeks and pleading expression. "Did you think we'd be upset? Like you're cheating on us?"

"No, no, it's just that it's so new. It's like I still have the training wheels on. Or something."

Struggling in private with something new is one thing. Admitting it to my friends or family—especially Dad and Nat—is just... I knew exactly what I was doing for the past ten years, even when I was trying something new. Now I don't know what I'm doing no matter what I try. Everything is a new frontier. If Alex were in my brain he'd probably come up with some *Star Trek* joke again.

"That's so nice of him," Sunny says, turning around for a second to pick up speed.

The cove is ahead and appears empty. We paddle for a minute or so before Sunny gives it up and turns around again, in full squint and not from the high morning sun. "Are we sure he doesn't want more? I mean, coaching you has to be time-consuming, right?"

I nod. "Well, yeah."

"*Well, yeah*, he wants more, or *well, yeah*, it takes time? Or both? Please tell me you're not trading him, *you know*, to learn how to hit a softball or something."

You know—sex. I swear my ears are bleeding. "God, no, what?"

Sunny is unmoved. "As gym mom, I have to ask."

"No!" I shake my head so hard my balance falters, which is saying something given my bouquet of beam titles. "Nothing untoward is going on."

"Then why are you blushing?" She shoots a raised brow at Peregrine. "Why is she blushing? And using words like 'untoward'?" Sunny nearly stands up courtroom-style and points an accusatory finger. "Something is going on! And both of you are in on it!"

We've entered the mouth of the cove, and now we're basically cornered.

Sunny fixes her stance on her board and glares us down, grinning at our silence. "Spill."

This is on me. Gripping my paddle for support, I force myself to look deep into Sunny's dark eyes. Wishing we were close enough that I could grab her hand, I take a steadying breath and complete my betrayal of my brother's best friend.

"Alex Zavala has a crush on you, Sunny."

16

Once the truth of Alex's heart is out in the July air, I swear I can't breathe. Not daring to inhale, exhale, or even blink, I just stare at Sunny as she processes a secret I can't take back.

And I really, really hope it's worth it.

As we float into the body of the cove, Sunny's face goes almost entirely blank like one of those gifs where a character is thinking so hard numbers and equations swirl in the ether around their head. "A crush? On me?"

I nod. "Since freshman year. I mean, your sophomore year." Then I clarify. "Mathletics."

The invisible mental equations fall into the green-blue lake water beneath our boards. "Seriously?"

"Yes."

In the pause that follows, I'm fairly certain Sunny and I are in a race to see who can blush the most. Her tan skin flushes a perfect sweeping rose, while I'm likely imitating a lobster mid-boil.

Sunny sinks to her board and dangles her feet in the water. Peregrine and I silently follow suit, our paddles slung across our laps. Sunny's attention swings to Peregrine, eyes narrowing. "You knew this too?"

Peregrine tips her head at a mischievous angle. "You think I got the idea *on my own* to steer you toward the farmers' market when I've never done that before?"

Sunny's lips drop open. At first I think it's a surprise to her that the two of us could conspire in such a way, but then I realize she's actually horrified. "Don't tell me Alex knew I'd be there."

"He didn't," I rush in to say, a little too loud and hard. "And, for what it's worth, he called me out on it on the run home. He knew it was a total setup."

A light springs on over Sunny's head. "You're setting me up?"

"Yes. Poorly."

"Why?" Sunny almost looks offended. She actually manages to get her hands on both hips and not tip her paddle straight into the water.

"Because . . . you're a catch and deserve a boyfriend?" Peregrine answers, *Jeopardy!* style.

"You've always taken good care of us," I add. Gah, why didn't I practice this yesterday? "You haven't dated since, what, last summer? And you've got to admit, Alex fits your type based on your last guy—tall, dark, handsome, athletic, all that."

Peregrine nods. We both remember football dude Timmy Chow picking Sunny up at practice on Fridays before she had a car of her own.

"You *mother* us," Peregrine says more gently than I expect, "but that doesn't mean we can't take care of you."

Sunny presses her face to her hands.

My stomach is dangling somewhere near my ankles. I'm never going to set up anyone ever again. I've learned my lesson. "Sun, I'm sorry. I thought it would be good for you and had it all worked out in my head, and that's not fair to you or Alex and—"

"It's just—I'm actually..."

Sunny is never one to be at a loss for words—that's possibly the only thing she and Nat have in common. "You're actually...?" Peregrine prompts her, leaning in like she can will the words from Sunny's throat.

Our senior sister suddenly looks so much younger as she blinks through her thoughts and wets her lips. Deep breath. "I'm actually worried having a boyfriend would be a problem?"

Peregrine squints at her. "A problem as in someone else would openly adore you and kiss you on the mouth?"

"That...would be a good problem," I venture. Because, well, unless we count the hot minute I "dated" Clay Washington in seventh grade, this is not a problem I know much about.

"I can only focus on so much." All the light that is Sunny is narrowed in on getting these words right—the same tunnel vision she gets staring down a dismount. I'm not sure she even realizes she's doing it. "I quit high school to focus on gymnastics. I quit seeing my friends, broke up with Tim. Quit going to dances, doing extracurricular stuff—mathletics, debate, student council—to focus on gymnastics." She switches into her spot-on Olga impression: "Trade your now for your future and you'll never regret it."

We're silent. Not even nodding.

Sunny presses her hands to her forehead, shimmery nail polish static. "It seemed like the right decision, and it got results—a ticket to nationals twice over, top twenty placement, a spot on the national team, a scholarship offer. I got that by focusing on gymnastics and stripping away everything else." Her hands drop. "Adding anything back in that pulls focus? I worry that I'll be off the rails before I finish the season."

The season—senior season, which leads up to UCLA. And maybe an international trip with the national team, but definitely not if she spins out of control.

Peregrine's current expression could grind every diamond ring in existence to pulp. "Alex is great, but I think you're giving him or *any* boy/girl/person too much credit. Sun, *you* are the reason you were able to accomplish all those things."

Sunny squeezes her eyes shut and scrunches up her nose. "Yeah, but...if I have my attention divided..."

"Then you're *human*, Sunny." I wedge my board as close to hers as I can get and put my hand on her arm. "There's nothing written in our genetic code that says we have to be alone to do great things."

Peregrine follows my lead and pulls up on Sunny's other side. She gets her hand on Sunny's wrist and now we have her sandwiched with intentions. "We've seen the movies, read the books, been indoctrinated with the idea that love is so engrossing it's worth everything. But if dating someone distracts you from the biggest things in your life, then you're with the wrong person. Love and friendship should enhance what's already there, not kill it. That's the definition of toxic."

I'm nodding super hard and piggyback off Peregrine's amazing breakdown. "The point is that we're *your friends*. We want you to succeed. We want you to be happy on *all* levels. You don't need to head into your senior year alone to make your dreams come true. If you want to date, we will absolutely warn you if we see any signs that any sort of relationship has distracted you from your gymnastics goals."

"Boy. Girl. They. Anyone. Nail polish. Baby watermelons.

Cinnamon Orbit. Whatever. Any relationship that's toxic goes." Peregrine makes a slicing motion across her throat.

Sunny coughs out a sad laugh. The almost-noon sun bathes her in perfect light between the clouds. After a moment, she swallows and looks between us. "And you *both* think Alex Zavala might be a good start?"

I nod viciously. "I've known him since I was in diapers. I would never set you up with anyone who didn't check all the best boxes. Plus, I have literal verbal confirmation that he has had a crush on you lingering under his cool exterior for the past two years."

Sunny's white teeth flash between lips that are totally curling at the corners. "You make it sound like an infection."

"Okay, we've all come to terms with the fact that my metaphor capacity is currently terrible," I admit. "But that doesn't mean I'm wrong."

"Cosigned," Peregrine adds. "Also, I concur that Alex is a stand-up guy, *if* you're interested. Neat, friendly, built like a tank with dimples, good family, never smarmy, holds down a job so he can maintain a car he paid for with his own damn money." My stomach squelches as I have the stunning realization that Peregrine has not only noticed this but cataloged it. And she's still going. "Not to mention he offered to help out Caroline with finding new sports without ever expecting anything in return. Stand. Up. Guy." Then she adds, "He had nothing to do with the setup except for the fact that he was brave enough to tell Caroline the truth about how he felt."

Sunny is silent. After a solid moment, her chin dips toward me and the volume of her voice lowers with it. It seems now that she's holding my hands more than I'm holding hers.

"Caroline, please be honest with me. Are you sure you're not interested in Alex?"

My gut trembles. "Sunny, he likes *you*."

Sunny reads my face longer than is comfortable. "I'll think about it."

17

When we make it back to the cabin, lunch is ready and waiting. The whole spread smells of charcoal and sunshine. We have our pick of perfectly cooked veggie burgers and whole-grain buns, sweet corn, the farmers' market watermelon, mixed berries, and a salad of roasted summer delights: red peppers, onions, pineapple, cherry tomatoes.

The whole thing is vegetarian yet Nat doesn't complain a lick, just makes all the right noises of thanks and piles his plate with a bite of literally everything. Bizarre, yes—Nat's charm button is stuck in the *on* position today and I have no idea why, but it's also causing him to be polite, so awesome.

Artemis asks if it's all right if they eat on the dock and Sunny says sure, and then she and Nat leave us be, trading the shady deck for the full sun of the dock. Sunny's parents split too, for where I'm not sure, and it's the three of us girls on the deck. Alone. Again.

I crack open a LimonCello LaCroix and squint toward the dock. "Okay, yeah, everyone totally thinks we stink."

"No," Sunny says, cracking open her own drink and dropping into a seat at the umbrella-covered café table, "they think we're just going to talk about boys and don't want to hear it."

Peregrine glances across the table to me, a hundred percent mischievous. "I know a boy we can talk about."

Sunny picks just that moment to take a *very long pull* from her KeyLime LaCroix.

And *just* when I'm about to broach the subject of Alex again, a peal of laughter and a splash come from the dock. I stand for a better look, and so do the other girls—I mean, we're all very petite—and we squint over the railing and through the trees toward the dock, where my brother is climbing out of the water. Artemis is laughing over her plate. I can't tell if she actually pushed him in like I predicted or if he dunked himself for entertainment's value. But of course, my brother is undeterred by his sopping-wet state, and predictably peels off his shirt, discards it on the planks, and *feeds her* a strawberry from his plate.

"Oh dear God, what the hell." Peregrine literally lowers her sunglasses to make sure she's seeing it right. "Are college boys really that bad, or is Nat suddenly not annoying?"

"A little of column *A* and a little of column *B*?" Sunny guesses.

"Nat's always annoying, but maybe his brand of annoying is now cute?" I tap Peregrine's arm. "You heard them in the car—they were giving each other shit the whole time. It's like the teenage equivalent of boys chasing girls around the playground. They torment because their hormones tell them to. They flirted the whole way. And probably during that whole canoe ride. And definitely now because my brother is probably intentionally shirtless."

"That is totally intentional," Sunny deadpans, making me laugh. But then the girl nearly takes my head off with a stunning side-eye. "Caroline Kepler, did you set them up?" My lips drop open to answer, but whatever I was going to say flames up with her searing facial expression. "Like, to prove you have some sort of latent gift for matchmaking?"

Peregrine joins the assault with a professional-grade head tilt. "If you say yes, you're an extremely underhanded evil genius because even I didn't know."

"I'm not evil, and I'm just as surprised as you are!" I fling a hand out toward Nat and Artemis. "Whatever the hell that is I will confirm is one hundred percent organic from my point of view." I try to throw a decent side-eye right back at both of them and completely fail. "Unless Peregrine orchestrated the whole thing."

Peregrine coughs out a rough laugh. "If you think Artemis would ever take a single suggestion from me, you fell on your head one too many times at Balan's." Then, as beautifully as she executes a salto transition from the high bar to the low, Peregrine pivots back to Alex. "Okay, pulling it back to *where we were*—Sunny, now that we're all situated and alone *and* you've had time to think about it: Do you have questions for Caroline about Alex?"

Sunny's side-eye flickers and her lips press together.

"Like about how well she knows him really? Or about his own sports goals?" Peregrine suggests forcefully. "Or maybe you want to do a lightning round of his faves to check compatibility—favorite color, favorite band, favorite food, all the favorites?"

Sunny pinches the bridge of her nose. Shovels the remains of her lunch around her plate. Tears the pop-top off her fizzy water. Peregrine and I watch patiently, applying pressure precisely by saying exactly nothing. She is better than us at nearly everything, but our powers combined in this way can bend even Sunny.

"A lightning round is not necessary." Her eyes flick open. "I . . . I just don't want to make a mistake."

Peregrine hauls her posture from slouching to pin straight. "There's absolutely no need to rehash the same conversation we had in the cove. Adding romance into a life that's successful on every other level isn't a distraction—it's *balancing*."

I nod. "And you know what? You don't have to add it to the scales if you don't want to. Going to dinner once isn't going to be a speed bump in your big senior year. A dinner date isn't a lifetime commitment. Heck, you don't even have to make it to the actual meal if the small talk sucks. It won't, but if it does, I'll personally borrow Nat's Jeep and pick you up myself."

"Or you could meet him there and drive your own self away when you're ready," Peregrine adds. This is true. And probably a better idea than me violating the terms of my driver's permit.

"Bonus, if you don't like him, you are literally under no obligation to see him again." My smile freezes as my heart speeds up. "You don't work together, don't live next door to each other, don't have five classes together at Northland. You can see if he's right for you and walk away if you want to."

"You both are really making it sound like it won't work out."

"Noooo." I shake my head, jumping in maybe too quickly. "We're just trying to stress your personal choice in the matter, because it's important, especially given your oft-stated reasons for concern."

Peregrine nods, and we resume our double-barreled patient stare. Sunny's eyes flick down to her plate, then away to the lake, where Artemis and Nat are either laughing or finally fighting for real—there's no in between.

After about a minute, Sunny draws in a deep breath. "Send him my number."

18

"Chicken wings are tiny morsels of genetically engineered perfection," Nat announces through spice-stained lips before discarding the bony remains of yet another tiny drumette onto a teetering pile of bird appendages.

It is seriously ridiculous how much this boy can eat, especially considering how little of it contains fiber to move things along. I'm not a doctor but eventually that's going to be a problem.

"Incorrect, my son," Dad says, cracking open his second beer of the holiday. He's a little loopy from the double whammy of a twelve-hour shift and putting the finishing touches on the dinner now plated before us under the shade of the big oak that leans over our deck. "The chicken wing is the perfectly engineered vehicle for the Kepler family spice blend."

"Jimmy, while I do commend you for this meal," Olga starts over her plate, which is ninety percent the salad I made and three afterthought chicken wings, "I do not understand the American obsession with spices. Anyone can spice something properly."

Nat lifts a brow. "Olga, have you met most Americans? We under-season everything, add salt to overcompensate, and then

136

die of hypertension because we never learned how damn good smoked paprika is on its own."

"What even is this conversation?" I hold up a hand over my plate, which looks very much like my former coach's, because, well, I'm me. "Olga, you know this is literally the only meal Dad can make consistently, and I could replace Nat's personal frozen pizzas with cheese-covered cardboard for a week and he wouldn't notice. They are not experts on food, American or otherwise. All they know is how to eat it." I catch Nat with a sharp look. "Or demolish it."

"Hey, I ate actual vegetables for lunch today," Nat says, aiming a wing glistening with fatty juices at me. What is with him and food as pointing aids? "I earned these."

Good God. "Oh come on, you only forced down those vegetables to look good to a certain soon-to-be college sophomore."

Olga catches my drift faster than Nat can deflect it. "Artemis came with you girls today?"

"Not only did she come with us, but she and Nat hung out the whole time," I inform them. Dad and Olga exchange a glance that makes me so satisfied, I dig in further. Sorry/not sorry, big bro. "Even shared a canoe instead of doing stand-up paddleboarding with the rest of us because they wanted to be *close.*"

My brother blushes. "Not like that." Mmm-hmmm. "It's not like we'd hang out with the three of you, that'd be weird."

I gesture to the table. "Yes, because spending time with family is so unusual."

As Nat scoffs, Olga touches my wrist. "How is your back, Caroline? Stand-up paddleboarding can be...strenuous."

Oh. Nat sinks his teeth into another poor bird limb while I've got the full weight of both Olga's and Dad's attention on me.

"It was fine." And it was. "Didn't even really think about it."

Olga takes a sip of her wine. "Have you been doing anything else?"

This is the perfect opportunity to tell them about my time with Alex—what we've tried so far, what we still have yet to test out, what I think I'm good at. Instead I go vague, that strange feeling about sharing my time with Alex still thick and slimy in my chest. He didn't respond when I sent him Sunny's number at lunch, and that makes me squirm with another layer of unease for some reason. "Running, yoga, stretching. Might start lifting weights, if that's cool with you, Dad?" The weight bench and squat rack in the garage are technically Dad's even though Nat's the one who set them up and uses them the most.

"Oh yeah, sure," Dad says.

Nat drops another wing bone to his plate and it immediately tumbles down the side and stains the white tablecloth that was a bad choice but very Martha Stewart of Dad. "Tried to get Caro to go out for cheerleading but she's too good for us."

I expect Olga to shoot that idea down for me—she's had more than one girl come to the gym to rehab after being dropped by a meathead like Nat—but instead she reaches across the table and covers my hand with hers. "When the time is right, you'll figure out how you want to use all that talent of yours."

Suddenly there's a little something in my throat and I just blink at her and nod.

Someone has strung tiny white Christmas lights up the trunks of all the trees of the park, giving our everyday recreation pocket a fairy-tale feel. I have no idea who to thank for this magic, but I love the new addition.

I spread out the quilt Nat and I hauled over here to watch the city fireworks display. Like most everyone in the neighborhood, we come here every year. The park isn't huge—still there's probably a hundred people or so, blanketing the grass as it slopes down toward the lake and away from the basketball and four-square courts.

Dad and Olga are settled in on a quilt next to ours—which Nat is hogging, by the way, his phone screen two inches from his face as he thumb-types at a rapid speed...I suppose his charm switch is currently in the off position. At least physically. Anyway, both Dad and Olga are perked up, squinting through the still-milling bodies to find Elena and her boyfriend, Chad, who said they'd meet us here.

I pop to my feet. "Which way were they coming from?" I ask, knowing that they'd planned to walk over after dinner with Chad's parents. Wherever that may have been. "I'll go see if I can find them."

"Would you, Caroline?" Olga smiles and her teeth are bright white in the near dark. "They should be coming from over there."

She gestures in a general northeasterly direction—up the hill, across the basketball courts, toward the rosebushes and the street that I've walked or run on almost every day this week. There are plenty of people in that direction, clumped in groups, and it's just dark enough that it's tough to truly make out anyone with absolute certainty from our current vantage point.

"No problem."

I start walking that way with a laser focus on each couple

because I know if I look hard enough I'll find Elena—probably along with someone else I know—and, accordingly, I don't even make it to the basketball courts before I feel a tap on my shoulder. I turn around, half expecting Elena finding me first, *or* Nat, ready to chide me for showing him up in the helpful child department.

Instead I get Alex.

"The fireworks are this way, Caro." He's got a smile on his face bright enough to make me question the light. It's possible he looks perfect at all times of day.

I sock him on the shoulder. "I know that! I'm trying to find somebody." Alex's brows scrunch together in the low light and suddenly I realize he thinks I'm being purposefully vague. Like I'm looking for a guy or something. I wave my hand and rush out an explanation before that train in Alex's head can leave the station. "Olga's daughter, Elena, and her boyfriend, Chad."

"Chad Chianti?"

"I, uh..." I haven't met Chad. I sweep a hand in the general direction I was walking, searching faces and shadows for Elena. "His parents live this way. I assume he's older than us because Elena's in college..."

Wow, I sound ill-prepared.

"Well, if it is Chad Chianti, he and his girlfriend are over there." He points over his shoulder toward a section of lawn where someone has set up a volleyball net. That is indeed Elena talking to a dude who most definitely could be Chad. Alex reads the confirmation on my face before I can say it, adding, "His parents' house backs up to ours."

A light bulb goes on over my head, because that sort of relationship totally makes sense given the direction I was walking, and Alex laughs. I turn around, ready to go their way, when I see Elena whip out her phone, screen bright in the night. She grabs Chad and begins angling toward our blankets. I suppose Olga got to her before I did, and I didn't even find her—Alex did.

We start moseying back toward the crowd and Alex says, "Hey, so I was just going to text you...."

"You were?" I squint up at him, all expectant. This is when I'll hear that I've achieved matchmaking glory and Sunny and Alex have officially connected. I will bask in the glow of the perfect setup for two seconds before probably having to admit that I spilled the contents of Alex's heart into Lake Dabinawa, but we'll cross that bridge when we get there.

"Uh, yeah, but then I saw you hauling butt across the park like a girl on a mission and figured I might as well try to catch you."

"Annnnnd?" I ask, head cocked to the side, prodding. Is he going to make me ask directly? Come on.

"I know it's late notice, but what are you doing tomorrow night?"

I. Uh. My schedule is about as open as a virgin bullet journal, but...that was not what I was expecting. "What time?" I ask, like it matters. It doesn't.

"Five thirty?"

"I could do five thirty. But...what...?"

His dimples wink as we pass a light-wrapped tree. "New sport."

Okay. I page through Alex's list, trying to figure out what would need a specific last-minute slot in the schedule, but then he answers for me. "I was going to keep it a surprise, just to see the reactions you'd get in one of your loud tank tops, but I should warn you it's golf."

Golf. I don't know why that surprises me, but it does.

"My dad has a standing driving range slot on Mondays but

tweaked his shoulder playing volleyball this afternoon." I immediately wince as he gestures toward the court that was set up for
today's festivities—likely with all the proper permitting, knowing
Alex's civil engineer dad. "I'd been trying to get us a time this
week and failing. So his injury is our gain?"

"Is he all right?"

"Yeah. Just old. So he says. We'll see what happens when the
extra-strength ibuprofen wears off tomorrow."

"I mean, I feel bad for your dad, but yeah, I can totally do that."

"Cool. I'll have to meet you at Northfield, if you don't mind
getting a ride or—"

"No problem."

That settles it. A hush descends over us as we get to the natural fork in the grass—his family by the fated volleyball court, mine
down the hill toward the duck pond. Our gait slows, and I take a
deep breath because I know it'll be even weirder if I ask tomorrow.
"Hey, um . . . did you get my text earlier? With Sunny's number?"

Alex stops walking altogether and I can't read his face. "Yeah.
Thanks."

It's right on the tip of my tongue to directly ask—if he's texted
her, if he's asked her out. What's the plan? But all of that just feels
overly invasive and maybe even a little creepy. Actually, I shouldn't
have even brought it up. He was with his family all day—he wasn't
exactly in a spot to text back. Or text her. In fact, he's with his
family now. But he's also talking to me. Who is overthinking all of
this. But I can't stop.

I should stop.

This must be where so many fictional and real matchmak-
ers go wrong. They get too involved. They try to force things

beyond the initial setup. Alex and Sunny aren't puppets, and I was never holding any strings to begin with. I really should've done my research on how to be successful in setting people up instead of wistfully just hoping it would all work out based on sheer will and my basic knowledge of Jane Austen characters.

I'm shifting my balance to sidestep away with a little wave good night when one of his big hands lands gently on my shoulder. It's then that I see his eyes are pinned on the face of his watch. "It should start in three, two, one..."

The first explosion goes off in a shattering white light above the treetops. An opening salvo meant to make a statement. And it does.

I can't help it, I literally jump.

And Alex, the statue full of cinnamon rolls, is right there, solidly tamping down my shock with a second hand on my other shoulder—his arm nearly draped across my back on the diagonal. "And here I thought you weren't afraid of anything, Caroline."

"I'm not afraid—I'm surprised."

"You're at a fireworks show, and I literally counted down the seconds."

"Okay, *Nat*—"

Another furious line of fireworks streams in after that, in rat-a-tat-tat succession. We both are stunned still. Electric blues, brilliant reds, more flashes of star-like white ebb and flow into the night sky. There's a music to them, and it reminds me of every floor routine I've ever watched or done myself—starting with a bang, then a low and slow moment before building, building, building, into something bright and beautiful and emotional.

Time stands still as our world becomes the canvas of the

city-dark sky and the show, which is told in flashes and sentences and even paragraphs. The choreography is exquisite, telling a tale, playing to our expectations, toying with our feelings.

There's a dramatic pause, the big finale up next, and I glance at Alex and mouth, "Wow."

Alex's teeth flash and suddenly I realize how close we are. His hands are still on my shoulders, warm and solid. His body is at a polite distance, and rather than standing directly behind me, he's off to the side. Still, we're close—so close I can smell the gel he puts in his hair and catch the glitter of the twinkle lights in the deep chocolate of his eyes.

And his mouth is *right there.*

The same moment I realize we're still touching, he seems to realize it too. He drops one hand and then the other from my shoulders and stuffs them safely in the pockets of his shorts, inadvertently making his phone light up.

I've spent nearly the whole show tangled up with Alex.

The warmth of his palms still sits on my shoulders, his fingertips gone but the memory marking the bare skin around my tank top. I look up at him, not knowing what to say, but then think better of it because my eyes immediately zero in on his mouth. Still so close.

Too close.

"I should go back..." I gesture in the general direction of my blanket. Nat's probably sprawled out on the whole thing, elbows and knees and all pointy things in my way.

Alex nods. "Me too."

As the big finale lights up the night above and the summer-dry grass crunches beneath my feet, I walk away, a chill brushing my shoulders despite the heavy ninety-degree air.

Just a trick of the night.

As I spy our blankets ahead—and get a surprise when I see Nat has gamely relegated himself to a corner so that Elena and Chad can have more room—my phone buzzes.

I pull it out. Alex's name and a text.

See you tomorrow.

19

I have no idea what to wear for golf.

I've never owned a pair of khaki shorts in my life. A quick Google of the best players is somewhat comforting because it confirms sleek khaki knee-dusters aren't the only appropriate attire of choice. So I spring for my single skort—the one I wore playing tennis. It's black, not khaki, but we're going to go with it. Most of the girls on the tour are wearing some sort of polo—basically, at least a single button. I don't own anything that looks like a polo shirt (because why would I), but in continuing my theme of tank tops or bust, I do have some sort of weird sea-green Henley-style sleeveless shirt that Mom sent in a random box of back-to-school clothes two months early. Better than two months late, I guess.

Even with a ponytail, I'm dressed differently enough for my dad or brother to notice, and that, combined with the idea of seeing Alex, makes my stomach flip. I don't know why—both of them want me to be trying new things. It feels different from explaining myself to Peregrine and Sunny. And my insides curdle at the idea of tripping over explaining away Alex's niceness. They've both known him forever and a day, yet when you're a teenage girl and a teenage boy is going out of his way for you...it changes the way friends and family see things. Obviously.

Dad's got the night off and he's taking Olga to dinner and a movie. The gymnasts aren't the only ones with more time in the evenings during the summer—the coaches get that time back too. At a quarter of five, he's in the shower sprucing up, and Nat's still playing ball, possibly with Alex. Some preplanned game that's the reason Alex has to meet me there, I guess—I have no idea. All I know is, this seems like an excellent time to start walking toward the country club to completely avoid any intersection of Dad-Nat-Alex and the target it puts over the strange feeling in my stomach.

I head out the door into the oven that is late afternoon in early July and point myself in the general direction of the club. I could take the road that runs past the park and hang a right like we did on our Saturday run to the market, but instead, I snake down the warren of side streets that leads from our neighborhood to the back of Northfield. Shorter, shadier, and far less likely anyone I know will see me and wonder why the hell I'm dressed like this.

Ten minutes out, I group text Dad and Nat to tell them I'm headed in the direction of Peregrine's. This isn't a lie in the literal sense, because it's more in the direction of her house than anyone else's. Next comes a text to Alex that I'm on the way.

I seriously cannot wait until September, when I have my driver's license and the most difficult logistics will be getting Nat to actually share the Jeep that he calls his but is one hundred percent in Dad's name.

Alex's reply comes in first. Meet you at the employee entrance?

Oh right. I'm not a member. It's private property. I can't just walk up to the golf course like I own the place. I'm not even allowed to be on the grounds without a member/employee like Alex.

When I arrive, Alex is already there and waiting by the gatehouse. His Royals hat is in place, but otherwise he's flexing a fashion muscle I haven't yet seen. His golf polo is legit Lacoste, little alligator on the chest and everything—it's crimson red and crisp at the corners despite the heat. Moreover, Alex Zavala *does* own khaki shorts, and they're clean and pressed too. He even has on an honest-to-God belt. Rather than his basketball shoes, he's wearing some fresh Nike numbers. The boy is nothing if not a breathing brand advertisement for all his favorites.

He arches an eyebrow at me. "Let me guess, you walked because you didn't think you'd get enough of a workout with golf?"

We'll go with that—I don't want to get into the fact that I didn't ask Dad or Nat for a ride. "It doesn't exactly seem strenuous when you've spent your entire life purposefully ping-ponging your full body weight into the air over and over again."

Alex manually raises the arm on the swing gate. I walk underneath, no awkward limbo required.

"There are different types of strength, Caro."

The smallest adult clubs at the rental shack are too big, and the kiddie-size ones are all checked out for some sort of mommy-and-me event on the other side of the links. This doesn't concern Alex in the least, and I try to take that energy with me as I shoulder my driver and follow him in the direction of the driving range.

Our assigned tee box is at the end of a row, bracketed by a tree to one side. The sun is striking hard at an angle, the light white and intense, salmon streaks still at least an hour away.

Alex sets up the tees and balls and goes through a short introduction. The gist—let's see if I even like the macro-level stuff before we try putting, etcetera. Makes sense. Next, he runs through the components of a golf swing: the address, backswing, downswing, impact, follow-through.

I mirror each component. Then he demonstrates what they look like put together. First without a ball, then with. He nails the poor thing and it goes flying past the 175-yard sign set up in the distance along with other markers, each at a twenty-five-yard interval. We stare after it as it falls to the nicely clipped grass.

Alex nods to me. "Okay, show me what you can do."

I set my feet exactly as Alex did. Shoulder width. The club is too big, but I think I've got my hands in the right place. Not to brag, but I can mimic a body position super easily. Even in midair, because of course. But Alex is staring at me in a way that stops me cold. "What?"

There's the hint of a smile on his face. "You look like you're trying to strangle the metal."

"I'm . . . just holding it?"

"Remind me never to wrestle you."

"Wrestling was on the list," I remind him.

"You're right." He discards his club and steps toe to toe with me, the ball sandwiched between us. My breath stalls as Alex places both hands on each of mine. I freeze, and I know he feels it. "Golf tonight. One sport at a time."

"Yes. Golf." I say the words but I can barely hear them outside my own head as he pries my grip off the club and reapplies it with gentle pressure.

When he removes his hands to sit back on his heels and check his handiwork, I'm immediately at a loss. It's probably ninety-five out here in the sun, I've been sweating for at least a solid hour, and somehow I crave that heat.

Alex leans forward and taps my right kneecap. "A little softer."

I'm good at taking this kind of direction and immediately adjust.

"Great, now the other side," he says without touching my left knee.

Obedient, I bend the joint to mirror its companion. Years of practice making myself appear exactly as Olga requests means this is a reflex more than a choice.

Alex squints. He taps his lips with a forefinger. They are nice lips. "Given the size of the club, I think that's okay."

"Uh, can I try now?"

"Yes. Just the swing. Inch back to clear the ball."

I move back and reset the same as before. When he doesn't correct me, I swing, mindful of my body position—using all those years of practice to send a carbon copy of his swing into the space-time continuum.

When I freeze again on the follow-through, he nods in my periphery. "That's a good imitation of a swing."

"It *is* a swing?"

"Yeah, *my* swing. Not *your* swing."

I... *What?* I glance up at him, and I know better than to look as confused as I feel. I mean, of course it's his swing. I'm copying him. But I'm also the one doing it, so how can it be an imitation?

Something about my reaction makes his lips quirk. "Here, wait," he says, popping up to his full height. "Stay still."

Again I go rigid. He touches one hand, like someone tapping a fence post—there and it's gone. But that renewed sense of loss I feel doesn't last long, because now he's come around behind me

150

and his hands return. Just like during the fireworks display, his body is at a respectable distance—nothing touches me but his hands. Palms, fingertips, the heel of his hand fading into the supple turn of his wrists.

But his presence is everything.

Something new and heavy, and more tangible than last night, hangs in the charged sliver of air between us, its heft growing as my mind races to catalog everything. The general warmth of his body, the swell of his chest just inches from my back. He has to duck to line his hands up with mine, his chin almost level with my ear.

My heart contracts. My cheeks blaze. My breath stalls.

Why is this... *what* is this?

It's so disorienting. And it's spreading. My entire body flames as my knees sag. It's only pure core strength that keeps me from completely pitching over.

"Eye on the ball," Alex instructs.

I stare at it so hard I'm about to excavate the crest of every little dimple on its surface. I'm not blinking, I'm not breathing, I'm still as stone.

Slight pressure on my wrists, Alex slowly draws back my swing. Guiding but not forcefully directing. He's letting me lead—the angle, the speed.

"There you go," he says when the driver crests, my shoulder flexibility paying off as much as my core strength. I'm staring at the ball so hard it's become nothing but a pinpoint. Alex lets go as gently as if he's turned my face for the perfect portrait. "Now follow through."

I do.

With a whoosh, the object of my focus is hurtling through

the sky. With it, everything I was holding back comes rushing forward.

The warmth of his body.

The gentle weight of his hand on mine.

The repeated squeeze and release of my heart as it threatens to burst out of my chest.

"That's gorgeous!"

God, his excitement. With a zing, I realize I could live on it for days and not miss my morning hit of caffeine.

This is Alex. This is Alex. This is Alex.

"Thanks," I say. I think. It's impossible to tell because to punctuate his exclamation, his full hand has landed on my shoulder. The driver above our heads quivers in my grip, and I swing it down, mindful of his proximity.

When my ball drops somewhere between the 125- and 150-yard markers, Alex's palm disappears from the curve of my shoulder. He steps away to grab another ball, and my nerve endings sizzle and smoke with the sudden heat displacement.

"Nice job on that follow-through. You want to keep it just as still as that. You're a natural."

I find my voice just in time to accuse him of not telling the truth. "You've said that with every sport."

"Didn't with basketball." He tosses the ball my way. It's a looping, gentle arc, and I catch it easily.

"I'll remind you we played *horse*, which is not technically basketball as defined by KSHSAA rules, but simply a playground game to improve shooting skills."

Alex points his driver at me accusingly. "You just want to steal the title of world's shortest point guard from Nat."

"Hey, if he's good at basketball, it tracks that I might be good at it too."

"I've seen his attempts at cartwheels and I can firmly say that he doesn't have your talent in gymnastics..."

He doesn't say I'd be terrible at basketball, but he doesn't have to. I make a face. "That's because Nat doesn't want to be good at gymnastics. You know how many times people have asked him if he's a gymnast too and then proceed to point out that he has *the perfect body* for it?"

"I may have been present for a few of those awkward conversations, yes."

"I guarantee that if he ever develops a crush on one of the cheerleaders he spends all his non-basketball time with, his latent tumbling talent will magically appear." Or maybe even with a former cheerleader like Artemis. But Alex doesn't know about the flirty lake trip as far as I know, so I don't mention it.

"You might be right." Alex tips his chin at the ball I've dropped into place in front of me. "Okay, show me that form again."

He's a good three feet from me, his driver resting lightly in one hand. "You sure you don't want to go again?"

"I don't think you need me to demonstrate anymore."

I squint at him. "Okay, but I *do* want to play with you."

"Ten swings and then we alternate."

"Fine." I settle into my stance, soften my knees, square my hips. His eyes sit on my body, checking the angles, the technique. Consciously, I know he's trying to spot problems before they begin in exactly the same way Olga has for more than half my life. Perfecting, perfecting, perfecting. But his eyes sit differently on me. Or maybe, just like when he was close—that's my own visceral reaction.

With the setup of each drive, my mind chants yet another reminder to the blood in my veins rushing around, turning my cheeks pink, my neck flush, my hands and arms and drop of my stomach hot.

This is Alex. It's his job to look at you. To help you. He's just doing what he said he would do.

I'm calming down. My nerve endings will stop overreacting. My mind will stop hurtling down the dark tunnel toward what... my visceral reaction could mean.

On the seventh drive, Alex takes a step forward. "Wait—please."

Blessedly, he's toe to toe with me, not stepping behind.

"Look up."

I move my eyes but keep my face down, head and neck sort of afraid to move from *the stance* that I've learned.

Alex laughs so softly I think I imagine it. A hooked forefinger touches my chin. He tips my face up. "You're tilting your head slightly toward the target. It's inhibiting your swing—you want your spine neutral." His hands sweep to either side of my face and he gently straightens it. The difference is so minuscule, but the way he's concentrating it must mean nearly everything. "I did this too when I started. You need to feel a little stretch here," he says, running two fingertips down the side of my neck, "until you get used to it."

Alex's eyes meet mine and for a moment, time is frozen as I stare into them. I've known these eyes all my life. Hell, I very recently sold these eyes to Sunny.

And yet, somehow they're different now. Or maybe it's my perspective. Good God, I hope the heat in my skin hasn't translated to me full-on blushing, because the way he's watching me he would most definitely notice.

I shake myself into answering him with a little nod of understanding, careful not to ruin his adjustment. My swing chambers and then unloads.

When I look up, I somehow made it nearly to the 150-yard sign. My longest drive yet.

"Damn, Caro."

I lower my club, and now I'm really blushing. "Thanks."

Alex nods at the bucket of balls, but his attention never leaves my face. "Let's finish 'em."

20

Our tee time goes so fast I don't even realize it's over until a couple of bro-dudes with cocktails start hovering near the tree dividing our tee box from the course proper. My cheeks hurt from laughing and my back is a tad stiff from all the rotation, but it's not late yet and maybe it's the charge of the sun, or the fact that I realize I'd been looking forward to this moment since his fireworks text, but I . . . don't want it to end.

Not yet. Not at all, really.

So as we're walking up the concrete path to the club rental, I flip around and walk backward facing Alex, who holds our clubs in one big hand. "You know, how about some tennis? Do you think we can do that?"

"Tennis?"

Yep. Something with distance. Where my heart doesn't do that thing it did when we worked on my stance. I might combust if it happens again. No, I *will* combust. And then the rich people will be pissed and Alex will likely have to clean it up because he brought the exploding riffraff onto the grounds of Northfield.

"Sure."

He says it like it's no big deal, but there's a hint of something else in his voice. Exhaustion? Doubt?

"Or we could just go home?" I give him an out. He spends so much time practicing when he's not working or with Nat. "You know, if you're sick of the courts."

"Never sick of it. Just not sure about availability."

This place with its timing and rules. You'd think there'd be a bell clang at the top of the hour just to keep everyone moving.

I turn back around so we're walking the same direction. My hand accidentally brushes his on the whirl, and I go back to clutching the empty ball bucket in a double grip like it's full of gold bars or something.

Court two is available, because a lesson ended early and nothing else is scheduled.

Alex and I grab his gear and Lily Jane's racket from his car. Unlike the pair of courts shoehorned into the green in front of one of Northland's *many* additions, the Northfield courts are a world unto themselves, bordered with beautiful hedges that make it look like we're entering an English garden maze instead of a wonder of American concrete in the heart of Kansas City. It's not as disorienting as that crushing wave of whatever that was during our golf lesson, but considering my height deficiency, it's close.

I'm so busy gawking at the fancy greenery that I don't notice someone waving until we're nearly right in front of them. I wait for Alex to return the gesture, maybe smile and call out a name. But he doesn't. Instead, he asks, "Someone you know?"

The man has on a tennis visor, racket bag over his shoulder, and water bottle cupped in a hand. He's silhouetted by the sun in such a way that he's backlit.

"Caroline Kepler, is that you?"

My stomach completely flips. Internally I sigh. I can't blame him for what happened, but I'm frustrated about the ball he started rolling in the direction of my retirement. "Um, hi, Dr. Kennedy."

"Jimmy didn't tell me you were members." Jimmy, my dad, right.

"I'm—we're not." I point to Alex. "He is. Alex Zavala. Reigning club tennis champion."

Recognition sparks in Dr. Kennedy's eyes. "Zavala? You're the kid who was the runner-up in the Orange Bowl last year, aren't you?"

He nods politely. "Yep, that's me."

Alex doesn't seem to want to expand on his tennis greatness, and I don't really want to get into the fact that this man fixed Nat's knee but didn't even try to fix me. Still, I grasp for what to say, when a tall woman with a smooth sun-kissed ponytail enters the chat—er, conversation.

"My most modest student is also my most talented. Hard to believe, eh, Graham?" She smiles in the most elegant way possible, lean arms snaking across her chest in a flash of tan skin and perfect pale polish.

Coach Bev. That's who this has to be. Alex's longtime tennis coach. The one he literally ran to see on Saturday. She appeared from the same court as Dr. Kennedy. It doesn't take much to put two and two together that their lesson just ended on the court next to ours.

Dr. Kennedy laughs and gives her a more genuine smile than I saw from him when he was breaking my heart in his office. "I think both of us know from our chosen careers that modesty and talent are not often friends, Bev."

Coach Bev's eyes crinkle delicately. It's the only thing about her that hints she might be my dad's age. Maybe older. She strides forward, and suddenly I feel immeasurably short. This woman has to be five ten and change, and Dr. Kennedy is not as tall as Alex but somewhere in between.

Coach Bev gently taps Alex in the chest with the racket that had been under her arm. "This one has too much of both. *Yes*, he was the runner-up in the Orange Bowl last year."

"That's big time, man, congrats." There's a gleam in the doctor's eye and I wonder if he's hoping to get a referral out of this conversation.

Coach Bev holds up a hand and gestures to Alex like he's a car in a showroom. "Yeah, please tell him that, because that notoriety has led to at least four ATP-level hard court wild cards that he's turned down this spring and summer. The Northfield tournament will be his first one of the year, because he decided he'd rather cream no-names in the 6A state tournament than pick on kids at his own level."

That sentence has an edge to it, and Alex's face snaps into a reflexive grin as he rubs the back of his neck. "That was a title defense too." Then he glances from me to Dr. Kennedy. "I wanted to spend time with my friends."

The answer is so honest and pure and so very Alex, but both their expressions waver with something like disappointment. Or sadness? It's so strange.

"Is that what you're doing tonight?" Coach Bev asks, finally dropping her gaze to meet mine, a foot below her airspace. "I thought tonight was soccer drills. Or is Monday basketball?" She waves a hand. "I can't keep all your other ambitions straight."

That—that sounded like a backhanded compliment? Or just a very sharp passive-aggressive dig? My lips drop open to defend him even though I don't understand his crime. But then Alex comes in with a calm, straightforward answer.

"Nope, tennis tonight." He puts a hand on my shoulder, arm draping across my neck. "Teaching my friend Caroline the ropes."

I give a small wave by way of accepting his introduction.

"Caroline is one of my clients—a very talented gymnast," Kennedy says, leaving it vague because we might all be on a first-name basis here, but HIPAA is still a thing and he knows I know it, thanks to Dad.

I'm actually grateful enough for his discretion that I explain. "*Was* a talented gymnast—I'm very recently retired. Alex gamely offered to help me find a better pastime than wallowing about the house."

For some reason this is easier than I had it all built up in my head to be. And it must make sense because Coach Bev glances between us at the end of my explanation. "Sounds like Alex."

"Not the sport I would've picked, Caroline," the doctor says. "Twisting motion okay?"

He means it to be nice, but the immediately negative attitude toward my choices sparks irritation. I smile sweetly as my insides sour. "Fine so far."

"Trying out anything else?"

With his second prodding question that highlights the fact that he thinks he knows more about my body than I do, that sourness within me completely curdles. It's all I can do to keep a smile plastered on my face. I don't know if it's because I'm small, or if it's because I'm sarcastic, or a combination of the two, but so many people, even my own brother, seem to discount my feelings. Which leads me to grand, bull-headed gestures to be heard, like rushing out of a restaurant and walking home or one final, life-changing Arabian. I smile politely. "Everything I've missed out on for the last ten years."

"That's the spirit," Kennedy says, more enthusiastic than I expected. "Be careful. Don't want to see you sooner than I have to."

Likewise.

"Have a good night," I say, grabbing Alex's hand off my shoulder and pulling him toward the court. Alex echoes with goodbyes to both of them and a guarantee he'll see Coach Bev tomorrow.

As they walk away, we take three steps toward our court before the weight of what is in my palm hits me, and I nearly fling it away because clutching Alex Zavala's hand in mine was not a great life choice.

Especially after that golf lesson.

I really need to practice at least a three-foot social distance situation from Alex because my body clearly has a mind of its own tonight.

Heart palpitations, hand-holding—I mean, really.

Almost as if he has no idea how ridiculous I'm being, Alex grabs *my* hand to pause my momentum. When I turn around, he's searching my expression. "You still want to play?"

"More than ever."

"Stubborn Caro is my favorite Caro." Alex pulls out a special key that'll give us access to court two. "So are you thinking tennis might be it? For a sport?"

I nod. "It's a strong contender. And *despite what Dr. Kennedy says,*

I think my back does okay with it. Could be the cortisone talking, but I don't think so."

"Fair enough."

Alex steps aside and gestures for me to enter ahead of him. I do, and it's like I've stumbled into a secret garden or something. Court two is markedly different from the high school ones. The playing surface is a fancy blue rather than the cracked mallard green at Northland, and even the fencing is nicer—newer, and coated a shiny rubberized black. This court has some sort of privacy mesh, though not all of them have that—I know for a fact I saw actual nonshaded bodies playing when we came for volleyball.

I step in—enforcing my new social distance protocol of three feet or more between us—and wait as he gently shuts the gate behind him.

"So this is where you spend all your time?" I ask as he hands me Lily Jane's racket. I extend my other hand for a ball, and Alex offers one...but withholds it until I look up. When I do, his dimples flash with a teasing smile.

"Yeah, when I'm not with you."

I have to glance down. Backpedal. Pretend I didn't find yet another rich chocolate shade in his eyes. "Or Nat. The whole family, really."

"Caro."

I walk to my side of the court like I haven't heard him.

"Caroline."

I examine the racket strings. I have no idea what I'm looking for, but that's what the pros are always doing on TV so it seems like a legit way to ignore him.

Alex clears his throat and I half expect the ball in his hand to strike my feet at a full Zavala-serve speed in a bid to make me face his criticism. But for the millionth time, Alex reminds me that he's not Nat Kepler. "If stubborn Caro is my favorite Caro, my *least favorite* is when Caroline Kepler diminishes her own worth before my very eyes. You're suggesting I'm only helping you because of Nat."

I can't look at him. "I wasn't."

Alex doesn't buy it. "Why do you do that?"

"I'm not doing anything."

"Yes you are. I'm coaching you. Don't make excuses for why I want to hang out with you. I want to hang out with you because you are my *friend*."

He lets the last word hang.

And then he keeps going.

"My friend," he repeats. "Not because you're Nat's sister. Not because I have a crush on your friend. Not because I promised I would coach you. I promised to coach you because of you. All those other things are tangential. I spend my time here. I *also* spend my time with you. I never expected anything out of it and I don't want anything other than the experience itself."

I swallow and force myself to make eye contact. Like his voice, his stance isn't angry or frustrated as much as it is matter-of-fact.

"Okay."

"Now," he says, "why do you do that?"

I blink at him.

He waits. Dribbles the ball. Waits some more.

The flaming light of sunset sits on his shoulders as he stands there, all six feet plus of him, patient and calm. Just open and waiting for an answer.

I shift on my feet. "I . . . I don't know. Reflex?"

"I'm not trying to psychoanalyze you," he clarifies, probably suddenly aware that he might sound a tad like his own mother. "I just...being self-effacing is something but it makes those who love you feel like shit."

Those. Who. Love. You.

We're ten feet apart and suddenly I feel like he's close enough to hear my heartbeat.

I don't have the words to explain to him that self-effacement isn't just a reflex—it's a survival skill. Honed over years of working very hard to be perfect and knowing it's nearly impossible to do so. Everyone has their ways of surviving perfection, and joking about my flaws is one of my best-proven defenses. And yet I had no idea the mark it could put on someone outside of the gym.

"Be proud in who you are and those who care for you."

Care. For. You.

"Okay."

Alex dribbles the ball again before picking it up and spreading his arms wide, racket gesturing to the majestic courts. "Yes, Caroline, this is where I spend all my time." Then he smiles across the space. "When I'm not with you."

He's said it before. Recently. All the other people and places he spends time with flit through my mind.

Work. Tennis practice. Hoops with Nat. Soccer drills. Stadium stairs. His family.

I clamp down that reflex to mention them. Stretch my stumpy wingspan reaching for something new to say.

Glad you showed me the Northfield courts.

Glad you let your worlds collide.

Glad I'm here with you.

Instead, I say: "Serve, Zavala."

And he does.

21

The good kind of exhaustion hangs over me—my muscles supple, sweat drying tightly on my skin, my heart happy. I'll sleep well tonight.

Alex already has towels laid out on the Challenger's seats, and as I slide onto the soft fabric, my stomach audibly growls. So loud it nearly echoes within the confines of the big muscle car.

"My thoughts exactly," Alex says as I fight the urge to cover my sweaty face with equally sweaty hands—my skin wouldn't be able to take it. So I just laugh.

"So embarrassing."

Alex turns the key in answer, and the engine's own growl roars into the night. "No, I mean, I'm starving too. Want to grab a bite?"

It's an innocent ask, and my stomach will not allow me to deny my hunger.

I check my phone and it's 8:02 p.m. No texts from Dad or Nat. So, I'm free. But also, I'm SOL. "I didn't bring money."

"Don't care."

"You know my guilt complex."

"Don't care," he repeats. And suddenly I realize we're toeing the same line I crossed when we set foot on court two.

Just go with the flow. Enjoy the experience.

Let Alex be your friend, Caroline.

My stomach growls a second time—quieter over the engine purr and slip of tires as we navigate the employee access road, but still audible. Goddammit. "Sure."

Alex's smile is illuminated by the glow of the newly lit dashboard. "Your enthusiasm bowls me over."

"Hunger skews how I display enthusiasm."

"I'm sure it does, but I think this is more about that overactive debt complex of yours."

Caught. "Maybe."

"How about I pick where we go? Does that mute your wailing guilt banshee?"

He's not wrong that it's always a three-alarm siren in my brain when I'm being let off easy. "A tiny bit, yes."

Alex laughs. "Okay, Bruno's?" The pizza place appears on our left like he summoned it, even though it's been holding down the same strip mall since our neighborhood was some farmer's field. Then he adds: "They have salad."

"Despite Nat's opinions, it is possible to eat more than salad even if you like it the best and gravitate toward it. I love pizza." Then, I add for extra emphasis, "Cheese is not the enemy."

"I'm putting that on a T-shirt."

"If it comes in a tank, I'll buy it." I toss him a grin. "And add a tip—thus paying you back for dinner."

"Knew that was coming."

We park and step into the night, which seems so much darker than five minutes ago—everything a pewter gray, the lightning bugs swirling despite our strip mall location. Walking next to him, even with a wide berth, seems to put our hands too close—height difference and all. I feel my stride slow so that I'm a half step behind Alex, despite my hunger.

Alex either doesn't notice or doesn't care about our hands. He opens the door and pointedly takes a step back, making it clear I'm supposed to go through first. I duck my head in thanks, while going so far around the open stance of his body that I inadvertently bang my shoulder into the doorframe upon entering.

Like my stomach growl, it's a noise I can't play off.

"Oh! Are you okay?" The hostess jumps into action from behind her little station after hearing the audible clang as I bounce into her restaurant, a self-made pinball.

My cheeks flame—I made a successful and long career out of my knack for controlling my body. "Yep. Uh-huh, fine." One open door mixed with Alex Zavala and I'm suddenly a klutz. "Two, please? On the patio if you have room?" I add, because I refuse to embarrass myself further by leaving a sweat stain the shape of the backs of my thighs on the faux-leather seating, which is even more of an embarrassing prospect than the leather over at Burger Fu. Yes, I am very much obsessed with these types of sweaty scenarios— I've spent my life working out, but I don't want to leave *proof* of it everywhere on pieces of furniture that aren't mine. Gross.

The patio is available and pretty quiet, most everyone settling up with checks or boxes for leftovers. The hostess tucks us in the far corner, between the wrought iron fence bordering the patio and some sort of clipped-bush topiary that's big enough to be a Halloween costume for someone like me.

We take a seat and our waitress appears with a pitcher and two massive plastic cups that she fills with a beverage that's more ice than water. Peregrine would toss the drink straight into the bush if she were here.

"So, tell me about Dr. Kennedy," Alex says, bringing the ice-filled cup to his lips.

I'm surprised by the subject matter. Tonight was a roller coaster on my end, and our run-in with the doctor wasn't the most thrilling part. Not that I want to discuss the swing guidance at the driving range, or my complete inability to accept Alex's kindness as genuine when aimed at me.

I frown.

Alex doesn't know the whole story. Not really. He clearly pieced together enough during our run-in, fueled by Nat's fantastic description at Burger Fu—*Caroline's back is shit and Dad made her quit gymnastics*—and whatever else my brother has shared when prodded.

"Dr. Kennedy fixed Nat's knee but took one look at me and announced I should retire at fifteen, approximately four hours before I face-planted and earned myself a trip to the ER for the double career death blow of a lumbar strain and spinal stenosis diagnosis." I hold up a hand. "Let me say for the record that despite the good doctor's *suggestion*, I left his office with my career intact and a steroid shot. It's not his fault that my back is screwed up. It's not. I know that." My hand drops and smacks the table. "*But* I blame him for preying upon that stubbornness that amuses you so very much, because I might not have face-planted at the next practice and bought myself a little more time until the stenosis diagnosis and Dad's kibosh on *my life*."

I expect Alex to point out I've blamed literally everyone but myself in that *hanger*-fueled rant. Instead he leans heavily into his dining chair, removes his hat, and runs a big hand through his dark hair. He doesn't smile. "I wouldn't have been that nice to him."

Somehow this makes me feel better even if I'm suspicious

about it being true. For the next several minutes Alex gives me all the space I need to rant more. About the timeline, the injury, how close I was to being elite, and how far I am now from who I was literally a month ago. He nods along before adjusting his ball cap as he puts it back in its place, and then, finally, pulling out his phone. "Two thirty to four thirty."

My head snaps up from where my vision had gone soft while staring at the menu but not actually reading it. "What?"

"That's our new practice schedule until August 1. Up at school so we're guaranteed a court. If tennis is your thing, you've got work to do."

I'm so flabbergasted by this that all I can do is fumble for the deadline. "What is August 1?"

Alex flashes the screen at me, a growling Northland Tiger at the top. "The start of pre-tryout camp. Two-a-days with Coach Brandt and the other girls. Same schedule as the other fall sports."

Ah. Soccer starts that day too.

August 1 is a little more than three weeks away. That seems like we're cutting it ridiculously close. But we would've been any-way with any fall sport. I guess. How did summer just begin and seem like it's over already?

Alex's next suggestion is a total curveball. "And I suggest you sign up for the Northfield Tennis Championships. It'd be a great chance for you to get some match play under your belt before the high school season starts."

"I—I've played tennis twice with you and you think I'm ready for a tournament?"

He lifts a brow, mischievous. "I think you're a trial-by-fire girl."

I smirk at him because it's true.

"There's a beginner's draw that's running parallel to the main draw at Northfield. It's mostly club members, but say the word and I'll get you in."

I hold up a hand. "Wait, so let me make sure I'm hearing you right. You're suggesting that we train every day for two hours, I sign up to play in a tournament, and that I'll then be ready to join the world of 6A high school tennis?"

"Yep. And before you go getting all weird about it, I can make two thirty to four thirty work without shifting my entire schedule. How I choose to fill it is up to me and this is what I want to do."

I turn skeptical. "Won't that interfere with your own practice? I mean, you've got a title to defend, soccer to prepare for..."

He shakes his head. "The Northfield tournament is always the last weekend in July. It times out perfectly so I can focus on soccer the next week. Not that Coach Bev is a fan of that."

No, no. I will not get him in trouble with the woman who molded him into a tennis star. "But that means you need to practice, and practicing with me is a cakewalk compared to what Coach Bev has planned for you."

Alex smirks. "Caroline, what do you think I do all day?" It's not a real question, though, because he scrolls over to his calendar. "Purple is work. Blue is tennis. Orange is soccer. Red is conditioning and hoops—basically code for Nat Kepler—and pink is Caroline."

I squint at the calendar.

The weekends are blocked off in solid walls of blue, with some other colors sprinkled in. The weekdays are a patchwork of color-coded bars, stacked one right after another like a particularly terrible game of Tetris. It's literally packed from sunup to sundown, but not necessarily how I imagined.

"You don't work until two?" All this time, I assumed he had the same grounds work schedule as Nat during the week: six to two. Nope. According to his color blocking, he actually works from six to ten in the morning, then practices with Coach Bev from ten to two in the afternoon. Nat's red color blocks of pickup games and stadium stairs are all over the place, and some days they're missing completely—another surprise. I guess maybe I just *thought* they spent all their time connected at the hip.

And of course he's already penciled me in for those two-hour blocks every remaining weekday.

"Alex . . . ," I start, because this is just too much, friend or not.

He stops me with a hand out like a stop sign. "I like being busy. Just let me work with you—I enjoy it."

I swallow. "Why?"

"Because . . ." Alex wets his lips, searching for the right words. Again. "Because you've reminded me why I like the sport."

I'm confused. "Tennis?"

He nods, and now he's the one fiddling with his straw. His big shoulders crowd the table, prompting my brain to again compare him to a Disney character, but this time, instead of Simba, he's the Beast—all in his feelings, except instead of rage bubbling under the surface, it's . . . exhaustion?

"It's a lot of pressure."

I wait, my hands clasped in my lap as he searches for whatever he's about to say. Vulnerable is not something I often associate with Alex, but that's exactly what he is here.

"My parents and Coach Bev think I can and should go pro after high school."

He's good enough. State champion. Beating the best in the city at the Northfield tournament—teens and full-grown adults alike. He's gone to national and regional tournaments. He's got scholarship letters arriving. Actually, he's a lot like Sunny—not on the national team, but hanging out in the wings, so close the spotlight glitters just feet away.

He tilts his head. "They would rather I drop soccer and basketball altogether because of the possibility of injury."

Okay. Sure. I get that. Suddenly, Coach Bev's passive-aggressive behavior makes perfect sense. "So...why don't you?" I know I don't need to tell him that from my personal experience, singular focus on only one thing outside of school is much easier than playing air traffic control with color-coded scheduling.

He sighs. And when he glances up, there's a sadness settling into his features that makes me want to scoot my chair next to his and place a hand on his slumping shoulders. My heart jumps in my throat, and my calves tense—I'm prepared to leap his way, no matter my new convenient-for-me rules.

"I did. For a season. After I made varsity soccer and basketball freshman year, they wanted me to focus full-time on tennis in the spring and summer and play up in 16s." He's getting all jargon-y but I know enough from my recent Wimbledon obsession to recognize he means the junior age categories—12s, 14s, 16s, 18s. "We compromised by letting me join the high school tennis squad freshman year and keep my slot on the mathletics team."

As he rolls through this turn of events, I page back, trying to remember how much I saw of him then. Not much? It's hard for me to figure out because I was doing my own training for thirty hours a week as an eighth grader and then freshman.

"But I dropped everything else and went out and did all the big junior hard court tournaments. Just as sophomore year started, I got invited as a wild card qualifier to the US Open junior tournament and made it three rounds in. It was cool being there, feet away from the big guns. After that, it rolled into the fall season, all the way up to the Orange Bowl, which is like *the* big year-end tournament in Florida." That's the one Dr. Kennedy mentioned. "All the best juniors go."

"And you were runner-up?"

"Yeah. But by then I was...sapped. Exhausted. Done." His eyes lift to the broad sky above. "Everything I loved about tennis became lost in the business of the pursuit. And worst, I was lonely. Constantly everywhere and nowhere. With Dad, Coach Bev, and my own head."

Alex bites his lip, more coming. I watch him, waiting—I'd known tangentially that he'd gone and done big things, but at that point I was going and doing big things too, moving up to the "optional" gymnastics levels—eight and above—where shit gets real.

Color rises in Alex's cheeks, and all those squishy insides I'd discovered when his crush surfaced are now tangible, and real, and out on the table. A mess of emotions and lessons learned.

"So, what I found out about myself is that while I might be good at tennis, I'm best when I also play sports with my friends." He putzes with his straw and hauls himself back up straight. "I mean, sure, I have friends on the tennis circuit, but it's...not the same as working toward a common goal with your best buds." He drops the straw. "I know you know what I mean."

"I do." Gymnastics competition is solitary—one girl, one routine at a time—but the experience is not.

"It's been clear to my coaches and family that tennis is my best shot. It's my college scholarship. It's maybe even a real career, with money involved, if I somehow decide to do the circuit again as a junior or even a senior, professional. You heard Coach—I've turned down wild cards and she thinks I'm dumb for doing it because it's not like they offer those to everybody." Alex smiles and it's sad. "They're afraid I'll look back and regret not making the most of my abilities. All because I want to just...be normal."

"You're not dumb. Being well-rounded isn't stupid. Taking time off isn't stupid." I think of Sunny—giving up regular high school, and apparently giving up on dating, simply because she didn't want to squander her shot. I understand that just as much as I understand those who love and push Alex. But...Alex is right. Aren't we more than our talents? A pang of guilt hits me as I envision Dad at my bedside in the ER, imploring me to understand that I'm more than my goals in the gym.

"But what if in trying to be normal...I blow my ACL in a soccer game? Or screw up my shoulder in basketball? Adverse effects, most especially to tennis, to my best shot—my *special* shot." He glances up from his hands and the pain in his eyes makes my heart lurch. We're two sides of the same coin, Alex and I—my body betrayed me when my brain told me to go on, and his brain is putting his body and his future in harm's way. "Can't I have all of it, Caroline? I'm hungry for all of it."

Our waitress magically appears at the word "hungry" like we've summoned her. For once, Alex is not on top of things, still vibrating with all the real-live Alex Zavala feelings he's laid out on the table before us.

I stare at him. "Want to share a pizza?"

He pauses mid-grab of the menu he hasn't looked at yet. Then he grins. "Never more in my life."

I don't break eye contact. "Large Mozza-Monster?"

His dimples flash. "Hell yes."

Our waitress flits off to get us the Bruno's equivalent of a "triple cheese," aka the least-like-salad food available other than, say, the Meat-a-Tarian, which is so laden with sausage et al. that it can only be consumed with a fork. Nat's fave. Obviously.

When she leaves, the tip of Alex's shoe gently tags my shin under the table. "Cheese is not the enemy, but it might consider you one, Caroline Kepler."

I laugh but then tilt my head. "Alex...about tennis. I appreciate your coaching me. I appreciate your encouraging me. But if working with me becomes too much—if you start to feel sapped or exhausted, or cheated out of the time you want to do all the things....please know that you've already given me so much."

I try very hard not to do that Midwestern thing where I shortchange what I'm saying with a laugh. And Alex nods and accepts what I've given. I glance down at his phone, wondering when or if he'll ever cash in on the only thing I feel like I was able to give him in return for his help. I don't say a word about Sunny or her number or anything else, but Alex's eyes dip to his phone too, and I know his line of thought is following mine.

I gather my courage and reach across the table and pat his giant hand with my much smaller one. "I want you to have it all." His eyes spring up to meet mine and I hope he gets what I'm not saying—subtlety is not my strong suit. "If anyone can have it all, it's you."

22

We're definitely a hit on some sort of worldwide cheese Interpol after demolishing the entire Mozza-Monster between the two of us. Okay, Alex did seventy-five percent of the demolishing (and agrees he's totally on an international most-wanted list) but I ate two large slices, which is most definitely way more than what I'd typically do on a pizza night with Dad and Nat.

My sweat's dried to the point where my skin itches and my clothes drape funny, but I'm more content than I've been in, well, months. My cheeks ache from smiling and my legs are sore from all the lateral motion. It feels good to be this bone-tired yet replenished. Relaxed. So much so that I only half-heartedly try to decline Alex's offer of a ride home. It's almost my curfew, and because Alex has insisted I take Lily Jane's racket with me until I get my own, I'd be a lone teenage girl wandering through dark neighborhoods with nothing but a cell phone and a tennis racket.

That said, I did convince him that it would be completely not necessary for him to pick me up every weekday ahead of our two-thirty practice. I can walk, or maybe even jog. Alex definitely thinks I should keep up a regular running schedule ahead of tennis camp, because if I actually make the team, that sort of cardiovascular strength will be a leg up in a match. But then I'd be the girl jogging in the hottest part of the afternoon with a tennis racket. So, yeah, maybe I should stick to mornings with that.

Anyhow, we've got it all worked out as Alex pulls up to my house. He sticks to the curb even though there's space in the driveway next to the Jeep. I don't ask why, but I'm grateful.

Alex cuts the engine and pops the trunk. Still distracted by the possibility that someone in my family will see that I'm with Alex and I'll have to explain things, I'm slow on the uptake of insisting that he doesn't have to get out, but he's already looping around the car. We meet askew—me up on the curb, heels in the grass, him down at street level, holding out the racket like it's a knight's beloved sword.

"See you at two thirty tomorrow," I say in acceptance of the racket. Knowing Alex, he got Lily Jane's approval to let me borrow it. I hope. I need to check my allowance against the price of getting my own. "Same court at the school?"

"You know it."

The melty feeling that possessed me on the driving range returns. Even though we're three feet apart. That smile spreading across his face in the shadows might as well be his clothing whispering against mine, for how hard my heart's driving. It thuds against my rib cage, punches my windpipe, so erratic and ready to escape into the night or his arms.

One of the two. Not fight or flight but embrace or escape.

I hug the racket to my chest, hoping that it'll dull the pounding. It doesn't.

I don't know how to end this. Because I'm on the curb, I'm closer to his height by a few inches, my equilibrium off.

He puts his hands in his pockets, chin tilted up, the cut of his jaw and his mouth catching all the light under the slashing shadow of his ball cap. I can't see his eyes but I desperately want to.

I also don't want him to walk away.

"See you tomorrow." It's redundant but I just...

A smile flashes across Alex's face.

"It's a date."

He says it oh so casually and steps away, leaving me frozen in a fog despite a night that's eighty-five degrees in the buggy pitch-black.

It is. It is a date.

And tonight...tonight felt like one too.

The Challenger roars to life, and as he swings out of the cul-de-sac and into the end of his night, I stand there, unmoving, hanging on to the racket for dear life while my heart taps out the truth I can no longer deny.

I have a crush on Alex Zavala.

23

It can't be.

But...my heart double beats, my cheeks are warm, and that whisper thread of contact from hours ago flips my stomach in a way that'll be highly problematic if it continues, considering that my gut is truly ninety-nine percent pizza at the moment.

I squeeze my eyes shut and stand there on the curb, racket pressed against my stuttering chest, feeling more than dizzy.

Alex *is* great. Which is why I've played matchmaker with Sunny.

My eyes fling open. The night's still there. Hot and sweet. The stars struggle to stand out in the darkness, the streetlamps blotting them out. I haven't moved an inch, but my heart's pounding as if I'd charged down the road, sprinting after him.

For what? Telling him will only make me feel worse. Will kill our tennis dates. Our energy. And I don't want to ruin it.

Kind actions + handsome boy + lots of time together + eye contact = crush. This has happened before. Plenty of times. It's only worse now simply because I've never had this much time to think about a boy. Or spend time with one who wasn't genetically related to me.

Of course, Alex probably makes *anyone's* heart pull pyrotechnics. He's just that type of guy. Charming, talented, genuinely nice. Literally no one, least of all me, could withstand a constant barrage of that combination of qualities for days on end without crushing too.

Peregrine even called it.

"Are you sure you don't have the slightest, tiniest, maybe-so-deep-you-don't-recognize-it crush on Alex?"

Maybe she has a tiny one too. She was quick to second his greatness.

Once he's with Sunny I'll stop feeling like a melted M&M, all gooey on the inside, polished outer shell failing.

Melt in your mouth not in your hand, my butt. I've eaten enough chocolate in the past month not to fall for that fallacy.

I swallow.

If all is right with the world, very soon Alex will be taken. Scooped off the market and into Sunny's capable, nicely manicured hands.

And then my heart will behave itself. Chemical reaction kaput. Dormant. Primed and ready to find someone else more appropriate to crush on.

Someone who is not my big brother's best friend.

Someone who does not have the hots for one of my best friends.

Someone who has not offered to coach me for hours a day in a purely platonic bid to see me succeed.

It wasn't a date.

It wasn't. And tomorrow's not one at all.

He's just using that as a phrase.

"Caroline?" Olga's coming down the front steps to the driveway, her nicest purse slung over her shoulder, a wrap dress with enough sequins to double as reflective gear twinkling in the porch light. On cue, the garage door sputters to life, revealing Dad's Prius.

Date night.

Which apparently was at home. Not dinner and the movies as planned.

Um.

"Oh, hey." I go in for a hug as a greeting, remembering the racket too late. I end up holding it out to the side, hugging Olga with one arm as she pulls me in with a full, unflinching embrace. "I was just at Peregrine's."

"That's what your dad said—"

"I said what?" Dad appears, stepping out of the garage, keys in hand. He always backs out for her so she doesn't have to squeeze past the teetering squat rack/home gym Nat set up in the second stall for reasons of both vanity and bum knee maintenance. "Is that a tennis racket?"

"Yeah, Artemis lent it to me. When she drove me home." The lie is out of my mouth before I can stop it. A continuation of my lying text, but in real time—I was with Peregrine, and driven home by her sister. For no reason other than if I say Alex's name right now I will burst. And blood splatter would go terribly with the number of sequins on Olga's date-night dress. About as poorly, actually, as Dad's requisite Dockers and boat shoes already do, but I digress.

"Hey, that's nice," Dad says, totally buying the whole thing hook, line, and sinker. "Maybe you can start playing?"

My guilt rises as he meets us on the driveway. Both of them are smiling at me, expectant. And maybe relieved? Actually, definitely relieved. "That's the plan."

"Edgar has been trying to get me into lessons at Northfield forever, but I've always put him off. He's trying to meet the ladies, you know." Of course Edgar the thrice-divorced Corn Nut–loving doctor suits up to meet ladies at the country club. I bet he joined after taking a trip with Alex's dad, Oscar, who's also a poker night regular. "But I'm not, obviously," Dad adds quickly, before an Olga elbow to his spleen. "Maybe we can do it together?"

"Sure thing, Dad." Eager to change the subject, I gesture with my non-racket hand. "Date night at home?"

"Dinner out, movie in," Dad answers, arm draped around Olga's shoulders.

She arches a steep eyebrow at me. It's buried in her bangs, but the intent is clear enough that I fork over a guess. "Dad forgot to reserve tickets?"

"Dad was too busy *saving lives* at work to reserve tickets," he answers before Olga does. "So sue me."

Olga could go in on Dad, but she doesn't. Instead, she dismisses him with a laugh. "The only thing I would've done differently is the dress. Very showy for the couch."

"I like that dress." Dad's response is almost defensive. Like how dare she reconsider it. Ugh, cute.

"Then it was worth it." She winks at him, and Dad sneaks a grin as he disappears back into the garage to get going. Olga and I backpedal past Nat's bumper, giving Dad the space not to run us over.

As I wait with her, Olga pushes a flyaway behind my ear. Her hand lingers and cradles my chin. "Two days in a row seeing you . . . I miss seeing you every day, Caro. Come by the gym sometime. I can't let your dad have me all to himself."

My heart stumbles in a much different way than it did minutes ago. We *have* seen each other more than just the past two days... but it's been awkward, with my walls up and history a river between us. I don't know why I didn't cross the divide sooner—better. It feels so nice to be in Olga's orbit again.

I'm incapable of words, tears pressing hot against my eyes, and so I just hug her.

24

I back into the house with a wave more to Olga than to Dad as
they perform almost the same three-point turn Alex did moments
earlier. Olga doesn't live far—she shares a townhouse with Elena
on the other side of Balan's. It's a newer place than ours, and more of
a crash pad. Olga spends all her time at the gym. She doesn't even
own a TV, so hosting movie night is sort of out of the question.

"How was your night with Alex?"

I spin around, and there's my brother, standing in the hall,
smirk cartoonishly drawn on his face—he doesn't want me to miss
it. His arms are crossed, tan forearms bulging at me.

Nat's eyes narrow as I fumble to dislodge the thing in my
throat.

"Alex? I was at Peregrine's." I fiddle with the little zipper cover
of the racket. And really hope in the low light he can't see my
tears because that'll make this one hundred percent worse. "Artemis gave me this racket too. Isn't it nice?"

Nat guffaws, baring his teeth. There's something mean in his
eyes. "Don't give me that. Artemis drives a Toyota Corolla. Even
with a racing package—which she does *not* have—it would never
sound like that." He steals the racket from my hand and I let him.

"Plus I saw this exact racket in Alex's trunk when he grabbed an extra basketball the other day." He turns it over, and there, in Sharpie at the bottom of the handle, are the initials LJM. A smoking gun in tidy teenage girl strokes. "Lily Jane Mack. Also known as Alex's half sister."

"*Sister*. Don't be a prick. Use what they prefer. Even when Alex and LJ aren't around."

His lips twist further. "How did Peregrine's sister get Alex's sister's racket?"

"They're friends." That is not a lie. Artemis was on cheer squad with Lily Jane.

But Nat was on that particular squad too. "They were *teammates*. Not friends. And a friend doesn't give away another friend's stuff without asking."

I—*shit*.

I'm caught, and Nat knows it. His smirk slides into a true smile as he does the mental gymnastics for me. "Are you going to tell me that Lily Jane was over at Peregrine's too? And then Alex picked her up, even though she's got her own car, and drove you back because it was stupid of Artemis to take you, and then Lily Jane gave you her racket out of the back of her brother's car?" He pokes me in the stomach with the racket and I steal it back. "So I'll ask again. How was your night with Alex?"

"It's not like that."

"What's it like, then?" Nat asks, challenging my pushback. "You better tell me or I'm going to start *assuming* things."

My lips press tightly against my teeth.

"Things... like that you were with him for the past four hours."

Four hours? It *was* four hours. Shit.

"That you had dinner together, because literally everyone,

including you, leaves Bruno's smelling like they could kill a vampire." Nat tips his head to the side, watching me like prey. "That *after dinner* he gave you a present literally only he could give you unless Lily Jane was hiding in his trunk the whole time—which I highly doubt because she left for a cheer clinic in St. Louis this morning."

Hell. Of course she did. And of course he'd know.

I can't get past Nat and his boulder shoulders in this narrow hallway. And I can't back up unless I attempt to retreat from the house, which is definitely an option because I'm wearing running shoes and Nat is barefoot... but then also, why do I want to lie so badly? Why have I lied already? And so easily.

The proof's cradled in my arms, and it's not like Alex isn't a text away on the phone in Nat's pocket.

It's just... neither of us have said a thing to Nat. And I like it that way.

So much of Alex is Nat's and this is my first piece of it.

I need to keep my sliver of Alex.

"Remember how you demanded I find a new sport? Well, Alex offered to help me find one. Volleyball, tennis, golf, running—and I guess basketball if you count that one game of horse. But I like tennis the best, and so... racket."

Nat is incredulous. "You played tennis tonight?"

"Yeah. Golf too."

Now he's getting it. "At the country club?"

"Yeah."

Nat just stares at me. "If that's what happened... why lie about it?"

"Because..."

I don't want to share this "gym class" experiment with anyone else.

I made a deal to set him up with my friend.

I have a crush on him.

Nat's big brother bullshit detector is running hot as he watches me fumble for a way to explain why I've been spending so much time with his best friend and neither of us have said anything about it. "Because it's...embarrassing." His smirk wavers. Encouraging. "Look, you were right. Dad was right. I need to do something with my time. Alex felt bad and offered to help me. So, in summary: You were right, I was wrong, and it's embarrassing."

Nat absorbs my attempt at a compliment without a flicker of smugness. That's not promising. "And so there's nothing going on between you two?"

"No!" I snap, in pretty much the same defensive way I did with Sunny and Peregrine, but it feels different because now *I feel different*. And I'm talking to Nat. So I add a distinguished/anguished, "*Gross*." I try to look properly horrified, though my heart slides into a new, laughing rhythm. There is literally nothing gross about that boy, and even Nat knows it.

My brother reads my body language as closely as a gymnastics judge evaluates for execution. I stay still, sticking my horrified little sister face as well as any dismount. My muscles twitch from my extended attempt at a wrinkled nose and puckered mouth.

Finally, Nat drops his arms to his sides, posture relaxing. "Good. Because if he put the moves on you, I'd take two inches off his vertical through his kneecap."

For extra emphasis, he steals back my racket and mimes going in, Nancy Kerrigan injury-style, on my left leg. I squirm away and steal back the racket, finally getting past him and down the hall. Roadblock averted. "No you wouldn't. If he can't rebound, Northland is screwed. And you hate to lose."

"Caroline, I think you're underestimating how pissed I'd be if anyone, even Alexander Oscar Zavala, came at my little sister with unwanted attentions."

I almost tell Nat about Sunny. About how I orchestrated a setup, and he just needs to pull the trigger—it would clear Alex of any suspicions, but it would also mean betraying his trust with his best friend, and I've already done enough betraying with that information. So I don't. Instead I say, "Everyone knows not to mess with you, Nat."

25

The next day, I arrive at the Northland tennis courts ten minutes early. Alex is already there, sitting in his car. I come up on him and rap two knuckles on the window. The second I move my hand out of the way, knock finished, is the second I realize that Alex Zavala is shirtless.

The swoop of his throat. Pecs. Nipples. Abs. Happy trail. Holy hell.

I was slightly too distracted to notice, but he's not necessarily shirtless as much as he is mid-shirt change. A fresh tank top is tangled between his upper arms—which just happens to leave his entire torso exposed.

To me. The idiot who didn't look before she knocked.

His abs contract under a layer of golden skin as he tenses at the sight of me, standing literally a foot away, gaping at his driver's-side window.

Alex hustles to complete the maneuver, and I try but can't tear my eyes away as the fabric skims his body. My cheeks are warming, and I'm pretty sure my mouth hangs ajar.

He finishes with the shirt and the door pops open. My body finally reacts, and I step back and away, my eyes flying to the grass, the tree overhead, the high school beyond. Anywhere but him.

"You're early," he says.

"Yep." I force myself to look at him. "Also blind. Should've looked before I knocked. Sorry."

He grins. "My protein shake exploded." Oh. An accident. He spilled on his clothes. He nods at my tank top, one of Nastia Liukin in her all-around pink leo from Beijing with a sparkly scroll underneath. *Gold medal if you're Nast-y.* "I don't have endless tank tops like you."

"You're going to have to up your game, Zavala."

"With you? I know, Caro, I know." Alex reaches back into the car for his hat—discarded along with his original shirt, apparently—and heads to the trunk for his racket bag. I spy a couple of basketballs in there.

"Um," I start. "So Nat knows about the coaching."

Alex pauses, hands overhead and curled around the lip of his trunk. I can't see his expression. "Yeah, he made that much clear before I'd even cut the engine in the staff parking lot this morning."

His voice is a little uneven—surprising.

"I told him you were just being nice. I was too embarrassed to say anything earlier." It's the third time I've said that to someone and though I know it's the truth, it still comes out weak every time. "It's hard to admit you're starting over...even when you have help."

Alex nods with a little shrug. "Well, I didn't tell him either."

I want to know why, but Alex doesn't appear to want to elaborate. He shuts the trunk with a satisfying clang. And when he turns, he's looking at his keys, fumbling for the locking clicker. Not looking at me. Actually, looking anywhere but me. "Nat's a good big brother. He's not always the best at expressing himself without sounding like a total jackass, but he means well."

"Ain't that the truth."

Alex pauses. Shifts his feet. His face darkens beneath his cap.

How much of a jackass was Nat exactly?

They've been the best of friends since literal diapers, our dads former college roommates. Last night, I told every bit of truth to Nat except for the Sunny side of it. And Nat was still a little peeved but didn't question me. Except for the whole initial lie of it, which, yeah, he had every reason to be suspicious about.

Alex begins to walk toward the court and I follow, Lily Jane's racket swinging loosely in my grip. "Anyhow, he wasn't in much of a listening mood," he admits as we slide through the opening in the chain-link fence surrounding the court. "So when you see him maybe you can put his mind at ease and inform him that Sunny and I are going to dinner on Friday?"

"You *are?*" I grab Alex's arm and swing in front of him. He's blushing, so he's definitely not bluffing. Wow—and she didn't tell me first? I would be pissed if I weren't so pleased that my repayment has come to fruition. "Why didn't you lead with that?!"

"I expected *you* to lead with it."

I mean, I would have. I have a serious itch to whip out my phone and fire off a subtle DO YOU HAVE SOMETHING TO TELL ME text to Sunny, but I have at least some tiny modicum of restraint. Life is full of happy surprises. Maybe I *am* a slightly better match-maker than Emma Woodhouse. However, my stomach swings low, my heart stuttering. My fingers shake. I'm too warm and though I pump enthusiasm into my voice, I only demand details because I'm supposed to. I don't really want to know. At all. "Tell me, tell me, tell me."

It must work because Alex's blush is spreading. This is a good sign. He literally sits down on the courtside bench—another new development. Suddenly I need to sit down too.

"Well, um," he starts, and I grip the bench as hard as possible. "Let's just say that after my conversation with Nat this morning, I got up the courage to text her."

Now that makes sense. I swallow. "And you're confirmed for Friday?"

He squints at me. "That's all you have to say? You're not going to toot your own horn? Give me a rundown of how you've been working the angle from the other side? Declare victory over your overdeveloped sense of debt?"

I deadpan. "I'm not Nat."

He surrenders a little smile.

"No, you're not." Alex stands. "Let's get down to business, *not Nat*. Warm-up and service drills."

26

I text our Sunny-Peregrine-Caroline group thread as I walk
home from practice, sweat ringing all parts of my body where fabric starts and stops—the tabbed ankles of my socks, the hems of my shorts and waistband, and, of course, the neck and arm holes of my Nastia tank. I've got my racket under my arm, the handle resting on my curved elbow, a water bottle from Nat's endless collection of Northland Basketball knockoff Nalgenes dangling almost empty from one thumb-typing hand.

Um, Sun, I hear you have PLANS for Friday night?!

They're not out of practice for a few minutes, so I slip my phone back into the side-holster pocket on my shorts and turn off the main drag and toward our neighborhood, the park about a half mile ahead. After a few minutes, my phone vibrates, and when I rearrange all I'm carrying to draw it from my pocket, it's no surprise that Peregrine replies first. I picture her standing two feet from Sunny, typing as they literally congregate at their lockers, practice finished for the day.

Oh REALLY. She caps it off with the staring, disembodied eyes emoji.

Pretty sure the same sort of side-eye is happening in real time and tinged with chalk-caked sweat. Sunny's little typing bubbles seem to last forever. Stopping and starting. Likely telling Peregrine everything in real time. A pang of sadness claws at my chest. How I wish I were there to watch this unfold in person, not through blinking dots on my phone.

And then it occurs to me that I might be helpless at being there as a gymnast, but I'm perfectly capable of getting the low-down in real time without being two feet away.

I hit the video button on Sunny's contact and all of a sudden we're FaceTiming.

Sunny answers, the screen jostling as she literally scampers out of the building, away from the prying ears of Olga and Elena. "I was going to tell you guys!" she scream-whispers, first to my face, then to Peregrine, who is jostling her bag, flip-flops, and phone.

"Holdout!" Peregrine crows accusingly, coming into frame.

I add, "Spill!"

"*You* spill!" Sunny orders me, ducking into the shade of one of the few trees in the parking lot. She glances up and gives a little wave as admirers come and go during the practice-time change-over—I mean, if you're an elite with a national track record, everyone wants to say hi to you all the time. That's the curse of being Sunny. "Alex said something?"

"Not much before he turned red and started barking drills to avoid my many questions. Just that he'd texted you and a date on Friday was the result."

"Yes—I know that means no girls' dinner..." We'd just adjusted to Fridays because that truly did work the best for all of us most consistently. "Maybe I should change it?"

I furiously shake my head. "No, no. His calendar is a Tetris board. If he came up with the time, roll with it."

"We can handle ourselves," Peregrine adds with a side-eye to me that says YES we are hanging together, waiting for updates on Friday night. I almost mouth, "Your place or mine?" when Sunny's face suddenly takes up the whole screen, eyes wide.

"I'm supposed to pick the restaurant—what's he like to eat?"

"He's a teenage boy. He'll eat literally anything you put in front of him," Peregrine answers.

"Uh, Caro, can you help pare down Peregrine's very sage advice, please?"

Bruno's immediately pops into my head, but if he took two girls there in the span of a little more than a week, the waitstaff would certainly notice. I mean, they're going to remember him—who wouldn't? Burger Fu would do, except that Sunny doesn't eat half the food there. "How about Eomma?" I ask. "It's cute, we know exactly how busy it is on a Friday, and I'd imagine he could probably put away some bibimbap in a major way."

My view quakes as Peregrine smacks Sunny on the arm. "That's it. Perfect." Peregrine's lips twist. "And you can impress him with your ability to magically make extra kimchi appear. The ability to conjure free food is likely high on the list of traits in a good mate."

Sunny immediately shields the majority of her horrified face with a hand. "Did you have to use the term *mate*?"

Peregrine smirks. "No, I just wanted to see you make exactly that face."

"Jesus Christ, you two," Sunny exclaims, hand sliding down her features, which are as red as if she'd been working handstands for the last forty-five minutes. "There will be no mating. Only bibimbap!"

"Mmm-hmmm." Peregrine's got an incredulous brow that is perfection.

Sunny sighs and resets, the color still high in her cheeks. "That said, Eomma's a good idea. That's a place where we can have *polite conversation*. And get to know each other."

"I mean, we know him. Do you want a crash course ahead of time?" Peregrine asks.

"Oh yeah, I'm sure I can swing a PowerPoint presentation complete with ancient photos by Friday," I add.

"That won't be necessary," Sunny insists, making full eye contact with both of us one at a time to drive home her point. "I don't want to come in creepy. I'd rather get to know him organically. No crash course, no PowerPoint, no nada."

"Fine, but you will tell us how it goes, right?" I ask, halting in the shade of a tree that edges the rosebush border of the park. The basketball court is empty, which is surprising—I very much expected to see Nat and maybe even Alex shooting hoops.

Sunny purses her lips. "Only if you tell me how it went for him."

I glance away, trying my hardest not to cringe. What if Alex asks the same thing? I've gone from matchmaker to double agent. I don't know that I can manage the embarrassment of sharing with both sides without exposing the way I really feel.

But Sunny's got Olga's stare powers, and my face seems to warm from it through the phone, so I shrug and say, "Sure thing."

I'm too chicken to ask Alex what he's thinking about the date. So chicken, in fact, that I have no idea how I'm going to keep my promise long enough to even attempt asking him how it actually went.

I don't want him thinking that I'm talking with Sunny behind his back, even though I sort of am.

And not to mention my own heart's been having a heck of a time this week, running wind sprints between being thrilled about this possible love connection and also crushed by, you know, my crush.

But all that's bottled inside me, compartmentalized as much as any extracurricular thoughts I had during a judged routine. Tunnel vision is in my skill set and nothing says I can't use it here.

And so, every tennis practice this week is the same: business as usual.

Alex asking me if I ran in the morning. (The answer is always yes.)

Alex grinning and saying, "Sweet."

And then: Drills. Drills. Drills.

I'm improving as far as getting a racket on every return... but I'm still marginal at getting the ball within the lines, let alone where I want it to actually go.

Hand-eye coordination and ball sports, man.

By Thursday I still haven't uttered a single word about the date. Toward the end of our session, I'm chugging water and trying to figure out if I should say something or save it for tomorrow. It's hot as all get-out and my mind is fuzzy, which isn't so great for decision-making. I'm probably extra sweaty because I wore black—I've got on my Nadia Comaneci tank again, her smiling teen face angling for the sun.

As I come up for air, my stomach suddenly very full of water, Alex chin checks Nadia. "Hey, so remember when you offered to show me gymnastics videos? With Nadia and the Amanar?"

I stare at him. I mean, I said those words. And he said cool, but then I showed him that video of Sunny doing her Amanar and I thought that's where it had ended.

"Um, yes." I literally have no idea where this is going.

"Would you be up for...playing historian for a crash course in modern gymnastics? I don't want to sound like an idiot to Sunny, but I also have no idea where to start. The cache of gymnastics videos on YouTube is...overwhelming." He pauses, a deep flush rising on his tan cheeks. Alex must realize he's going the direction of a candy apple, because he rubs his neck as if it'll erase the color.

The vulnerability. Again.

Dear lord.

"Are you kidding!? Of course I will." I almost add that there's pretty much no way on Simone Biles's beautiful earth that Sunny will spend the entirety of dinner quizzing him on the evolution of modern gymnastics, but I will take the chance to help Alex Zavala with literally anything. "When?"

"Do you have time...tonight?"

"I can go right now." I sound a little too eager, but in my defense, it *is* four thirty, and we have a lot of ground to cover.

Alex laughs. "Slow down there, sparky. I don't know about you, but I need a shower." He glances at his watch, then away, thinking. "Six? At my place? I can order pizza and pick it up when I get you."

"How about six at your place, I walk, and *I* pay for delivery? You're always doing stuff for me. Take your shower. Chill. I've got this." His lips drop open to fight me. I put my hands on my hips. "Alex Zavala, king of nice things, please let me do this for you.

I can handle a Mozza-Monster and a five-minute walk with wet hair."

His hand drops from his neck, and all that fight of his slips away into a smile.

"Deal, Caro. Deal."

27

I arrive at Alex's house a few minutes early, perspiration threatening my freshly cleaned skin on yet another summer night. But it's cloudy and the wind's kicked up—good ole Midwestern thunderstorms a possibility—take that, sixth-driest summer on record.

Rather than wearing one of my millions of tank tops, I'm standing in a sundress, the light blue fabric making even me look a little tan. The tennis and running probably have something to do with that too.

Either way, Alex is surprised—and not by the pop of color on pale me.

"A dress? You're not going to troll me with that one tank top with all the names on it?" Alex grins as he opens the door. And he's one to talk—instead of his own endless supply of workout tanks and tech fabric shirts, he's wearing a polo and shorts. His hair is drier than mine. Whatever product he puts in it to seal in the perfection smells really nice.

"I didn't want to spot you a cheat sheet. Plus, this dress has pockets big enough for my phone. No purse for the win."

He laughs. "Come on in."

I grab the door instead of ducking under his polite wingspan.

Confusion breaks across his face, but no sir, I will not set my hormones up for the sort of roller coaster we had at Bruno's.

I'm here. As a friend. Helping him ace his date.

I'm not selling Sunny's deepest, darkest secrets or giving him creepy amounts of detail. I'm just teaching him about the sport that was my life, and then letting him use his newfound knowledge (or not) while devouring bibimbap and that addictive kimchi.

We sweep down the entry hall toward the kitchen. "Pizza will be here in twenty—though I ordered it thirty minutes ago," I say. "Just a long wait—but it's paid up. Except for the tip." I pat my pocket. "I've got cash for the guy."

Alex nods. "Awesome, thank you. Water?"

"Sure."

He gets the glasses, and as he does, I glance around. Music plays softly from somewhere. Bon Iver or a knockoff—I'm terrible at identifying anything that wouldn't be played over the gym stereo. Alex has a laptop out on the coffee table, the wall-mounted TV across from both it and the sectional couch showing his screensaver, the setup ready for video viewing. He's just as prepared for this as he is for all his practices.

He hands me the water, ice clinking in the glass. "Need a snack ahead of Mozza-Monster?"

"No thanks." I trail him as he heads to the couch.

"I actually had a bet going with myself that you would show up with a pan of your brownies."

I sink into the down-stuffed ridiculousness of their family room couch. "What was the over-under on that bet?"

"Sixty-forty. Mostly because I wasn't sure you'd have time to get them cool enough to carry."

The couch claims him too, and we both slide toward the middle as it accepts our collective weight. I try to right myself, but he weighs more than me and it's not going to work. I scoot over a good half foot but it's helpless. "I actually was going to bring you some brownies, as both an appetizer and a dessert, when I found out the wait time. But I was missing a key ingredient." He raises a questioning brow. And so I tell him. "Don't laugh—beans."

"They . . . *beans*, beans?"

I nod. "Like the kind you would put in a burrito."

Alex's lips form an O.

"That sort of recipe was popular a few years ago, and I guess I never let go of it. I should probably try the almond flour ones or something . . . probably less . . . potentially problematic." *Ohmygod*, I've now brought up both "ball sports" and an allusion to poo in front of this perfect person. *Shut up, Caroline.* "And stuff."

I brace for his thoughts on this but because he's an angel, he simply says, "That's a lot of fiber."

Bless him. "Don't tell Nat. It's probably the only fiber he regularly gets in his system."

"He's never seen you make them? Didn't notice cans of beans in the recycling?"

I shrug. "You've seen what he forces upon his digestive system. Do you really think he cares how anything is made?"

"I. Uh. No." His knee knocks mine, and I try to escape the couch's clutches long enough to slide out of its clearance. And then, because *beans*, I change the subject.

"Okay, so gymnastics?"

In answer he shifts the laptop my way. "You can airplay from your phone if you want. I just thought this might be easier."

"It's perfect." My fingers hover over the keys. He's got YouTube pulled up, and apparently the kind you pay for without ads. Fancy. "So, shall we start in the modern era and go chronologically?"

"Seems reasonable."

I start to type. Vera Caslavska and Cathy Rigby come to mind as probably the oldest good footage available. And indeed—a few rare pieces from the 1968 Mexico City Olympics pop up. I really should've been Alex-level prepared and created a playlist. Oh well.

That's when I realize . . . "Where is everyone?"

"The country club. Trivia night. Well, trivia for Mom and Dad, pool time for LJ and her friends." Huh, Lily Jane must be back from St. Louis. "They leech themselves onto my parents to score one-for-one entry on trivia night and then sneak out."

"Oh. Do you usually go?"

Alex grins over the rim of his glass. "No. I'm at that club enough."

Fair. "Okay, well, you'll be enjoying only the finest pizza and ice water at the gymnastics club tonight. Shall we?"

In answer, Alex sits back, crosses one ankle over his opposite knee, and drapes one arm over the couch. It's the side opposite me, which repairs the couch's cushy equilibrium a little.

"Okay, so, for your reference, the modern women's gymnastics era started in 1928, because that's when women began to compete in the Olympic Games. That said, the golden age really began in the 1960s."

Alex nods. "Television really upped the ante, huh?"

"You bet. The games weren't televised until 1960 in the United States. And for gymnastics, the real highlights came in 1968 at Mexico City. Not that the sport wasn't great before then, but the talent wasn't as widely appreciated."

"Plus there's not much in the way of video from before then?"

"Yep. Larisa Latynina was the first big star. She won fourteen Olympic medals between 1956 and 1964. Then came Vera Caslavska and Cathy Rigby—"

"*Peter Pan!*"

I stare at him. "Um, yes, Cathy Rigby played Peter Pan."

Alex settles into a self-satisfied smirk that he surely learned from my brother. "You know I know *Hamilton*—why are you surprised that I know *Peter Pan*?"

My mouth is hanging open. "Because it wasn't widely available on a streaming service?"

He laughs at my literal jaw drop before tapping my chin with a knuckle to correct it. "Gramps has an old VHS tape of it. Watched it probably ten times a month as a kid." He shakes his head. "Boys are allowed to love musicals, Caroline, and I love them just as much as Gramps—and Dad too. Want me to regale you with the time I made a recording of 'Agony' from *Into the Woods* for LJ when she broke up with the asswipe she dated before Topps? Perhaps you'll appreciate it more than she did at the time."

I blink. "*I love that song.*"

I've seen the movie version more times than should be allowed. "Giants in the Sky" was Peregrine's floor music the first year of optionals—and the Chris Pine/Billy What's-His-Name version of "Agony" is my favorite part. I literally have no idea what to say because over the past two weeks Alex's human-esque qualities have just trickled out, and now the dam's busted and the mushy insides of Alex are threatening to take me away. Marble statue stuffed full of cinnamon rolls indeed. Alex Zavala is a true *music theater nerd* and I had no idea.

"It's the best kind of stage sarcasm," Alex is saying. "Even the movie version is great—"

The doorbell rings and cuts him off. He hops up to get it. I shoot to my feet and chase after him, because the order's in my name.

"Caroline?" I hear the pizza guy ask as I zip around the corner.

Alex hands the guy a five, shuts the door, and blocks the hall-way to keep me from squeaking through with my own tip.

"Hey. The pizza was mine to get."

"And you did. If I promise to eat at least one more piece than you, will you refrain from chasing that guy down the street to trade my tip for yours?"

I steal the pizza from him. "Though I have improved my speed with those track workouts you prescribed, it would definitely be more efficient to toss my money at you."

"Remember the cabana? Same rules apply here. Your money's no good."

Alex grabs a couple of plates and makes sure to very obviously pile four pieces onto his. I, meanwhile, start with two. I fiddle with the napkins as he heads over to the couch first, eating as he goes. Sure that his back is turned, I haul out my own five and stuff it underneath the pizza box to surprise him later.

My money is good here if I say it's good here.

Perhaps I am a tiny bit like Nat.

28

I step back into the living room, and Alex has changed the Bon Iver/knockoff Bon Iver soundtrack to a very familiar *Ohh, I do, I do, I do.* "Is that 'Helpless'?"

He grins. "Yep." He tips his phone in my direction. A curated "Broadway Songs" playlist scrolls across his screen. He brings a hand to his mouth as if he's telling me a secret. "I run to this."

My eyes grow wide. "You're kidding."

Dimples flash. "Dead serious—don't tell anyone or I'm using the beans against you."

I mouth, "Oh my God."

And he laughs. "We've got eight songs until an 'Agony' dramatic belt-along. Enough time? Or do you want me to hit shuffle and shock the clock?"

"Straight through." I swallow a bite of pizza and it's even better than the other night—the cheese is melted perfection, and the crust is not too crisp and not too soft. "Does Nat know about the Broadway addiction?"

"He knows enough to completely avoid referencing it because he's far too embarrassed by the cheese factor."

For someone who goes out of his way to embarrass himself,

Nat can also be completely finicky about the embarrassment he will weather for others. "Checks out." I dust cornmeal off my fingers and pick up where I'd left off. "Okay, so I was going to show you Vera, but let's start with Cathy." I pull up a beam routine where she's all blond pigtails and sass. "I think it's safe to say she was the first darling of American gymnastics." It's easy to see why. The California-girl glow, the petite body, big smile, high energy, and the fact that she won—not at the Olympics, but at the world championships when she took home the United States's first-ever international competition medal, a silver on beam.

I relay this to Alex and pull up another gymnast who defined the early televised era—Olga Korbut. She's also pigtails and sass but with the added bonus of her absolutely insane "Korbut Flip." I search for her 1972 Olympics bars routine to make sure Alex sees the flip—a move so risky that Alex momentarily forgot he was chewing and nearly choked on some super-delicious Bruno's crust.

"Did...she...back dive...off the bar?" he asks between hacks, covering his mouth with his wrist for a moment, eyes watering. I hand him his cup and he takes a long drink. By the time he's cleared the offending crust and is breathing normally, I have the video skipped forward to a modern slow-mo capture that clearly demonstrates that, yes, she literally crouched atop the high bar, sprung up, and boomeranged back down to catch the bar before pinballing to and around the low bar and flying back to the high bar.

Alex sits forward, elbows on his knees, rewinding it and pausing it to the very moment she's flying straight down before her body curves around to get fingertips on the bar. "That. Is. Terrifying."

"Terrifying and *banned*, actually."

"Look at that." He traces the line of her body. "If she misses, it's a swan dive straight onto her head from—how many feet up is that?"

"The bar's eight feet, but she clearly jumps higher while performing the Korbut Flip."

"Jesus."

"Okay, so now you can speak eloquently about the subject of Olga Korbut and her banned move." I skip Ludmilla Tourischeva and just head straight for Nadia Comaneci and the 1976 Olympics. "Let's watch some perfection, shall we?"

The second I begin typing her name, Alex is on it. "The girl from your shirt."

"Yes! She got the first perfect ten in the Olympics, and then got six more."

"I think I've heard of this."

"As a jock who's not dumb and also doesn't have his head up his own butt, I'm sure you've inadvertently seen an Olympic-year vignette or two about great performances."

"You've described me perfectly."

"Okay, more perfection!" I cue up a video featuring Nadia's perfect performances. Alex is still leaning in, watching on the close computer screen instead of the big screen behind it. His knee brushes mine. I expect him to adjust, but when he doesn't, I don't either, letting my skin warm with the contact.

When the video's over, he doesn't reset. He meets my eyes with utter awe. "That was incredible."

It's so nice that he can see it too.

The 1980s are all power and pomp from Mary Lou Retton and stoic conformity from all the Communist countries prized for their skills and artistry. We make a hard turn into the 1990s, and the Americans begin to control the stage like no other.

Kim Zmeskal. Shannon Miller. Dominique Dawes. Kerri Strug. The 1992 Barcelona team slides into the 1996 Magnificent Seven. Alex has seen Strug's famed one-legged vault, but he hasn't seen the run-up to it. So I find a video of Dominique Moceanu's uncharacteristic falls that add to the tension of that famed moment.

"Afterward, the story became that the equipment wasn't set up right—that's why they fell," I say, trying to tell the tale without getting so technical that I ruin it. "Rules kept Bela Karolyi off the floor, and he usually set the height of the vault and distance of the board for both of them. Not sure if it's really true or if it was just plain nerves or even bad luck, but it's what happened. In real time, on prime time, in the host country, which is super dramatic and incredible."

"Wow. Yeah." By now, Alex has heard the Karolyi name a few times—the famed coaches who trained Nadia and Mary Lou. They also trained several other big American gymnasts in the 1990s and ran USA Gymnastics before fading away to retirement as the Larry Nassar allegations came to light.

We move ahead to the early 2000s. Carly Patterson, Shawn Johnson, Nastia Liukin—Alex remembers my tank top from earlier this week too, so gold star!—into the Gabby Douglas and Aly Raisman era before the run-up to the dominance of Simone Biles.

"We could watch clips of her all day," I say of Simone.

Alex jokingly scrolls down the sidebar on YouTube, where there are literally endless clips of Simone, her performances, training clips, tutorials, and just on and on. Alex scrolls as if he's spinning the dice. "Here's one that's not just her. We'd get to it at like four in the morning if we let it play through." He clicks on it—a video entitled "Best Saves!"

It starts with Kerri Strug's vault, obviously. Moves on to

fingertip saves on bars, and then, more than half the video is comprised of saves on beam. The beam burns pile up and I realize the education part of the night is over. And yet, even though Alex can now easily have a conversation with Sunny about gymnastics, it seems he's not done either.

He's really enjoying the incredible talents of these girls in real time. Even save after save.

Of course, with about a minute left, Chellsie Memmel flashes on the screen. "Oh! She's had two kids and totally went back into training and competing after eight years of retirement, even in her thirties." I scramble for my phone in my deep dress pockets. "Let me see—"

My vision narrows on the screen, because I realize exactly what move World Champion–era Chellsie is doing.

A standing Arabian.

I stiffen and glance away, hoping Alex won't notice.

But of course he does. "What?"

I shake my head, and he hits pause on the video and waits. I swallow. This is stupid. It's not like I can't watch this move. That would mean never watching a televised gymnastics event again, or even my own friends—Sunny has had an Arabian in her beam routine for more than a year.

I meet his eyes. "That was the move I hurt myself on." Breathing carefully, I rewind the video and slow it down. "Blind landing. You can't see where you're going, and sometimes you're falling before you even realize it. This time I realized it, but everything was already out of my control, and, well. I fell apart in the worst possible way."

I smile, mostly because it might keep the tears pressing against the backs of my eyes from spilling over. Alex may have shown me he's a human being over the last few weeks, but I've shown him I'm an emotional trash fire more than once. I press my hands together in my lap, a tremble in my fingers. I don't let Chellsie flail, keeping her reaching for the beam, reaching for the hope of a stick that's not coming.

I force myself to glance up at Alex. "A millimeter either way and maybe I...maybe I wouldn't be here."

Here.

This is the second time I've teared up at this word in his presence, trying to describe the state of me. The first when starting over. And now, when reflecting on where I was. Where I've been.

As much of a struggle as it was during those first weeks after my career ended, and the strangeness of trying new things...I like being *here*. In this new chapter with a lifelong recurring character. In the surprise and delight of it all. The changing landscape, sands shifting under our feet with each new experience.

My life previously was about repetition, perfection, the safety in knowing exactly what's coming, how to do it, how to save it. Even as we've settled into a routine, I still never know what to expect from myself or Alex. And the hope of it all, of each new breath piling onto the next and making time enough to be called an experience is just...exhilarating.

And Alex makes it that way. A hundred percent.

I squeeze my hands tighter together, pressing them into my thighs, the fabric of my dress flattening across my knees. Yet my fingers still shake, my lips tremble now too, and a hot tear spills over as I try to cover a sob.

Alex sweeps his thumb to my cheek, stopping the tear in its tracks. Blunting it with the softest of touches. That thumb sweeps the wetness away but then stays, warm against my cheek. "Don't cry, Caroline."

At the sound of his voice, my eyes lift from my lap and stop on his mouth. There's no tightness to it, his lips held as softly as his fingers touch my face. Supple—that's the word for them.

Supple. Inviting. Close.

I tear my attention away from his lips but only succeed in meeting his eyes. Chocolate brown and warm, trying to read my face.

Tension increases between his fingertips and my skin. I'm disoriented and crying, but in this haze I swear he's drawn me closer. Our knees knock together, the downy cushions and gravity doing their work. Alex's other hand cups the double fist I have in my lap, calming the tremble I can't shake on my own.

We're bare inches apart now, and everything in me wants to close the distance.

I want to kiss him.

I want to toss away every fear about the aftermath. With Alex. With Sunny. With Nat. With this new life of mine.

That tension in his fingers has only grown, and now he has a true cradling grip on the side of my face, his fingertips splayed in my hair.

I watch his eyes, his mouth, confirming that he isn't saying no to this.

He hasn't budged. Hasn't pulled back. Hasn't telegraphed any signal that I'm reading him wrong. He's all warmth and strength and skin on skin.

The consequences hang between us, a veil between before and after.

And for once I don't care.

My lips part. I lean into his hand, an invitation of my own.

Alex's beautiful eyes flutter shut, and I swear he's nearly closed the distance. But that kiss is still a promise just out of reach.

My wet lashes touch and I tilt toward him.

Toward the promise of his warmth and his choices, and the safety of satisfying the want churning in my gut and the consequences that come—

All at once, the garage door rumbles to life and the front door slams open. The collective slap and step of more than one set of sandals echoes down the entry hall.

Lily Jane's voice crashes into my consciousness. "Alex! Nat's here, looking for Caroline. Is she—"

We jolt apart.

Lily Jane appears, hair wet, a sundress not so different from my own draped across her frame. Over each of her shoulders stands a gape-mouthed boy: her boyfriend, Topps, and my brother.

Topps looks like he's dodged a bullet.

Nat looks like he swallowed that bullet and it's caught in his windpipe.

Shit.

I shoot to standing, my water glass tipping over as my knee catches the lip of the coffee table hard.

Alex scoops the laptop up safely in his arms. In the jostling, Chellsie spins back into motion, falling into an acrobatic save before some other unfortunate girl appears to be lining up a different move and a new way to almost fall. "You guys are back early," Alex says way more coolly than I could possibly do right now.

Lily Jane's eyes narrow, the faint scent of chlorine wafting our direction as both she and Nat run through older sibling bullshit detector protocol in tandem. Their eyes swing from us to the couch, to the crust-and-crumb-covered plates to the speakers, to the current space between us, to the laptop cradled against Alex's chest, to the mirrored video on the big screen—a girl in what amounts to a long-sleeved swimsuit prancing across a four-inch apparatus hauled four feet off the ground.

Under their twin scrutiny, my knees soften enough that I sway. The spilled water dribbles off the edge of the table and onto my lower calf and ankle. It's not a bucket of cold water over my head, but it might as well be as I blink at them, the ultimate picture of *doing nothing wrong.*

"We're back at the same time we were last week," Lily Jane says finally. Her brows thread together and the beginnings of a laugh puff past her lips. "Alex, is that 'Agony'?"

Obviously it is. Neither of us says anything, the arrogant princes growing more blindly entitled as the vocal duel of one-upmanship goes on.

Topps's cheeks glow astronomically red as if in pity for us. My brother, however, looks more confused than anybody, even though his presence means he was expecting some sort of gotcha-type confrontation. He was at the basketball court. He might have seen me. He clearly figured it out. And now...

"You're watching gymnastics videos to...show tunes?" Nat tips his head at a vicious angle, as if attempting to match the lines on an impressionist painting with what the description says it should be. "Why?"

I want to glance back at Alex. To plead for him to say some-thing, to keep me from betraying his trust about his date with Sunny. Maybe Lily Jane already knows, and if she does, I wish she'd put two and two together like right the hell now.

"Because that's what all the cool kids do," Alex's mom says as she comes in from the garage. His dad trails her, both of them in navy and white like that's the Northfield Country Club's official trivia night uniform. And maybe it is. They sort of pause in the no-man's-land between the eat-in portion of the kitchen—aka right smack dab in the middle between where Alex and I stand—awkward and frozen as our siblings form a wall of suspicion.

"Oscar, I need your help with something," Mrs. Zavala says, snagging Mr. Zavala's wrist from behind her back, dragging him toward the hall, and escaping up the stairs.

They disappear and Topps looks like he regrets ever entering the house. "LJ, maybe I should head home early tonight."

"No, maybe you should stay and Alex should explain this very random scene."

Topps does as he's told but makes it a point to completely ignore us and help himself to the leftover pizza on the counter. The box shifts out of the way and I hear him ask a soft question: "A fiver?"

I step farther away from Alex, from the very obvious, very close dents we've left in the voluminous footprint of the sectional. Around the coffee table. There's now at least six feet between us and I can see him in my periphery because he moves forward, almost presenting the laptop as proof.

"This is completely embarrassing—"

"Um, obviously," Lily Jane answers, squinting at her big little brother.

Alex draws in a deep breath. "I have a date with Sunny Chavez tomorrow night." He nods my direction. "Caroline made it happen and is giving me a crash course in gymnastics so I don't look like a dope."

I twist my hands in front of me and nod in both confirmation and relief, even though my cheek is still warm from his touch. I hope to God that my eyes aren't as red as they feel and Alex's thumb truly blotted away any trace of that tear.

"Wait. Sunny from mathletics?" Topps asks, brushing pizza crumbs out of his adult-sized beard.

"Oh my God, you *still* have a crush on her?" Lily Jane asks, eyes lighting up. "I remember you sniffing around, asking questions about her forever ago."

"Well, he didn't ask me," Nat says. "And I had direct access to her. By way of Caroline, but still." Nat's gaze shifts to me. "Is this what you girls were being all weird about at the lake house?"

I nod. "We didn't think you would even notice our weirdness, given what fun you were having with Artemis." I clear my throat in hopes that others will get my drift, but all of this has zero effect on my brother, who doesn't flinch or turn red or in any other way reveal that, yeah, he spent all day flirting with Peregrine's older sister, who all three of them definitely know. "And, well, it's weird now, so I guess we failed."

"Not going to lie, gymnastics videos to show tunes classifies as weirder than 'Hey, that girl I had a crush on two years ago? We got set up!'" Nat scoffs, and I breathe a sigh of relief.

In the background, the horrific scream at the beginning of "Stay with Me" reverberates around the room, and Alex lunges to cut the song.

"Okay, with that, I think it's time to head home. Caroline, are you ready?"

My immediate reaction is to tell Nat I'll walk. That I need the fresh air. But I also need to get out of here as cleanly as possible.

Away from what nearly happened.

How I feel about it.

How Alex must feel about it.

Away.

And like it or not, Nat appears to be one hundred percent less suspicious now *and* the easiest way to get from point A to point B.

I turn to Alex and force out a smile. I should say something like, *"See you tomorrow."* But that feels like it'll invite questions from Lily Jane when I'm gone. I wonder if she actually knows I have her racket or not.

Alex's lips draw into a tight smile, his body language closed off as he palms the laptop. "Thanks, Caroline. For everything."

I sweep past Lily Jane, catching my brother's forearm so that he spins around to face the door with me, and then we're gone.

29

We step into the night and it smells like rain, the humidity heavy despite wind gusting enough to pick up the uneven hem of my wet/dry dress. Nat's Jeep isn't out front as I glance around, but when Nat makes a hard right onto the sidewalk, I don't need to ask—we're walking. Lightning spiders across the sky, the earlier promise of a thunderstorm finally coming to fruition.

I would normally start jogging—flip-flops and dress and all—to make sure I made it home mostly dry, but in that very moment the promise of the night being washed away sounds pretty good.

We hit the end of the street and make a left turn to head past the park and toward our cul-de-sac. Nat's got his hands in his pockets and has been uncharacteristically silent, eyes pointed down. He doesn't sneak a peek at me, eyes combing the cracks in the sidewalk as we shuttle past the rosebushes that line the park. My brother is not like this—like Alex. Calm and thoughtful and introspective.

A peal of thunder shakes across the sky. I realize then that I didn't ask how he knew I was with Alex. My initial thought was that he saw me walking over but what if it's more? Maybe Alex said more to him than I know when Nat confronted him at work.

Maybe there's a text thread between them not unlike the one I have going with Sunny and Peregrine, not talking about girls, but full of words unsaid in front of others at work.

Words that made Alex text Sunny more than twenty-four hours after I gave him her number.

I can't let myself wrap hope into that waiting period. Just like I can't hold on to what almost happened on the couch.

Alex has a date with Sunny.

That's happening. And now everyone knows it.

Nat's Adam's apple bobs after a moment. We make the turn to our street, our house ahead dark and empty. I'm relieved Dad isn't home yet. I'm relieved Nat isn't interrogating me further. I'm relieved it's all out in the open now. Everything but what lives within my chest, my head, the memory on my skin.

"Caro, did you really set Alex up with Sunny?"

My emotions swoop out of my gut and toward the pinch point of my throat. I nod.

"Any reason why?"

"They're perfect for each other."

Nat shoves his hands into his pockets. "I realize I'm talking to someone who sought literal perfection for years on end..." He glances at me before pulling in a deep breath. "But have you ever considered perfect isn't always best?"

I stop on a dime. After all this, is he suggesting that *I'm* the better match?

"Oh no you don't." My anger flares along with my stubbornness. "You don't get to go all hard-ass about how you're going to bash in Alex's knees if he tried anything with me and then question my decision to play matchmaker like you give a shit about my feelings."

I expect Nat's arms to be thrown wide, his head back, as he ratchets up a response that'll make porch lights flick on. My big brother with his big responses. But he's just as stationary as me, his voice level, none of his usual push-button attitude evident in the calm lines of his summer-tan face. "I reacted the way I did both earlier this week and tonight because I was in the dark. I thought the worst because *both of you* were keeping quiet about your training plans. Not to mention, you were both quiet *and* lied to my face about it."

Nat pauses and I nod to confirm that, yeah, I did. I lied to him, and lied to myself and stuffed down everything that came into the open in that few seconds on the couch.

"I'll admit that I was partially pissed because I was jealous," Nat says. This time his eyes are on the silver shadows that creep along the edge of the sidewalk. "I'm the big brother. You should be coming to me for help, and instead you went to him."

Oh shit. Nat did offer to help—well, it was more that he was trying to shove cheerleading with a side of fries down my throat, but from his point of view, that was definitely something he saw as a kindness.

"Maybe," he says, "to make myself feel better, I wanted reasons not to buy it and . . . well, I may have offered to ruin more than just his kneecaps."

I want to press my hands to my face and hide but don't.

"And so I also thought the worst when I realized that you'd gone to Alex's house and not Peregrine's."

I'm silent. He's right. And I'm terrified that his correctness is being presented in a calm, orderly way. He's never been like Dad; he's always been like Mom. She's all sass and walking out with middle fingers, and he didn't fall far from the tree. Now I'm standing in the shade of him, the moon at his back. And his reaction is so dramatic it doesn't even telegraph with his normal scale. "Listen, you don't have to say it out loud, but I get it all now."

Okay, now my hands are on my face.

Nat went from confronting me, confronting Alex, and following me to . . . at least appearing as if he understands?

"Look, if you *don't* want to keep training with him—I'll help you cover it, and train with you if you want to keep doing tennis or whatever." He does understand. He completely understands. And is being subtle about it. "If you *do* want to train with him just to hang out—I promise I'll stay out of it. For real. I won't ask you about it. I won't ask him. I won't push."

My throat is full again, hot tears pressing against my lash line, compounded by the pressure from my fingers shielding whatever I can from my brother, the moon, any armchair snoops drawing back curtains for a look.

"I know sometimes I'm about as bad at showing it as Mom, but I love you and I want you to succeed. And, you know, not be pressured into things by dudes with muscle cars and access to the country club, even if he's my friend." It's a repeat of his stance the other night but now it feels different. Like everything else. Nat palms the top of my head like it's one of his basketballs, more gently I guess, but the intent is the same—*I've got you.* "But you weren't pressured. That much was clear on both of your faces."

Both of our faces? What does Alex want? I only know what he's said:

He confirmed he had a long-festering crush on Sunny.

He said yes to a reintroduction.

He said yes to my meet-cute payment plan.

He said yes to a date.

And yet...he would've let me kiss him just minutes ago. I think.

Actions speak louder than words, but we never completed the action, just the run-up. And after that, he confirmed his date with Sunny. Publicly. That was a choice—an action—too.

I know I could just toss everything to the wind and ask him. I could. But we all know how shitty I am at hand-to-ball coordination—I'd probably take off Alex's very handsome head with my forty-five-pound bag of emotional confusion.

My eyes skip to Nat's face, hoping he'll make it clear what he saw of us, frozen there, not touching, literal "Agony" lilting in the air.

He doesn't. Instead, a smirk inches across his face, confident tilt back to his chin. "And...if you change your mind on everything and you need me to take him out at the knees, I will. I wasn't kidding."

Nat turns and walks up the drive. Leaving me standing in the creeping shadows and moonlight with my thoughts, the whisper of Alex's touch still warm on my face.

And, as the storm door slides to a pneumatic close, the skies open up and it finally rains.

30

When I wake up Friday, it's to the sound of more rain. Heavy rain. Fits my mood—dreary and dark, even though it's past dawn.

When I stumble into the kitchen, I find Nat devouring a scone as big as his fist. "CAWFEE IN DA FRIDGE."

He motions toward the refrigerator with a half-drunk massive Frappuccino topped with enough cream to ski across. As I open the door to find my very own cold brew—though Nat's name is scrawled across it, of course—he swallows enough scone to provide an explanation on his sudden bout of caffeine-fueled kindness. "They sent us home. Can't do grounds work when it's pouring buckets. But they told us we'd be paid for a full day, and if that's not worth dropping twenty dollars on breakfast, I don't know what is."

I tear the paper off my straw and take a deep pull of perfect coconut milk cold brew bliss. "Thanks for including me in your money-for-nothing celebration."

Nat studies his scone like he just realized he ordered that and not some bacon-filled breakfast sandwich. "I figured you could use a pick-me-up after last night."

I don't know what to say. Are we having this conversation?

Like, did Nat see Alex at Northfield before they were sent home? Did they talk about last night? And *what* would they talk about, exactly? Nat isn't the most subtle person on earth. If he wanted to try to have a nuanced conversation about my feelings, Alex's feelings, and Alex's date tonight with Sunny, well...that conversation would likely be even more embarrassing than our siblings walking in on a situation that very much felt like it could've amounted to a kiss.

Well, I mean, at least that's where *my* brain was.

"So...," Nat says, ripping off part of the scone and handing it to me. I won't turn it down even though I'm shocked he would share. Maybe he already had a breakfast sandwich and this was a sugar-dusted afterthought. "The date's tonight?"

Mouth full of scone, I nod.

"And...you're fine with that?"

I just shrug and continue chewing.

Nat's eyes narrow under his Northfield-sanctioned ball cap. "And are you supposed to practice with him today?"

Last night, Nat said he'd stay out of it. I could stiff-arm him with a reminder, but it doesn't matter. He's asking me all the questions I should ask myself.

"I mean, yeah?" If I'm really going to do this tennis thing, I have to take all the practice I can get. Plus, if I don't act normal after last night, will Alex know I wanted to kiss him as badly as I did? Ignorance is bliss.

To my surprise, Nat's lips pull up in a sugar-crusted half smile and he points the remainder of his scone at me. "You really are a glutton for punishment."

I swallow. Guilty as charged.

Though, come to think of it, it's like Nat's stolen metaphor of the elephant sitting between us at Burger Fu. Maybe I don't just want to ignore the elephant between Alex and me.

Maybe I just want to eat the elephant to be rid of it entirely.

Over text, Alex cancels our training session because of the rain. He gives me some drills as homework over the weekend.

I give him a thumbs-up.

We don't discuss the date. I don't even wish him good luck.

I don't know what's wrong with me. But I do know that the rain has me covered. It's a mood, and it's perfect, and it hangs around all weekend. It's at once hot and sticky and damp, the pressure change applying a vise to my prefrontal cortex and holding on tight. I use the headache to beg off the plans Peregrine and I had to wait out the date together.

As Friday spreads into Saturday, then Sunday, and the rain batters the windows, Sunny doesn't text me. Alex doesn't text me. Even Peregrine doesn't prod me with a well-placed Have you heard?

On Monday at lunch the rain is gone, and I stare at my phone, alternately wondering if it's broken or if the pair of them hit it off so well that they fractured the time-space continuum and I'm stuck floating by myself in negative space without knowing it.

Of course then Nat comes home from work and begins microwaving three-quarters of a bag of frozen chicken nuggets. I expect him to ask me if I finished the ketchup (I didn't, but Dad did) when I walk into the kitchen in my tennis gear and find him standing at the counter eating the nuggets dry (ew). Without a word, I drop a couple of ice cubes into a clean water bottle and begin to fill it, the ice crackling under the pressure of the liquid and thwacking the sides of yet another fake Nalgene.

Nat swallows and coughs, but rather than admit defeat and grab his own water, he takes a moment and clears his throat. "Did you hear from Sunny?"

I shake my head.

"Alex?"

I shake my head.

Nat shifts on his feet. And for once he goes the extra mile and doesn't make me ask. "He was at work but didn't mention it. At all." Nat notices my clothes. "Are you going to meet him? Now? Still?"

I nod. Tighten the lid on the water bottle.

Nat inspects a chicken nugget. "Do you want me to head to the school? I'm always good for some extra stadium stairs."

He'd probably have an excellent view of the tennis courts from the top of the Northland stadium. Actually, from pretty much anywhere on the track or infield.

I swallow and shake my head and readjust the racket, which has slid down from its original position pinned between my upper arm, rib cage, and armpit. This is the grave I dug. I set up my friends and developed a crush on one in the process. I can handle this. I will handle this.

Nat sets his plate on the counter. His eyes weigh on me, and I don't meet them, staring instead at the toes of my suddenly beloved Nikes. Finally, he lets me go without a fight. "Okay, well, text if you need me."

That might be literally the most subtle my brother has ever been when it comes to my feelings as a human being.

Alex is there when I arrive—already changed into a clean tank, already on the court, bag on the bench, yet another blue hat (this one sporting a swooshy KU logo) shading his face as he digs through his bag, hauling out cans of balls, hand towels, racket tape.

My heart ratchets up from the relatively normal beat of a brisk walking pace to an all-out pound as I make my way to the court. My knees soften and the whole thing feels like a slog. Like I'm pushing through time and space. And yet here I am, no coward, ready to face this boy who makes my heart double beat, after his date with one of my best friends.

I really wonder at what point Emma Woodhouse felt like she was going to pass out just addressing Knightley. Because I am *there* and Jane Austen did not make that abundantly clear.

"Hey," I punch out, just so I make the first move. It's weak and barely lands, as I'm still going through the little jog in the fence to get to the court.

But Alex hears it anyway.

Glances up.

A smile crosses his face and it's almost as if he's happy to see me.

Like I didn't make it obvious I wanted to kiss him the last time we saw each other.

Like I didn't avoid texting him all weekend. Today.

Like...we're normal?

His dimples wink. "Hey, how was your weekend?"

I stop my advance several feet from him. Set my water bottle on the opposite end of the bench. "Um, good?"

"Did you practice? Do your homework?"

I nod. Between the pop-up storms and the headaches, I did. I ran, I took the racket and ball to the park, found a wall, and did exactly as he said. Every single day I didn't see him.

"Good, because I have something for you."

Another thing I don't expect. "For me?"

Alex nods, unzips a side pocket, and pulls out a stapled packet. "Your paperwork for the Northfield Championships." A sheepish grin flashes across his face. Maybe there *is* a rip in the space-time continuum, and we're in an alternate universe where he didn't just go to dinner with Sunny. Or not. "You're official. Two weeks and you'll be in your first tournament."

The paper hangs between us. I don't take it. "What if . . . if I decide I'm not ready?"

"If you don't want to play, it's okay. It'll just be a bye for your opponents. Your entry still gets you in." Then he adds, "You can come watch my matches if you want. And bring a friend. Perks."

My smile wavers, but I snag the paper. "Okay, so what now?"

"We spend the next two weeks simulating play, that's what."

I nod. "Okay, let's do it."

31

At the end of practice, Alex and I walk toward his car slower than usual. We also played longer than usual—it's closer to five than to four thirty, and traffic is picking up accordingly between Northland's front lawn and Eomma across the street.

I'm clutching the entry paperwork like it might fly away, my eyes pinned to my grip on the stapled sheets, mostly so I don't look up at Alex. Of course he notices. Of course he does.

"You're going to do great, Caro. My matches shouldn't conflict, so I can watch you." There's a dimple flash from under his hat. "It's going to be awesome."

And that's when I realize...he was right—I'm his friend. In tennis. I'm the buddy he's doing it with. He's not alone.

My heart flickers and I tell it to shut up. This is as good as things are going to get for me when it comes to Alex Zavala. Eventually there will be someone else who makes my heart do this and the pining will be over. I'll be like Nat—hopping from out-of-reach Liv Rodinsky to unexpectedly interesting Artemis Liu. The clouds will part, the sun will shine, and suddenly I'll be doing whatever my equivalent is to eating vegetables and manning a two-person canoe. "So, um, how was Friday?"

"Oh . . . um, good. Eomma was packed for a party, so we ended up at Burger Fu."

He doesn't say Sunny's name. "Caprese-and-arugula salad for one, and a Bunny Fu Fu for you?"

Alex doesn't look at me. "Actually, salad for both."

Huh. Perhaps boys gravitate toward vegetables when they like a girl. Someone should study that.

"Cool." I force myself back into the friend zone and elbow his rib cage. "Did you regale her with your knowledge of Cathy Rigby's entire career from the Olympics to Broadway?"

All my fear about dipping a toe back into what happened on his couch falls away with his immediate laugh. "Nope. Didn't even come up, but I'll be ready if it ever does."

Ever implies a follow-up date. Or time spent together. This is what I wanted, I remind myself.

His eyes meet mine. "Thank you."

I glance away. I'm not sure I can really enjoy those beautiful brown eyes from close range anymore. "Of course."

He stops at his car. "Hey, do you want a ride home?"

I do. But I don't. Before I can even shake my head and make my exit, Alex's phone actually starts *ringing*. We're both so stunned that he fishes it out of his bag, inspects the screen, and—it's Sunny. Alex immediately reddens about the ears, and because it's my role, I waggle my eyebrows and gently punch him on the shoulder with a knowing twist to my lips. "See you tomorrow."

Our deal is done. Successful. He did his job. I did mine. Everything from here on out is a consequence.

My emotions are a total jumble as I walk home. It's ridiculously hot, blistering waves hovering over the asphalt, but a chill has settled in my spine, pooling into my stomach. All at once I feel cold and sloshy.

Alex and Sunny went out, and now she's calling him. They'll probably meet up for a dinner date that will have everyone in a ten-foot radius falling over from sugar shock at the sweetness of it all.

This is what I wanted. And clutched in my hand is the paperwork for what I got out of the deal besides bragging rights in making the most perfect match ever.

A new beginning.

As I move in toward the rosebushes and the park beyond, I spy Nat on the basketball court. The weird hot-cold feeling within me seems to even out at the sight of him, and my heartbeat smooths into a fast but predictable rhythm. Without really meaning to, I veer past the park boundary and cut up the lawn toward the court.

Too late I realize that he's not shooting hoops alone. He's got a partner, a dark-haired boy who makes me do a double take.

The clothes aren't right. The build's not either. And there's not a blue Challenger, or actually a single car at all, in the four-spot lot edging the opposite end of the park.

Ryan Rodinsky?

Perhaps I'm not the only one learning a new sport.

Ryan notices me first and waves. Which is the perfect popular boy move—I know more about him than he likely knows about me, but he's the affable kind of popular who at least pretends we're all on the same level.

"Caroline, hey," he says, trapping the ball against his chest. "What's up?"

"What's up with you? This doesn't look like stadium stairs." As far as I know that's their only real interaction, something they've kept going ever since Nat used it as an excuse to talk with Ryan's older sister.

Ryan grins and shrugs, squeezing the ball between both palms, elbows straight out to the side. "I'm no one-trick pony. I like to play."

I shoot a glance at my brother. "You're recruiting him."

"Kid's got talent. And we need more depth at forward."

Forward. Alex's position.

They might be almost interchangeable on the soccer field, but in basketball Ryan needs to add about twenty pounds, six inches, and a whole lot of court time to get anywhere near Alex on the depth chart. "Hey, Ryan, can I borrow my brother a second?"

"Sure thing," he says, automatically dribbling his way under the basket for what looks to be layup work.

Without a word, Nat meets me where I'm toeing the edge of the court.

"Hey, so you know the Northfield Tennis Championships?"

"Do I? They had us weed every single bed in the place this week in preparation for several truckloads of mulch they're delivering Sunday. Then it'll be fresh pebbles and stringing lights and testing bulbs. I fear for next week. Think I should quit a couple weeks early? You know, to save my knees?"

I ignore his plight. "So, about that." I extend the packet toward him. "Alex entered me in the beginner's bracket. We're allowed to bring a friend—would you want to be my plus one?"

Nat continues to build on the nuance he somehow discovered in the past week and plucks the paper from my hands, taking the time to scan the whole entry description and rules before answering me. "That was nice of him."

I can't read his tone. "It was. So...would you be in?" I could ask Dad. Olga. Peregrine. Sunny. But my gut wants Nat to be there. I don't know if that's because I want him to see that I've actually been working really hard, not just hanging out with Alex, or if it's because I need someone who will tell me like it is, no matter what the score says.

But maybe he's also my preferred buffer. Someone who can stand between my heart and Alex while also being firmly at my side. Nat thinks for a moment, eyes shaded. I'm about to summarize his commitment and emphasize that it won't be too much—a match Friday, the next match or the loser's bracket on Saturday. Maybe something Sunday, but not likely. He wouldn't have to go to the end-of-tournament gala on Sunday night with me. Heck, I might not go at all—

"Of course," Nat says. I try to steal back the entry paper, thinking that's it, but he whips it away from me. "But on one condition."

That is never a good addition when it comes to a deal with my brother.

"You allow me to buy you a new racket." He thumps the *LJM* on the bottom of my racket handle. "You've progressed past borrowed bits."

Well, that's unexpected. "I don't mind. No one knows it's borrowed—"

"*I* know. And I'm telling you I'll go if you let me buy you a new racket. It can be exactly like that one for all I care. If you're going to do this, let's do it right." My face melts into surprise I can't hide, which Nat actually reads. "This isn't a 'gotcha.' You won't owe me. It's...something I can do. Let me do it."

"Um. Okay."

He checks his watch. "We can get it done before dinner if we leave now."

"What about Ryan?"

Nat simply turns. "Hey, Rodinsky, I've gotta run. Stadium stairs tomorrow?"

Again Ryan says, "Sure thing," and grins like the freshman homecoming king he was last year—the sophomore crown is probably in the bag already. But then, as Nat jogs over to grab his water and extra ball, Ryan tosses me a curveball out of left field. Okay, I know that metaphor doesn't totally track and he's a soccer player currently holding a basketball, but it works. Promise. "Hey, Caroline...how's Peregrine?"

I halt. Ryan's standing there squeezing the ball again. This time, his confidence is propped up by his height and gleaming smile, any internal tension being channeled through his fingertips and palms as he crushes that poor ball.

He's holding on for dear life. But he's also not fighting his fight.

I don't know what to say—I'm not sure if Peregrine's really serious about him or not. So I just point out that this is his problem, not hers. "Why don't you ask her yourself? I hear you have her number."

I forget who he's supposed to be dating now—it's like the freshman cheerleaders each lined up for a turn with the star soccer player. But if Ryan's embarrassed, it's overpowered by another emotion: fear.

"I do. But I'm too intimidated to use it."

If I'm shocked Ryan would admit *that*, Nat is nonplussed. Actually, he's irritated. "If a girl gives you her number, you use it. Immediately." Ryan ducks his head and Nat squints at him. "*Wait.* How long have you had it?"

"Um..." Ryan fumbles.

"*March*," I answer as Ryan—popular, handsome, nice guy Ryan—looks like he wants to melt into the cracked asphalt Wicked Witch of the West–style. "He's had it since March."

"Oh, for fuck's sake," Nat exclaims, now irritated, disappointed, *and* pissed. "It's not the black lipstick you should be afraid of, it's that you've strung her along for five months. Jesus Christ, man."

Even *I'm* shocked when Nat grabs Ryan's phone off the bench and tosses it to him. Ryan drops the ball, angling to catch the phone.

"Open it," Nat orders, walking up to him. Ryan does, and Nat immediately steals it back, scrolls down, and begins typing.

It only takes a second, but then Nat's done. He stabs *send* and tosses the phone back to Ryan. "There you go, opening gambit. You're welcome."

Ryan's lips drop open as he reads the text "he" sent. "Hey, wanna get coffee?"

Nat finger-guns Ryan. "You're welcome, kid."

32

The week flies by. I see Alex every day, and we don't talk about Sunny.

I can't explain it, but for something that was my focus for *weeks*, the idea that Sunny and Alex are dating is now literally the last thing I want to think about or talk about.

I don't know if they've gone on more dates.

I don't know if they've gone from those dates to some sort of boyfriend-girlfriend relationship.

I don't know anything.

I haven't talked to Sunny about it. Peregrine either. It's like we've made a pact never to mention it. And that's fine. Meanwhile, I haven't talked to Alex about it except for our initial conversation about double caprese salads and gymnastics knowledge left unshared.

I'm lucky that given Alex's complete embarrassment by the whole forced setup I concocted, there's pretty much no way he's going to bring it up during the ten hours a week I'm guaranteed to see him.

And that's fine too.

Alex, sunshine, a workout. Day in and day out. Pretty damn good combination.

On Friday, though, my ignorance will officially come to an end. Well, a likely end. The girls and I made plans to meet at Eomma at six—I specifically asked for some time to get home after tennis and shower because the restaurant has no outside seating and I will not park my stinky self in their dining room. No way.

Meanwhile, as I spend the day girding myself for hearing about the perfection that was my setup, I get a surprise text from Alex.

Hey, would you be up for coming to Northfield for practice today? Same time. I can pick you up.

I do a bit of quick math in my head and decide that even though it's farther away, I should be able to make it home for a quick shower and still get to the restaurant on time. Sure. But I can walk. Then, because I know he has lessons with Coach Bev until two, I add: You're already there. Stay put!

Will do. Meet you at the staff gate at two thirty.

I grab my new racket—it's a hair smaller than Lily Jane's and works super well, *thanks, Nat*—and water bottle and head out at a good clip to make up the difference in distance. What I don't realize until I walk up is that I've gotten there way early. Like super early.

I'm standing at the little gatehouse nestled into the staff parking lot trying to decide if I can talk my way past the security guard by name-dropping Nat—who I must have just missed, because his car isn't here—or Alex, when the sound of a familiar elegant voice whips my head around.

"Ah, the one Alex spends all his time with. The gymnast."

My stomach plummets another peg as I turn around to find Coach Bev enveloped in a white tennis dress that highlights her flawless tan. She's got car keys in her hand and a bag over her shoulder—break time before the late-afternoon clients trickle in, if I had to guess.

"Caroline," I say as a reminder and smile. "Former gymnast."

"Ah yes, of course." She waves her hands and grins hard enough that eye crinkles sprout from the sides of her sporty sunglasses. "*Former* gymnast and *current* tennis player. Alex is getting the ball machine to court five for you."

"Oh." I figured he wanted to meet me here to get me familiar with the surroundings, but the access to equipment makes sense too.

"Your first match is in a week, is it not? And you've been playing for, what, a month?"

It's actually less, but I nod. "I don't exactly have Alex's pedigree, but I think it's worth it to give it a go ahead of tryouts—Alex says I have a good chance of making the Northland team."

Her eyes crinkle further. "That's because no one is ever cut from the Northland team."

But there are tryouts.

Alex even made a big deal about helping to prepare me for camp so I'd be ready for the team.

But maybe all I had to do was show up . . . did he know that? Or would he just not realize that no one is cut because he never really paid attention in his own tryouts—it's not like there are twenty Alex Zavalas wandering around Northland. Tennis isn't like Alex's other sports. Players aren't a dime a dozen.

My smile falls. It seems as if Coach Bev was waiting for exactly that, because she pointedly puts a hand on my forearm. "Oh, don't be discouraged by that. I've coached Alex for twelve years, and you know as well as I do that he would never mislead you. He comes by his enthusiasm honestly." Coach Bev straightens a bit. "He just has no idea that the player pipeline into Northland is set to a trickle."

I'm silent. And she continues, almost wistful. "He forgets that he's special. Often. Alex is the exception, not the rule—the kids who are his level don't play for their high schools. Most of them aren't even *in* a normal high school—they're at an academy or online." Or homeschooled like Sunny. "Easier to have a career that way. No distractions."

I realize *I'm* a distraction in her characterization. She said just as much in the first moment of this conversation.

"Ah, the one Alex spends all his time with. The gymnast."

Alex has constantly worked to ensure I didn't feel like a distraction or a burden, or an unnecessary use of his time. And yet, here I am, bundled up with ... what'd she call it before? Alex's other *ambitions*? I swallow, my stubbornness rising in Alex's defense. "What if he doesn't want a career?"

To my surprise Bev doesn't double down on all her sharp edges. Instead, she laughs, and it's just as elegant as everything else about her. "Oh, hon, I know Alex doesn't want one *now*. He's made that clear by turning down every invitation to the big leagues he's received this year. Do you know how many wild cards he's given up?" I'm about to answer "four" because that was the number she gave me when she complained about this when we first met, but she holds up a spread palm. "*Five*. Soon to be six, because one just came in at the end of August for a big tournament in Winston-Salem.

"These aren't just invitations—they're opportunities. Alex is a smart kid, but he won't realize what he's given up until they aren't piling on my desk anymore." She serves a brittle smile. "He wants to score goals and dump vats of Gatorade on his coaches and ride around in that ridiculous car of his in his three-sport letter jacket."

That's not at all what Alex wants. Or at least what he's told me he wants. I open my mouth to inform her that she's wrong, that he doesn't want the glory, he wants the *experience*, when her stark blue eyes pin me straight in the face from over the top of her sunglasses.

"Did that sound flip? I didn't mean it to sound flip. I just get frustrated..." She sighs, and for a hot second I think I see the person beyond all her gleaming armor. "Because he has no idea how many people would kill for the chances he has."

I think of Alex, just wanting to be normal. Not wanting the big career. I think of Sunny, giving up so much to focus in the way he's not.

Bev adjusts her bag and checks her watch. "Enjoy your time at Northfield today, Caroline."

Coach Bev's words won't leave me. They sit heavy on my chest through practice.

With every minute, every ball, every sip of water, every chunk of advice tossed my way by Alex, snippets of our conversation ring in my ears.

He forgets that he's special. Often.

These aren't just invitations—they're opportunities.

...he has no idea how many people would kill for the chances he has.

I can't escape the thought that I'm making things worse. Wondering if my fresh start made it that much harder for Alex's future to begin.

She may not have seen all the pink squares on his calendar, or all the time allotted to me that was not formally blocked out, but the subtext of Coach Bev's analysis is correct.

I spent basically the month of July being a huge distraction.

Alex wants to do it all, but he also can't say no. Not to helping me, not to being set up, not to anything.

I know that he was lonely on the road. That he was burnt out. That he just wanted time with his friends. I understand that and I get why he didn't want to roll right back into the way things were this summer.

But...but what if those opportunities stop coming?

What if I've made things irreparably worse for him? Blinded him from his focus? What if all the energy he poured into me hurts him more than it helps me? I'd been so focused on paying him back and yet I didn't know the true cost until tonight.

And now...what?

What do I do? What can I do? Or maybe most of all: What *should* I do?

Alex is free to make his own choices and do what he wants with his life. But Coach Bev's train of thought keeps rumbling through my head. If it's her job to make sure he doesn't regret his choices, isn't that my job as a friend too?

And if so, what do I do? Eliminate the distractions until he can see a path that's only for him?

I can't break up Alex and Sunny. That would be both cruel and worthless. It's only been a week but trying to forcibly cut her out of Alex's life now after working so hard to get them back in the same orbit would be seismically terrible for all three of us. And as far as distractions for Alex, I've been much worse than a budding romance with Sunny. *Ah, the one Alex spends all his time with. The gymnast.*

I'm not going to be a drag on his system much longer. In a little over a week I'll have the Northland coach to build on the tennis knowledge Alex gave me. And Alex will have his soccer bros back in his life, along with his regular sessions with Coach Bev and her watchful eye, and maybe Sunny too.

His color-coded Tetris of a schedule flashes in my mind, all busy and indistinct. Would it be possible for him to do it all—play soccer and basketball and slum it in 6A tennis *and* accept enough wild cards to keep things moving? Surely with Alex's having been varsity in every regular Northland sport, none of his coaches would keep him off a team simply because he wanted to attend a special tennis match or two?

And as the questions keep coming, I realize I'm doing it again. I'm trying to force things and tell Alex what's best for him, and push him toward the type of path and opportunity I wish I still had.

"Hey, want to hit up the snack bar?" Alex asks as we exit the maze of courts. Actually, it's not so much of a question as it is a warning, because we're walking that direction and he's already waving at the girl behind the counter even though she's several feet away.

I'm about to defer because I do have to get home to change and hit up Eomma. He knows I've got plans but won't be denied. "It's 105 in the shade and I happen to know for a fact that they *just* added frozen malts to the menu." His waving hand has switched to a static hold of two fingers—the boy is basically putting in our order. "You look like you could use some sugar."

I don't know what to say to that. I don't know what to say at all.

Seated on a stool in front of him with chocolate malt frozen bliss in my hot little hands, I realize that I've walked right into a trap. But when Alex raises a thoughtful brow over his own treat, wooden spoon frozen in his tan fingers, the question he asks is not what I expect.

"Are you nervous about next week?"

What. *Oh.* The Northfield tournament. The look of concern on his face is about to melt me faster than this heat. I study my rapidly liquefying treat before I become a puddle. "No, no."

Alex takes a quick bite. "You don't have to do it. Easy enough to pull out now. Even the hour before. Seriously—"

I cut him off with a hand to his wrist. We both freeze. "Alex, no it's not that."

"Is it your back? There's a trainer in the clubhouse who could take a look if you..."

I furiously shake my head and Alex's words trail off into a bite of chocolate malt that he's clearly forced upon himself to give me more time. But I'm not sure I need time as much as I need everything to realign in my brain and stop being a jumble. I'm so afraid this is going to come out wrong and controlling and like I'm entitled to his thoughts and choices. I yank my hand away from him because contact with Alex is definitely not helping me think. "How do I say this?"

I don't even realize I asked that question out loud until Alex glances down and says, "Caroline, if it's about Sunny—"

"I talked with Coach Bev before you met me at the gate," I blurt out so he won't finish the "Sunny" thought because the last thing I want is for him to feel guilty about that. My eyes fly up and he's looking at me, measured and still. I glance back down and fiddle with my little wooden spoon. "She was pretty honest about what she thinks you're giving up by not accepting those wild cards or doing any tournaments, except, well, this one."

He laughs and it's a little darker than I expect. "*This one*, which I'm basically being forced to play because it's my home tournament."

"And . . . maybe you should reconsider your time off."

He swallows. "Okay. . . ."

"I know how you feel about this." My eyes flash to his. "I'm not saying you should dive back in with two feet. I just . . . maybe keep a toe in the water? Accept one wild card. Go to one big tournament. And then come back and play your soccer games. Prep for basketball. Eat pizza and blow out your speakers with Broadway compilations. I just . . . you have the chance, and I think you can do the big-time junior tennis stuff *your way*."

He's silent and again my hand seeks to touch him, landing on the very solid meat of his forearm. Somehow this doesn't seem as intimate as his wrist, and I give him a supportive squeeze. "I meant what I said weeks ago. If anyone can have it all, it's you." I let that sit, the forced air of the fans mounted over the snack bar whipping my ponytail around my face.

Alex's expression gives away almost nothing, except for the high color rising in his cheekbones and the wink of a dimple as he worries his lip. Pensive looks better on him than it should on any human. It's really not fair.

I extract my hand from his forearm. The second I peel my fingers away I wish I hadn't. I drop my spoon into my cup and hold both hands up in the universal gesture for "all done."

"I've said my piece. I promise not to badger you one more second about it or to use my tale of injury woe to guilt you into continuing a path you're not sure you want to choose. I'll just stand here next to you as a vertically challenged defender of your perfectly reasonable life choices."

Alex's eyes meet mine and there's something in them that is so electric I almost fall off my chair. "Thank you, Caroline." His lips are rosy from the cold treat, and after a blink I swear they're closer. So close that even with his world-class reflexes, if I were the kind of person who would gamble not one friendship but two, I could steal the kiss I want more than nearly anything in this very moment.

Instead, I inch myself back from his mouth, lift my eyes, and remind myself verbally why this cannot be. I swallow and blessedly the words come out as I've directed them to. "I should go. I refuse to ruin the upholstery at Eomma with my sweaty self."

33

I'm late to Eomma.

Of course, Alex gives me a ride home without my asking.

Of course, I can't say no. It would've been both a logistically and vainly stupid move, especially given how I decided to exit our snack bar conversation.

And, of course, as we pull up to my house, he offers to wait around and drop me at the restaurant after I clean myself up. That's typical Alex-level nice, but...I just can't hog any more of his Friday night.

God, when I have my driver's license, I will just zoom away from every awkward interaction.

But because I'm fifteen and stubborn, I simply say goodbye to Alex, race through a shower, and hoof it the mile to the restaurant as I'd originally planned.

When I walk in, I spy Sunny in the back, cup of tea already nestled in her hand and an assortment of kimchi arranged in an elegant row before her. She's alone, and I breathe a sigh of relief that I've somehow managed to beat Peregrine in the late-to-dinner Olympics.

"I'm so sorry to keep you waiting." I tuck my napkin over my lap, take a quick sip of ice water, and turn my surprise into a question about our missing piece. "Wow, I really thought I'd be the last one here—Peregrine didn't ride with you?"

Sunny swallows her sip of tea. "Actually, I asked her to pop in at six thirty." It's ten after now, and as I'm trying to process this information and square it with the possibility that maybe that coffee text from Ryan actually went somewhere, Sunny gently sets down her teacup. "You and I have something delicate to discuss."

I can't read her expression. She's calm, yet...guarded? "I—er, what?" I stumble, unsure of what to say.

Of what this could be about other than, well, Alex.

Alex, who we haven't talked about all week, who seemed completely normal, almost *purposefully* normal all week. In fact, the only time something was amiss was when he was concerned for me tonight. "Did Alex...?" Did Alex *what?* I'm not sure how to reasonably finish my own question. Turn out to be a creep? Stand her up and lie to me about their date? Did...*what?* My mind is blanking out, and my panic is rising.

What don't I know?

"Alex—" Sunny says pointedly, picking up my sentence, "is everything you and Peregrine said he was."

I breathe a shallow sigh of relief. The panic in me crests and then recedes, but I can't ignore that it's still there. The feeling is exactly the same when you make a save on beam—you're still standing, but your confidence is shaken.

As Sunny continues, I know a true fall is coming. I'm just not sure if it's a simple slip or a total wipeout like my final, disastrous Arabian.

"He's kind, charming, level-headed, goal-oriented, and a perfect gentleman." She pauses. "Alex is exactly what you said he would be and exactly the type of guy I should date."

I brace for the crash of the coming, inevitable caveat, and Sunny must know it because she reaches out and covers my hand with hers. Her palm is warm from the teacup and roughly calloused from hours of bar work, and her nails sparkle with starry night glitter.

"But . . . ," I supply, my attention speared on our mingling hands.

"*But* . . . even though Alex is all those things, he simply isn't for me."

My mind whirs to a static-laced halt. Am I the one who has to tell him? That I got his hopes up, made it happen, and . . . it's not going to work out?

Maybe Coach Bev will be happy about one fewer distraction, but that won't make it any easier for Alex, and might actually help to prove her point about how he should only focus on tennis—everything else causes complications.

"Sunny, you don't have to explain at all. I'm sure it'll be fine. I'm sorry that you had to go through that exercise—I know you weren't sure about it and—"

"Caroline."

My lips snap shut and my eyes jump to hers.

Sunny smiles softly, her gaze unwavering. "Caroline, he's not for me because he's for you."

I—what.

I blink at her. She gives a little nod, her eyes furiously reading mine, searching for understanding that isn't there.

I gape long enough that she finally just continues with a squeeze of my hand. "Every moment I was with Alex, it was increasingly clear that though he may have once had a crush on me, he was only on that date because you wanted him to be. He only wanted to make you happy."

I start shaking my head. "No, no. That can't be..." My words trail off into the same void that's devoured all the others since this whiplash of a conversation started, but even as the words are falling out of my mouth, the way he looked at me on the couch—heck, the way he looked at me *an hour ago*—hits me like a ton of bricks.

"It is." Again Sunny catches my train of thought with the same sure confidence that she displays at the start of each and every competition routine. "I called him Monday. We met up after practice—and I told him my suspicions about his feelings, and after he nearly melted into his chair, I asked him point-blank how he felt about you."

I might melt into my chair hearing this—my cheeks burn and I should take another sip of water but I'm afraid my hand will tremble.

Sunny's expression doesn't shift. Doesn't let up. Her voice is low but sure and the only thing I can hear over the very loud drumbeat of *but but but but but but* in my head. "I won't tell you exactly what he said because I think you should hear it from him, but I can confirm that Alex Zavala *likes you* much more than he *previously* liked me."

I've spent so much time denying my feelings—at first because I was sure I didn't have them, and then because I *did* and didn't want to ruin the perfection that should've been Alex and Sunny—that I can't stop denying that this is happening.

No matter how stern Sunny is or how badly I really, really want to believe this is true.

Still, despite my internal knob set hard to *denial*, Sunny

continues, calmly. "I asked if he wanted to act on his feelings and that was a more complicated answer. He doesn't want to make things weird for you, especially with your focus on your first tournament and trying out for the Northland team. Not to mention the Nat factor, which I'm sure would be tough to navigate. And the expectations of his tennis coach, who really wishes he'd take a page from my playbook and go the homeschooled route."

She readjusts her grip on my hand, flipping it over and twining our fingers together between our water glasses and the kimchi. "And so he chose not to act—yet."

Yet? Or at all?

"We discussed keeping up appearances, making you think your matchmaking skills worked, at least through the end of Northland tryouts...but there was no way *I* could spend the next few weeks pretending that we were dating." Her eyes flick to mine. They're at once both clear and remorseful. "Because I went out with him for the same reason he went out with me—I wanted to make you happy. I ignored the fact that I could plainly see you thought the world of him and had your own feelings to work out."

My heart lurches as Sunny takes another measured sip of her tea.

"Now, I'd thought about playing matchmaker on my matchmaker—you know, some sort of purposeful pairing at my birthday party. And though that would be epic and involve swimsuits, the last thing I want to do is to put more pressure on you, Caroline. Or on Alex." She squeezes my fingers. "I'm here for you and I want to arm you with information that's yours to act on. You can wait for Alex to get up the courage, or you can take matters into your own hands. Or the both of you can do nothing. But for what it's worth, now you know."

I blink once. Twice. I seriously don't know what to say or where to start. "I was telling the truth a few weeks ago. I didn't have a thing for Alex."

Sunny's face breaks into one of her beautiful smiles. "I know. But that doesn't mean truths don't change."

I'd joked to myself about having more prowess than Emma Woodhouse, but maybe, just maybe, I'm both less successful and more emotionally dense than fictional Emma. Alex really is my Knightley, except way less old and broody.

Sunny squeezes my fingers one last time and then raises a hand in the air. Peregrine arrives, dropping into the empty chair. "You're both still here," she says, unsure. The black lipstick is back, matched with chartreuse eyeliner that only someone with Peregrine's fine motor skills could pull off. Summer goth in the flesh. "That's a good thing, right? Or is it a bad thing, because shouldn't Caro have barreled out of here and straight to Alex's doorstep?"

Sunny smiles gently. "We're going to let Caroline do whatever she wants."

Peregrine arches a dangerous brow. "And, if necessary, we're going to help her."

"Yes," Sunny says, and begins piling kimchi onto her plate before Peregrine claims half of it for herself. "But only when she asks and only when it's time. Until then she's driving the bus."

Honk, honk.

34

I spend the weekend planning my approach and then chicken-ing out.

First I think I might have Sunny drop me at Alex's house after dinner on Friday. Just stand there in his front yard, courage spiked by time with my girls and some really great bibimbap, and go for it.

Then I think I might run to his house and propose a farmers' market trip. Or maybe sneak into Northfield and ambush him before tennis practice. Or after, at his house. Or when he's scheduled to play basketball with Nat in the late afternoon. Sunday's plan is similar to Saturday's, because all but the farmers' market makes those days interchangeable in the overscheduled world of Alex Zavala.

Finally Monday comes, and the second-guesses begin to pile up with my abandoned plans. Maybe I should wait for him to make the move. If Peregrine can wait nearly five months for a text from Ryan, I can wait for Alex. Right? And I don't want to pull focus from the Northfield tournament. He told Sunny he didn't want to make things awkward between us as I prepare, but it's his championship to lose. And what about that wild card? And soccer tryouts next week? Distraction layered upon distraction from Coach Bev's point of view.

But then, as I try to soothe myself with a post-lunch stretch session on the deck, it hits me.

Alex already feels this way about me.

I already feel this way about him.

With all due respect to Coach Bev, the distraction is there, whether either of us acknowledge it or not.

In fact, it might take more of his "non-tennis" energy to navigate all of this if we leave it unsaid. That's the distraction.

And even though all of this is logical, even though it has me nodding to myself as I walk to Northland, a zip in my step, I'm still not sure I can be the one to put it out there.

I either take the leap or wait for Alex.

In the end, I decide that I *won't decide* until I see him for the first time since Sunny's gym-mom/let's-be-adults-about-this confession at Eomma.

So I arrive early at Northland. There's a little more activity at the school this week than last. Fall sports two-a-day camps start next week—girls' tennis, boys' soccer, football, cross-country, volleyball, girls' golf, and, of course, gymnastics and cheerleading. All those coaches have to be ready for all those kids, and there are more cars in the parking lot, and a couple of the school's exterior doors are propped open so people can easily come and go.

The tennis courts are empty, though, as they have been before. I enter the court we've used exclusively for all of July and drop my racket and water bottle on the bench. I should start stretching— but instead I just begin to pace. Words press against my teeth—how am I going to say how I feel? To Alex of all people? How—

"Caroline?"

I turn around at the sound of his voice, and when I see him, I nearly fall over. My famed balance is just gone. As are the words that were trying to bust their way past my teeth mere seconds ago.

Instead of anything I'd planned, or anything normal at all, I say, "Alex Zavala, I challenge you to a handstand contest."

He comes closer, confusion and amusement and concern all warring for control of his handsome features in the too bright light of the afternoon. Over his shoulder, I see his car parked where it usually is—how did I not hear it? How did he surprise me? Was I that out of it?

Does it matter? No.

"Handstand contest. Now."

A grin breaks across his face and he says, "I thought you'd never ask."

And before I can even tuck in my shirt, Alex is already kicking up. He's far more vertical and steady than he was all those weeks ago on the park basketball court.

"Have—have you been practicing?"

It's clear when Alex attempts to reply that the answer is yes. "Maybe." Simply the presence of an attempted, let alone successful, answer coming while he's inverted screams YES. He kicks down and smoothly stands up. "But just for this moment. Not for any other reason."

Wait. What?

And now he's driving the bus. "Ready?" Before I can answer or even move, he starts counting. "Three, two, one..."

He kicks up and I have to follow suit. My shirt's still not tucked in, but I don't give a shit, I just kick up, toes pointing in my tennis shoes. My fingers arch, working the cracking surface of the

Northland tennis court in the baking sun of the last week of July. All the heat it collected since sunup seeping through my palms and up my braced arms.

After a few seconds, I can feel Alex begin to go loose. He's learned to walk on his hands to save a handstand, but he goes too far and knocks straight into me.

In a flash, his warm legs touch mine, and then we're both tumbling toward the court.

Alex catches himself quickly enough to reach out for me. Of course I'm fine, managing to execute a quick pirouette into a front walkover to avoid landing on him. The lowest portion of my back stiffens, but I'm no stranger to that and arch through to complete the whole maneuver. I end up standing, facing him where he sits on the ground, one hand extended toward me, color high in his cheeks from being upside down.

Actually, he looks just like he did the day I offered to reintroduce him to Sunny. Red-faced and human and full of actual, heart-rattling emotions.

Feeling brave, I take his hand and sink to the ground. I wrap my other arm around my knees, hugging them tight to my chest. His hand is solid, holding me more than I'm holding on to him, our grip flipped. My heart leaps to my throat, threatening to cut off my air supply. Before it does, I use that bravery to put my heart on the line.

"Alex Zavala, I have a confession to make."

The flush at his cheeks deepens.

I open my mouth to tell him. That I do have a crush on him. That I shoved it down deep and tried to pretend my feelings weren't there, threatening to smother me from the inside out. That I really did think he was perfect for Sunny, and she was perfect for him. That in my quest for engineered romantic perfection, I completely discounted my own heart, and his and Sunny's in the process.

But nothing comes out.

He's watching me, his dark eyes as warm as the sun beating down and his hand in mine. My lips tremble and I tip a millimeter closer to him.

We're farther apart than that night on the couch, but this time, it's all the invitation he needs.

This time, Alex kisses me.

It's so hard and full of want that my hands fly up to clutch his face as I give back everything my heart has asked for in these past few weeks and more.

Our knees knock, and my eyes spring open. I find Alex watching me, his own eyes half-lidded. They appear . . . relieved? His fingers comb a lock of my hair behind my ear so gently, so calmly, we might as well be in an idyllic English meadow and not on our butts on the baseline of a high school tennis court.

I grin at him, dabbing the indentation of a dimple with the pad of my thumb. "My confession is I like you. A lot."

I swallow, the words making me feel just as vulnerable as that millimeter I closed before our kiss.

I want to kiss him again, but I also want to hear him say it. Say that his feelings match mine. Our actions are in the open, but words matter—and I need to hear them.

Alex leans in and kisses my left cheek. My right cheek. My forehead. His hands fall to mine, clutching them tight between us, our knees still another point touching. "I like you too." He boops my nose. "A lot."

I laugh because I didn't expect the nose boop, and then he

kisses me smack on the lips again, this time softer. His forehead touches mine when he pulls away just enough to speak. "I fell for you more every day we were together, until I was in so deep there was no climbing out."

Yes—that's exactly how I felt.

"Still, even when all I could see was you, I fought it. I was afraid of demolishing not only the friendship we'd built, but my relationship with Nat." He glances down at our hands, his thumbs moving swiftly over my knuckles. "Not to mention, you were already going through seismic change—I didn't want to break you."

Tears press against my eyes, but I don't look away. "I'm stronger than you think."

He laughs. "I know you could probably bench press your brother."

"Oh, most definitely." I swipe at my eyes with my bare shoulder, just so my hands don't leave his. "I don't want you to think I'm a terrible friend—Sunny told me about your conversation. She did exactly what I *didn't* do for her right away and I . . . I really just wanted to help you and Sunny be happy. And I should've known better, I should've—"

He presses the pad of his thumb to my lips, shutting off the faucet of all my regrets and didn't-mean-tos and every other hurdle I'd tossed up in my brain.

"How were you supposed to know? I didn't say anything." He smiles and yet I'm the one who sighs with relief. "I told you I liked Sunny. That was the information you had. And you wanted to help and went with it. And I let you."

This is . . . true. But . . . "No," I say, "you did what you set out to do. I needed a new sport, and I found one that I love—actually two, you were right about running."

Alex lights up further. "Told ya." We laugh, and as the sound dies, Alex tips my chin so that our eyes meet—his gaze is warm on my face.

I play with our hands, still entwined. "I needed a fresh start and a new outlook. You gave me both but you didn't push. I did. I'm sorry for trying to force you into something with Sunny. I really thought it was what was best and seemed perfect, and..." Nat's summer night big brother wisdom kicks into my brain. "And what's perfect on paper might not be in real life." I shake my head, glancing down. "It certainly wasn't perfect for me. Or Sunny. Or you."

"Caroline, that's not your fault. I was ready to go on dates until Sunny said no, just to make you happy. And I thought I'd screwed everything up before I even began. I scared myself shitless thinking I'd misunderstood you before LJ and Nat walked in."

I guess we're all capable of overthinking things. Even Alex Zavala.

"And because I didn't know what to do, I just went ahead and let you think everything with Sunny was great," he says, "when I should've addressed reality instead of just going on, business as usual. In truth, I was ready to do that today, tomorrow—as long as I could stand it. I didn't want to mess up your hard work."

"You know," I say, "I had the same thought. You've got your Northfield championship to defend, and a varsity soccer team to make after a year away, and not to mention the delights of junior year of high school..." I don't add the wild card stuff, just letting that arm of the existence of Alex Zavala sit between us.

"Yeah, all of that. But just so we're clear." He draws in a bracing breath and I stare into his dark eyes. "Sunny was everything I'd hoped she'd be and everything I thought I wanted." A grin pushes up in the corners of Alex's mouth. "But I don't want her. I want you."

I lift my hands from their tangled embrace and cradle his cheeks in my palms before speaking directly to his handsome, grinning face. "So we're clear: I want you too."

This time, I kiss him. And it's perfect.

35

Somehow the days have flown by in a blur of court time with Alex, rides home with Alex, Mozza-Monsters and bibimbap and caprese salads with Alex . . . and now it's the first day of the tournament and I'm about to vomit. It hasn't been *that* long since my last competitive outing, but my gut is acting like this is my first rodeo and I pregamed at an all-you-can-eat buffet.

My heart's no help either—it pounded all night, keeping me awake until I must have fallen asleep, though my only indication was jolting awake to the sound of my alarm. I rolled out of bed, showered, and took the same dose of preemptive ibuprofen I've lived on for years. My back isn't yelling at me, and I would like to avoid a single peep from it at all today, if possible. It's been stiff from all the hard training the past two weeks but not painful, if that makes sense.

I don't know that it does. My brain is day-old scrambled eggs.

I wander into the kitchen for some sustenance and am choking down some stomach-friendly dry cereal as Dad appears, dressed and chipper. He's been in a fine mood since I told him about tennis. Probably because he's regained his legendary status as "top moper" in the Kepler household. Not that he has much to complain about these days. "Check the fridge, Serena."

At least Dad's tennis references are clear enough that I don't have to think very hard. I do as directed, lugging the fridge open to find . . . my typical cold brew, as I like it, on the middle shelf, ice still wholly intact. My family really does know that the way to my heart is through perfectly chilled rocket fuel. "Nice surprise, thanks, Dad."

"Want another one?"

"Another . . . coffee?" I take a long drag in hopes my brain will jog to life. They don't sell this nitro cold brew in larger sizes than the one in my hands because it's *so* caffeinated.

"Another surprise," Dad clarifies.

"Um. Okay?"

"I'm going to be at your match today."

I blink at him as the caffeine hits my system. "You are? Instead of Nat?" Now I'm really confused, because Nat is already at work but he'd confirmed my draw time and asked to end his shift ahead of time—golf course maintenance and done.

"No, in addition to Nat. Oscar invited me." Oscar—Alex's dad. "I guess the whole Zavala-Mack clan can each bring a guest. Seems like the least Northfield can do for that arm and a leg they hack off with membership each year."

Oh.

This doesn't make my stomach feel much better. Dad will be there to see me suck. Nat will be there to see me suck. Alex will be there to see me suck and then kick ass on his own. Ugh.

"Cool."

Dad also, as it turns out, intends to drive me. We get in the car at seven thirty so I have time to check in, warm up, and be ready for my match, which is to take place in the second slot—not before ten o'clock. I text Alex that we'll meet him out front of the clubhouse.

When we roll up to the members' gate, we're magically admitted with a special pass Dad obtained from Mr. Zavala, who, from the way Alex talks, is clearly the de facto sports parent. As the clubhouse looms, Alex waves, as if we're going to miss the two very handsome men standing out front looking for Dad's car. Of course, to go along with the Northfield experience, a valet rushes around to take the car off our hands. I grab my racket from the trunk, its handle poking out of the backpack I have moonlighting as a tennis bag, an ode to my previous life—the backpack's black has gone gray with chalk I couldn't wash out, embroidered scroll across the flap: Team Balan.

"Hey there, Keplers," Mr. Zavala says. "Lookin' sharp."

And we are. Dad and Nat ganged up on me and insisted I get a couple of actual tennis skirts with pockets for balls. This one is black and swishy, and I paired it with an actual athletic top—a blue not so different from the competition leo I have stuffed in a drawer—plus a pink golf visor I picked out because it looked cute.

Meanwhile, Alex looks like he's ready for Wimbledon in tennis whites. Honestly, my heart skips a beat like it truly understands the phrase "angel on earth." Today's hat is one I've never seen before—it's white with a little green Lacoste gator across the front. His clothes are different too. Nike, but actual tennis clothes and a little matchy-matchy. Not the mishmash of labels and uses—basketball shorts, running shorts, soccer shorts—I've seen him wear all summer.

I guess we're both a little different on game day.

Or is it match day? I've only had meet days. What even is this?

It's different. That's what it is.

"We'll see you on the courts," Mr. Zavala says, shaking me from my blatant bout of staring at his son. "I want to hit up the bakery before the croissant offerings are picked over."

"Croissants?" For a moment Dad's blinded by the idea of a second breakfast, but then he remembers himself, pivots, and catches me in a fierce hug. "You're going to do great, Caro. See you out there."

I mumble something through my compressed breath and then the dads peace out, jogging up the steps like they've been unleashed to vanquish baked goods in a way that might save the world.

Alex adjusts the bag over his shoulder. "Are you ready?"

I grab his hand and kiss his shoulder. It's subtle, but his cheeks pink, and suddenly my stomach flips for an entirely different reason.

"As I'll ever be."

"Okay," Alex answers, placing a gentle palm on the small of my back. He guides me toward a set of doors I've never entered. "Players this way."

∽⟁⌒

The first match on my court is a rout—6–0, 6–0, aka a "double bagel," which is mean because it sounds like the losing player spent the match reclining with brunch in hand. Though, the most natural alternative for two 6–0 sets, "double love," might not actually be much of an improvement.

My biggest goal is not to win—I have no illusions about my talent and the timeline—but to get on the board.

Six–one, six–love, if it has to be—I don't care. I just want to avoid a shutout.

Alex leads me to the court and then runs off to page both our dads and Nat. Which leaves me with an empty court and my opponent. A girl who is possibly younger than me—our age bracket is fourteen to sixteen—but Alex warned me that some of the more talented girls play up—even in the beginners' draw. This girl has no hips but is also at least three or four inches taller than me, her legs indicating that past puberty she'll appear to be serving from a tree.

Still, you can't tell if someone has talent until you see them play.

I hope the same can be said for me.

Per warm-up rules, we take turns hitting serves, volleying from the baseline, and up at the net. By the time we've run through it all—me copying the other girl and always a half step behind—the meager stands on the side of the court are almost full.

Dad, Nat, Alex, and his dad sit in the front row. Alex is talking to a guy next to him who looks vaguely familiar. Does everyone belong to this club and I don't know it?

Alex nods at me. Mouths some words. "You've got this, Caroline."

I take a deep breath. The chair umpire climbs to her spot.

And we begin.

36

The first set is a graveyard of close calls but no points on the board for me. By the time my opponent—Marina—hits 5–0 on her own serve, I'm starting to really sweat that I won't make even my most basic goal.

Despite the scoreboard—or the score announcement, really... there's no actual board, just the chair umpire's running tally—I've been better than my "love bagel" indicates. No double faults. A couple of serves she couldn't return and dumped straight into the net. A few winners even, but more of my points have come on her mistakes than my successes and we both know it. If Dad and Nat know it, they don't care, cheering wildly at anything I do correctly. Also, somehow Olga snuck in—another surprise courtesy of Dad, the Zavala-Mack clan's ticket status, and likely Elena taking over the final hour of morning practice. It's great to see her, but somehow just her mere presence has me even more stressed than before.

Still. I can do this. I used to defy gravity on the regular. I can string together enough points to claim a game.

I can.

It's my serve. I hold the ball and back up to the service line.

Watching Marina, age twelve, waiting with a glare she clearly learned from bingeing tape after tape of Maria Sharapova's glory days.

I can do this.

Just get on the board. That's it.

I sneak a glance at Alex. He's sitting with his dad and the semi-familiar man, but his focus is completely on me. Alex nods and claps, and that's when, at his back, I spy the face of someone else I definitely know. Dr. Kennedy. He's squeezing in behind Dad and Olga. Most likely with a crack or two about my back. That old Kepler stubbornness ignites inside of me. I'm no longer "Flip," but I can still have the same calling card.

Watch this.

I launch into my serve, aiming as best I can for something that will go right into Marina's body. Her scowl seems to slow down her footwork (too much energy involved, I think), and predictably, she's terrible at getting out of the way. She gets a piece of the ball only by blocking it rather than hitting it. The ball pings off the racket strings guarding her midsection and dribbles to a rolling stop.

Fifteen–love.

My next serve is more of the same. Into the body. My fledgling aim fails me and it sails to her backhand side, but only just, and she has to scoot out of the way to avoid yet another block. This time, the ball angles wide, dumping into her side of the net.

Thirty–love.

Marina's anger is starting to show through her brooding mask. She aggressively adjusts strings on her racket, muttering to herself.

Fine. She's expecting that I'll change it up. That would be a typical strategy. But I'm not a typical player. I line up my shot.

Straight at the body.

This time, she doesn't even get her racket head on it, the ball bouncing off the Y between the head and handle.

Forty–love.

We switch, and I'm going to go for her forehand. She won't expect it. And with as far over as she is in the box, if I hit, she'll have to lunge to get it.

I wind up a serve . . . and dump it into the net.

Damn.

I grab a new ball from my pocket, my tennis skirt working perfectly.

Okay, I can do this. I toss the ball up and hit it with all my might.

The ball doesn't go anywhere I want it to go. Instead of angling toward her forehand, the ball barely catches the service line right near the tape dividing the two boxes. It bounces and skids out, almost in the dead center of the court.

Ace.

I hit an ace.

Claimed a game.

The score is now 5–1.

Dad, Nat, and Olga are on their feet like I've just won the whole thing. Alex and his dad hop up too. Even Dr. Kennedy and the semi-familiar guy clap.

This isn't a title, isn't a match, isn't even a set. But it's a huge step in the right direction.

And it's exactly what I need.

I lost the match. As I knew I would. But I put up a better fight than my opponent or I bargained for.

Six–one, six–three.

Yes, I won three whole games in the second set.

I am exuberant as I meet Marina at the net for a shake before each of us thanks the chair. I'm drenched in sweat but energized even in my exhaustion. Alex comes in like a jet plane.

"That serve!" He greets me with a hand up for a high five. "So awesome!"

"Good thing we worked on it all week, huh?" I have to jump to slap his hand. God, I want to kiss him right now, but I don't, because without context that would lead to a lot of sudden questions and not, you know, ones about me surviving my first-ever match.

Alex grins. "It's rule number one or you're never going to win a point."

"Well, she could break for a point, right?" Nat asks, always the devil's advocate.

"Yes. But no matter how many games you break, you can't win without holding serve at least once," Mr. Zavala answers, trying to be diplomatic. Nat's clearly doing the math when Alex's dad turns to me. "Great job, Caro."

"Seriously fabulous, Caro." Olga envelops me in a hug, strong and solid as Dad joins in with a pat on my head.

"See, I told you another sport would be good for you. Look at you! What gymnast? I see a tennis player."

Oh, Dad. My eyes prickle, hot. I can't cry. Not here. Not now.

"Really, you were great, Caroline." Alex lands one big paw on my arm. "And I'm not the only one who thinks so." Alex uses that wingspan of his and plops his other hand on the semi-familiar man I noticed. "Caro, you know Coach Brandt, right?"

Coach Brandt. I blink at him. "I'll be your fourth-hour chemistry teacher this year," he says. "And if you want, tennis coach. Camp starts Monday. I hope you'll come."

Oh my God. My first-ever tennis match was watched by not only my new boyfriend/coach, judgmental older brother, well-meaning dad, former coach/surrogate mother, and boyfriend's dad, but also the coach I wasn't planning on meeting until next week if I got up enough courage to attempt tryouts/training camp.

Cool. Cool. Cool.

I bobble my racket to get a hand out. "Hi, nice to meet you."

"Hey, I have to go get ready," Alex says. "You two talk, though. See you on court one?"

"I'll be there with bells."

"And lunch," Dad adds, going in for a hug before angling away with Nat, Olga, and Mr. Zavala. "We'll grab you something Caroline-approved from the crepe tent. Okay?"

They leave and I feel like I've been set up, though Coach Brandt smiles in that genuine way only teachers seem to be able to muster at awkward moments. "So, Alex tells me you were a really good gymnast? And need a change?"

I nod and force down a huge gulp of water, thinking about how best to talk about the past without spewing it out all over this man. "I got hurt and had to quit. Alex spent the past month helping me try to find something new—gymnastics was my life."

"Impossible to replace?" I nod as he sort of turns and we start walking toward the exit together. "I know that feeling. I was a football player. One too many concussions and it was over for me and contact sports. My older sister put a tennis racket in my hand, and that was that."

Huh. "How old were you?"

"Sixteen and stupid. Well, stupider than a kid like Alex."

"So like Nat, then?" I joke.

"Eh, a foot taller, but the same sort of package." He shrugs.

"Oh, and because I know you might be thinking of this—Alex didn't tell me to come scout you. Nat either, though he was also in fourth-hour chem last year. I hit up this event every year—Oscar, uh, Mr. Zavala, spots me his entry. I play in the geezer's bracket. My match is no earlier than four."

"Oh. Good luck."

He pauses at another court, where two girls are warming up. "One of my varsity girls is over here. Want to watch for a few minutes before Alex starts?"

I can only see the top of the girl's head—dyed a turquoise Peregrine would appreciate. And I do want to watch. But. "I should probably clean myself up," I say. I'm pretty rough and would prefer not to look like a drowned rat for the length of Alex's match . . . but really I just want to hang with my family and come down from this high. "Thanks for the invite, though."

"Not a problem. Maybe tomorrow?"

"You bet." Definitely.

I take another sip of water and Coach Brandt makes his pitch. "Anyway, please consider coming to the school on Monday. Camp starts promptly at seven. Break at ten thirty with another session going from two to five. I have a good group of girls, but we can always use more."

I nod. "Cool."

And it is.

37

Over the next two days, Alex predictably blazes through to the
Sunday championship.

I, predictably, do not.

With Olga watching along with Dad, Nat, and the Zavalas, I put
up a pretty good fight in my losers' bracket match on Saturday—
falling 6–4, 6–4. This time, I lose to a girl my own age, the one
Coach Brandt went to watch after my Friday match—Charlotte.

I actually spend my morning watching her in the losers'
bracket "championship" alongside Coach Brandt. It's 6–1, 3–6,
4–4 with Charlotte serving over Marina the twelve-year-old, who
lost yesterday, when my phone buzzes.

And it's Sunny. Hey: SURPRISE. Alex got us entry to the tournament! We'll be there in ten minutes! Come meet us!

Us—it's the group thread with Peregrine.

Of course he did. Of course he'd have entries to spare. Of
course.

This is the *best* surprise.

More typing bubbles. Peregrine pops in: I hope I didn't have to
dress up. My Cure shirt and leather chaps are cool, right?

Sunny sends a preemptive strike of an eye roll emoji followed by a separate line of text: She's wearing something appropriate. I promise. We won't embarrass you.

Honestly, I wouldn't even care if they arrived in leotards—I'm stoked that they're here—though I suspect they also had the option to be here yesterday when I was playing...but they didn't come because they didn't want to make me more nervous. I don't have to see the text thread to know that it was a likely consideration between Sunny and Alex.

With a quiet word to Coach Brandt, I slip out between points and book it toward my best friends with a singular focus. Charlotte's match is on court ten—one of the farthest from the entry to the courts—so I run the gauntlet past all the other courts and then around a hedge-lined curve that points toward the crepe and champagne tents and the merry tones of George and his very popular accordion.

Just as I'm past the massive hedge, though, I hear my name.

"Caroline."

I turn around half expecting a false alarm—some other Caroline being summoned—when I see Coach Bev standing there in an ensemble that likely costs more than Alex's car. I still have a good five minutes of race-walking across the grounds to meet Sunny and Peregrine, but I also have a baked-in respect for coaches, and this woman is so important to Alex, even if she totally doesn't get his desire to live a life that isn't tennis 24/7.

"Hey there, Coach," I say, the title sticking in my teeth. I'm not really sure if I can call her that or if I'm supposed to call her "Bev" or if maybe I need to eat something to get my thoughts to process. "How's the tournament gone for you? I'm really excited for the final today—Alex is just so amazing."

"*He* is amazing. On that we can agree. His play? I wouldn't call it *that* at this moment." She doesn't answer my question or ask me how my tournament went. Instead, she finishes that thought with a pointed tilt of her head. "He still seems very...distracted."

This time, she doesn't mean the soccer team. Or basketball. Or his job at this very club, which I'm sure she all-out hates too. It is very clear that Coach Bev means me.

I don't know if she knows Alex and I are a thing right now. I mean, we've purposefully not made a big deal out of it. But just like our families, it's not like she's completely oblivious to the way we interact.

Still, Alex has the biggest match of his year thus far in T-minus thirty minutes, this woman is likely on the way to the players' area to meet him and needs to be on top of her game, and my friends are waiting on me, so I simply smile sweetly and shrug. "Distracted? I don't know, he seems to be focused on the things that matter to him most."

Bev's posture tightens as if I've just served straight at her face, but before she can come up with an appropriate retort, we're overcome by a gaggle of women in Lilly Pulitzer. They descend upon us in a chatter, compliments tossed at Coach Bev as gracefully as rose petals at a wedding. She grins prettily, the Queen Bee among these expensive flowers, and when the women are gone in a puff of perfume and sloshing champagne flutes, Coach Bev returns her attention to me. *The distraction.*

"We'll see if that's a good strategy for him soon enough."

Again, I shrug with a smile on my face, trying very hard to make my argument without being argumentative. "I don't think it's a flaw to be well-rounded."

Her smile is a stagnant thing. "I agree, but the scoreboard might not."

"Good thing that's not all he cares about, then, huh?"

Point, Caroline.

Coach Bev knows I've scored off her—I brace as her features shift and sharpen with...appreciation? "Yes, I suppose so."

My phone buzzes—loud enough that Coach Bev's attention flicks to it. The girls are probably wondering where the hell I am. "Good luck, Coach. I'll see you in there."

Sunny and Peregrine aren't intimidated by much, but Northfield Country Club might have just been added to the very short list.

When I meet them outside, Sunny hands her keys to one of the two valets, eyes going wide with "ain't this the life" joy about two seconds after she pretends her keys go the valet route every single day.

"So fancy," Sunny whispers, stepping up the curb, where Peregrine and I have already exchanged obligatory hugs of greeting. They both smell delicious and are, as promised, completely country club appropriate in sundresses and sandals. Even Peregrine's lipstick has been toned back down to lavender instead of black.

I check my phone for the time, and three texts from Lily Jane blink on the screen too—an order, a thank you, and a line of emojis. "Alex should be warming up now—his family is saving us seats. I promised we'd grab their order from the crepe tent on our way back. Sound good?"

"Are there crepes in it for us?" Peregrine asks.

"Well, duh."

Peregrine arches a brow high over her sunglasses. "How much

will these fancy country club crepes cost me? More or less than a questionable airport turkey club?"

"They're free with your entry?" I did not expect free-food pushback.

"So only for the low, low price of my soul? Got it."

The unengaged valet is apparently eavesdropping because he bursts into a snicker, hiding it poorly because he's got to be our age.

Sunny drapes one arm around Peregrine's shoulders and starts steering her toward the stairs. "How is that any different than the concession-stand coupons we get at meets? Other than being five hundred times more delightful than nachos smothered in space cheese?"

"Sunny's got a point," I say, jogging up the steps to get the entry door so Sunny can steer Peregrine inside. "Crepes are just rich people's nachos."

"I would liken them more to a quesadilla," Peregrine argues.

"Holy jeez," Sunny answers, catching my eyes, "let's get some food in you, Hangry Falcon, before you steal a golf cart to drive yourself home."

"While I appreciate that you decided to use my superhero name in public, I would like to point out that if I were an *actual* falcon, I wouldn't have to drive anywhere, I could just fly—"

"Oh my God, in the building, now."

It's amazing what a good crepe can do. By the time we arrive at Northfield's largest-capacity court—court one, naturally—with armfuls of piping-hot Swiss-mushroom-spinach goodness, Peregrine's snark has completely evaporated.

"Okay, the French quesadilla is awesome," she admits with a grin, busting into hers before we even climb the baby risers to where the Zavala-Mack family is holding down two rows. "Why don't they have these at gymnastics meets?"

"I saw them at nationals," Sunny pipes in, grinning at Lily Jane, who has spotted us and is waving like we're navigating a giant arena and not four flights of bleachers. "Sushi too."

Peregrine rolls her eyes and elbows me. "Elites always get the best stuff—fame, fortune, access to the Olympics, and crepes. It's really not fair."

Okay, maybe her snark isn't completely drowned in Swiss cheese. Sunny doesn't dignify that with an answer, but I . . . I find myself being okay with the gymnastics joke. I'm not elite, and now I never will be, but the pain in my chest is so dull at this point that I can actually grin. Like, really.

"Oh, thank you, yum." Lily Jane lunges for one of the two paper boats and foil-wrapped goodies I'm holding—obviously hers because she asked for a side of kettle chips that will be annihilated by her hummingbird metabolism in two seconds flat.

As we get situated, Peregrine and I wave at the Zavalas. Sunny introduces herself and immediately compliments Mrs. Zavala's shirt, and they begin the kind of little chitchat of which both Peregrine and I are truly incapable. Peregrine situates herself on the end of the row and plows through the rest of her crepe with such singular focus that I know we should've gotten her two.

Meanwhile, I take the opportunity to get a decent look at the court. Alex is nearly through his warm-up with his opponent—a kid his age or maybe a little older. Today Alex is in white and blue, pristine Lacoste ball cap shading his face as he runs through his net shots. I decide to wave at him, and he immediately waves back. Alex never misses a thing. Of course, Coach Bev doesn't miss our interaction either, her sunglasses sliding down her nose over tightly pursed lips.

Well, fine. As much as I want her to see me as an ally and not an opponent for Alex's attention, I know that if he kicks butt the way he can, that will contain her concerns more than either of us can—

"Rematch of the 6A state final." Coach Brandt's voice startles me out of my thoughts. He's leaning over, eyeing the guy across the net—we've definitely hit it off the past few days, which is a relief, to say the least.

"That's the guy Alex beat in May?"

Coach Brandt nods. "Barrington Cassell from Jewel Academy— well, he was. He graduated. Scholarship to Mizzou."

I take a better look at the guy on the other side of the net— and even if I didn't know his school affiliation, I would be annoyed with him because though he's also in a ball cap, he's wearing it backward. Fine for neck protection, but completely stupid considering they're playing in the full sun of early afternoon in late July. I'd take actually being able to see properly and avoiding crow's feet over a red neck and whatever sort of cool factor he thinks he's pulling with that hat placement.

"Alex beat him in straight sets at state this year," Coach Brandt says, "and last year he was the defending champion of this tournament but had to bow out with an ankle injury the round before Alex won."

I suck in a hissing breath between my teeth. "So he wants this one bad."

"It'll be a challenge, for sure."

38

"Challenge" turns out to be an understatement to the tune of Barrington Backwards Hat going out like a bat out of hell, taking the first set 1–6 from Alex.

I literally had no words other than "no" when Sunny leaned over and asked, "Um, is he okay?" Because I had no explanation.

I'd never seen this Alex. This utterly human Alex, who, at least for a set, looked like he had taken a year off from tennis.

Shots that would normally catch lines went wide.

He double faulted (more than once).

Drop shots fell into the net or caught the tape and dumped back onto his side.

It was... not Alex-esque.

More than once I caught the sour scowl of Coach Bev as she tapped her temple, eyes on Alex, imploring him to think of other ways to win because what he was doing was not working.

At 4 all in the second set, Alex grabbed his towel, wiped his brow, and began a run that had him winning the set 6–4, pushing it to a third.

I was hoping the momentum would keep going, but that chip on Barrington's shoulder was not going to let him relent.

Instead, it's even closer than the second set, and every game is played to deuce, though somehow both of them have stayed on serve, not a single break.

By the time they're at 6 all and 4 all in the third set, I've gone from breathlessly explaining tiebreak rules to Sunny and Peregrine—I had no idea they used them in the deciding set here, a la the French Open—to squeezing my empty water bottle like a stress ball. Mr. Zavala has made more than one awkward joke about making a visit to the champagne tent to survive the tiebreak.

Movement catches my eye at the end of the row as both players wipe off their faces and arms with towels. "I'm bad luck. I should leave," Sunny whispers, one leg already reaching the long way down to the court concrete. She's yanking down her dress with one hand to avoid any indecency.

"We're *both* bad luck," Peregrine whispers back, "but we're going to distract him and make it worse if we leave. It's literally almost over no matter how it goes. Stay put."

Sunny grimaces and returns her leg to the bleacher step. "If he loses, the dude should never want to talk to us again." Her face is crumpled and braced at the same time, and I can see it all over her body language that the past two hours have only driven home the fact that adding a significant other to a serious sports career can have dire, dire consequences.

And honestly, I'm wondering the same thing. Because maybe it's not Sunny and Peregrine throwing him off...maybe it's me.

I know. I know.

Peregrine and I argued with Sunny that day at the lake that

she shouldn't worry about a relationship pulling focus from her dreams because no one should have that much power over the goals of someone like her, but she also eliminated everything else—regular school, extracurricular activities.

And I don't think I have that sort of unhealthy power over Alex...but...

It is *not* a flaw to be well-rounded, I really do believe that, but what if Coach Bev is kind of right? Maybe Alex can handle soccer and basketball and a job and his friends and family but I send him over the edge? Not as a *distraction*, but...what if rather than having it all with me, he has too much to handle?

Gah.

I don't know what's right. I just know that in this moment I feel like I should seep straight into the earth.

Attempting to muscle my way out of this mental nose-dive, I grimace out a smile when I whisper back an answer that is as much for me as it is for them: "*Should*, but he will talk to you guys, because he's Alex."

Peregrine nods. "He'll probably just want us to come to all his tournaments until his luck changes. Can't lose them all."

"Quiet, please," the chair umpire says into her microphone as Alex steps back up to the service line.

Peregrine's lips snap shut, cheeks pinking above the violet that's still going strong on her mouth despite her love affair with crepe-y goodness. (Peregrine does not skimp on her makeup quality.) Sunny adds a second hand to her face, glittery nails the only cheery thing about her as she blocks out her view of the court entirely. And I can't look anywhere but to Alex, who dribbles the ball in a well-practiced rhythm.

Come on, Alex. Come on. You do this every day.

He tosses the ball into the air, and at just the right moment, his racket crashes into it with a velocity I wish they measured here like they do on TV. The ball has so much speed and so much top spin that it catches Barrington Backwards Cap completely off guard and he has to backpedal just to get a piece of it. And that piece angles it wide.

It's 5–4.

Alex needs two more points to win the tiebreak. Well, unless his opponent wins the next two. It's confusing. He needs to get to seven points, but only if Barrington has five points or less. If he has six or more, Alex has to beat him by two.

This could be endless.

His opponent spits some choice words at his racket and stalks across the length of the baseline. Alex pays exactly zero attention and crosses to return serve. His mom and sister have twin knuckles kissing their lips, while his dad sits calmly with his arms crossed and still (no champagne yet). Coach Bev looks sour as shit, and Coach Brandt has locked arms drilled into place on either side of his seat, all his weight seemingly braced on his palms and the aluminum bleacher beneath him.

End it as soon as possible, Zavala. Come on.

Barrington dribbles the ball and sits back into his serve. He tosses the ball over his head, and it comes crashing back down with everything he's got.

"Fault!"

The ball was out.

Barrington moves forward as if checking for a mark—which is way harder to do on a hard court than other surfaces, from what I understand—but doesn't put up too much of a fight.

"Second service."

Barrington nods at the chair umpire, returning to his service spot. He takes a long look at Alex across the net—wide stance, racket forward, waiting for his chance at a response. Again, Barrington goes through his service ritual—dribbling, taking a controlled sit back, and then tossing the ball. And again, he crushes the ball, putting all his weight and frustration behind the movement.

This time, the ball's trajectory is completely off, and it dumps into the net on his side of the court.

"Double fault. Tiebreak is 6–4, Mr. Zavala. Match point."

Barrington lets off an aggrieved scream and swings his racket in a devastating arc toward the court, pulling up to avoid bending the frame only at the very last moment. His face is red, he's sweating like a pig, and he's pissed as all hell.

I don't blame him. But that's not Alex's fault.

My heart is in my throat as Alex readies for his turn to serve.

Sunny shrinks further into a ball, Peregrine's grip on her forearm is leaving marks, and my water bottle threatens to shatter.

Come on, Alex. Come on.

Though Alex is at the baseline and ready to go, ball bouncing, Barrington is still angrily making out with his towel and cursing himself. Asshole.

As soon as the intentional slowpoke is back in position, Alex leans back for his toss. For a moment he's as still as a statue, knees bent, trunk straight, arm extended toward the sky. He smashes the ball straight at Barrington's body this time, his aim eighty million times better than when I tried the same thing during my match on Friday.

But Barrington has seen this one from Alex before—in this match and so many others—and anticipates, swinging around to his forearm side. He goes for a winner, deep and angled to catch the very baseline corner that's crosscourt of where Alex is stationed. My teeth clench as I watch the ball's trajectory, Alex hunting it down with a straight-on sprint. The ball catches at the crosshatch of lines—in—and Alex slides in behind it, his long body stretching as his legs straddle outward, the foot closest to us sliding smoothly on the hard court as Alex gets as low as he can without diving.

Alex manages to get the ball back over the net. Immediately he rights himself, prepared for Barrington's return on an awkward ball that wasn't hit as hard as we all know he can.

Barrington lines up a smashing forehand, going for the opposite corner. Alex tracks it, sprinting, racket out. This time, though, he gets to it earlier and is able to get his full weight behind it. With a resounding thwack, his forehand connects and he shoots it straight down the line. No angles, no tricks, just raw power.

Barrington has to shift directions, running the opposite way. But the ball sails past him, thudding hard into the court wall behind.

A clean winner.

"Game, set, match, Mr. Zavala."

Alex raises his hands to the sky. His head is tossed so far back, his cap falls off as the crowd cheers. He bends down to scoop it up, dimples flashing. And then he spins toward his coaches, his parents, his sister, and us.

The chair continues, in a melodic voice that plays out as perfectly as a dream. "Please give your warmest congratulations to Alex Zavala, back-to-back Northfield Tennis Championships winner."

39

Everything after Alex's win is a dance known only by the people who have been here before—which is pretty much everyone but us.

Rather than with an on-court presentation, the trophy and runner-up plaque will be presented in the impressive air-conditioning of the clubhouse.

"This way, girls, I'll show ya." Lily Jane gestures to Sunny, Peregrine, and me when it's clear we don't know what to do. Alex's parents and Coach Brandt are deep in conversation with both Coach Bev and tournament officials, and Alex has been whisked away with a wave and a round of applause to...somewhere.

"They want him to shower before the presentation," Lily Jane says when she realizes we're all craning our necks around as we exit the court and dump out onto one of the designated paths that wind from the courts to the clubhouse. "Little old men can wear the same clothes two days in a row to golf and then while away the day over glass-bottle Coke in the clubhouse, but actual, hard-earned sweat? Not allowed. It'd look disgraceful in the pictures they'll take."

Sunny giggles. "Tell us how you really feel, LJ."

"You don't want that," Lily Jane warns.

"Uh . . ." Sunny bites her lip. "Why?"

"Because then I'll tell you that I was betting on Alex and Caroline all along—no offense." I'm floored. My jaw drops and I'm totally glad Lily Jane is locking eyes with Sunny, confirming that, apparently, she was always Team Caroline? Like, I didn't even know I was on a team until a few weeks ago. "From my point of view, this has been brewing with Alex for years—puppy love city, even though he tried to hide it. So when we caught them on the couch, I wasn't surprised."

"On your couch?" Peregrine asks, pointedly yanking off her sunglasses. "What happened on the *couch*, Caroline?"

I immediately turn red. Oh God, I didn't tell them about that.

"You know what? No offense taken, LJ." Sunny saves me by looping one of her arms in Lily Jane's and then snagging Peregrine and forcing us to keep walking four across. "In fact, I was hoping you and Topps and maybe the football crew might be interested in coming to a birthday bash I'm throwing at the lake next weekend. More the merrier, right, girls?"

"There's only one bathroom, but if you don't mind peeing in the lake, you'll be good to go," Peregrine adds tartly.

Luckily, LJ laughs. "You're going to wish you didn't say that, because the football team gets out at noon on Saturdays and every one of them is going to want to party after the first week of two-a-days."

Somehow, even after a day outside, Sunny is positively glowing when she answers. "I'm counting on it. Actually, tell them their significant others and family are okay too. Peregrine, you know Liv Rodinsky's younger brother right?"

"She sure does," I answer as Peregrine's mouth opens and closes idly with the knowledge that she's just been completely set up.

A sly grin crosses Lily Jane's lips—I'm sure that as a North-land squad leader she's refereed more than one catfight involving freshman cheerleaders in Ryan's rotation last year and would like nothing more than to solve that problem. "I'll see to it that Ryan makes it." She tugs hard on our little linked row of four. "Okay, let's hustle—the mini lobster rolls are to die for."

The clubhouse is packed with more people than those who watched Alex's match. The winners of every other bracket are here too, as are all their families, friends, followers.

Piano music tinkles in the air, booze flows freely—the champagne tent and George the accordion player have packed up and moved on—and Lily Jane was more than right: those lobster roll canapés are absolutely amazing.

Not that I got to convey my lobster roll enthusiasm to her, because we lost Lily Jane immediately to someone she knows from her trivia night visits. We lost Alex's whole team too, everyone splintering off for side conversations of his or her own. Pretty quickly, the three of us wedge ourselves between the end of the water table and the windows.

A half hour ago, Alex arrived and accepted his trophy, strolling up the dais as Tennis Alex in all his should-be-on-the-tour glory. His hair wet and tamed, a fresh white polo and pressed shorts. Alex has always been the kind of guy who gives off the impression that he smells as good as he looks, and he completely lives up to that reputation at this moment.

Not to be crass, but he looks utterly delicious.

Starting tomorrow he'll be Soccer Alex for a few months, and then Basketball Alex, but at this moment in time, he fits the part of a Wimbledon star, with crisp white edges to his clothes and a fancy watch I've never seen him wear dangling from his wrist.

But since the award ceremony, he's been stuck in the crowd, still up toward the dais. His stream of admirers doesn't seem to end. And in our corner, the three of us are sort of running out of things to talk about. Sunny and Peregrine have veered into gymnastics.

"Jada could totally make level ten before season," Sunny's saying. "She's really crushed it the past few weeks."

"She's crushed it but she's not consistent, and you know that's Olga's big thing." Peregrine pushes a lock of errant hair behind her ear. "It's not can you do it once, but can you do it over and over?"

"Okay, true, but the leaps and bounds that she's made this summer are just—"

"Hey, you guys want to wait outside? It's so crowded in here." I force a smile, but I'm already setting my drink down and pivoting away.

The girls follow after an exchanged glance that I don't miss. The patio is sparsely populated, the twinkle lights from the clubhouse making everything look like a fairy tale in the falling dusk. When we settle at a cocktail table near a balcony overlooking some golf hole I don't know, Sunny's brows pull tightly together, her fingers snagging mine as I attempt to scuttle away. "Sorry to talk about gymnastics."

"It's okay. It's not that—go on with what you guys were saying. Jada at level ten? What about Avalon?"

"Later," Peregrine says. "We can do better. Like, how do you feel about tomorrow? The tryouts?"

The girls didn't see me play. They also don't know that apparently anyone makes the team. Coach Brandt didn't confirm Coach Bev's assessment, and I'm not going to treat next week as if I'm already being fitted for a Northland uniform. We've spent so long being the best, pushing ourselves in a sport where it's really you against yourself. Sure, other people come into play, but it's not the same as a sport such as tennis when there's the filter of judges and rotations.

So, I simply say, "You know, I think it'll be good for me."

Sunny smiles, and Peregrine matches the sentiment with words. "We think so too."

Peregrine is facing the door, and the second her eyes light up, I know Alex has finally joined us. I turn around and gasp as I confirm he's the most handsome person I know. How did I not realize this until just now?

The lights of the clubhouse glow over his shoulder, the golden hour candlelight-soft on the edges of his hair, summer-tan skin, white polo. The shirt's top button is open, revealing the soft scoop of his throat. Just . . . wow.

"Thank you so much for coming," he says to Peregrine and Sunny, ever gracious.

"Thanks for inviting us," Sunny replies.

"Thanks for introducing me to the love of my life, the Swiss-and-mushroom crepe," Peregrine adds.

Alex laughs. "You guys are always on point."

"We are. And we know when to exit stage left," Sunny says, grabbing Peregrine's arm. "Good night, folks, and good luck at two-a-days!"

And they're out. Sunny's hauling Peregrine toward the path

that leads around to the front and the valets holding her car hostage.

Alex nods at their retreating forms. "I swear I showered."

I stand on my tippy-toes to tussle his still-wet hair. "Yeah, I don't think it was your hygiene."

I trail my fingers down from his hair to his jaw and cup it in my fingers. His hands encircle my waist, drawing me close.

"I'm so proud of you, Alex. You did great."

He kisses my nose with a self-effacing sigh. "I did good enough to win. Coach Bev's right, I'm rusty."

Rusty? Not distracted. That's an improvement that I don't question.

"I am obviously not an expert in tennis—yet—but I *am* an expert on being too hard on myself and I think you don't need to worry too much."

Alex wets his lips, teeth flashing white in the night, and raises a brow toward his perfectly curling hair. "Well, I better shake the rust off quickly, because Winston-Salem is in less than a month."

I slip my heels back to the ground to steady my stance and clutch his arms. "You took the wild card?"

"Sure did. You're right—I have the opportunity, I should at least attempt to do it my way."

I'm thrilled. Absolutely thrilled—and worried. "Alex...I'm sure you can balance tennis and soccer, but I want you to promise me that if I'm too much, that if this is too much—"

Alex cuts off my words with a kiss so hard and hungry that I nearly achieve liftoff. His mouth is minty and sweet, his skin still warm from the court hours and shower steam. After a moment, I pull away just enough to gaze into his eyes, swaying a little with him.

"The worst parts of my play today had everything to do with me and nothing to do with you." His dimples wink as he presses his forehead to mine. "The best parts of my play today, though, had everything to do with the fact that you were there in the stands."

I believe him. I believe in us. And I'm starting to believe in my own advice.

There's nothing written in our genetic code that says we have to be alone to do great things.

"Good, because I plan on watching every soccer match too. Which reminds me . . ." I reach into my bag and pull out a tissue-wrapped log. "For you."

It's slightly wilted from the heat, but of course Alex accepts my present like it's an object worth an international heist. I collect the tissue paper and string while he gently unwraps it. Once the paper is gone, it's very clear this is a men's sleeveless shirt in the same KC Royals blue he wears constantly. "Please tell me this is my 'Cheese is not the enemy' shirt."

I grin at him—if the Mozza-Monster becomes our signature meal, that'll be ordered next. "Not quite."

He unfolds it and holds it up. "That's how I roll," he reads aloud, and under the words are the balls for his three sports: tennis, soccer, basketball. There were a million designs with that saying and each of the balls separately, but I wanted to make sure every one of his athletic loves were in one place, just for him.

"I love it, Caroline." To prove it, he yanks it over his head, over his fancy polo, where it fits all weird but he still looks amazing. He spins around as if to prove it's perfect, and when he's back to facing me, he grins. "I suppose I'm lucky that you didn't do the same design with the phrase 'I do ball sports.'"

"I thought about it for a hot minute, not going to lie."

Alex scoops me close again, and his smile is just a breath away as he laughs with me, never at me. "Of course you did."

He closes the distance between us, and in that moment my new beginning feels exactly like a beginning for both of us.

40

Sunny's lakeside birthday bash is already in full swing when we pull up and spill out of Alex's Challenger. I elected to wait and head up to the cabin with Alex after his Saturday tennis training—Coach Bev modified his schedule to elongate the weekend sessions to make up for the time lost because of his soccer two-a-day preseason schedule. I actually think she likes torturing him for hours on end better than consistently over several days in a row.

"So, I guess the entire cheer squad and football team decided to take Sunny up on the offer she extended to Lily Jane?" I say, gaping—the number of cars is staggering.

Alex laughs, palming the volleyball his sister frantically asked him to bring via text. "It would appear so. Hope you're ready for some unfiltered hormones."

"Good practice for the return to school," I admit, and pointedly thread my fingers through his, balancing my potluck offering on my hip.

Following elaborately perfect directional signs set up to keep guests from tromping through the cabin itself, we use the easement path and walk around the side. And as we do, the scene below unfolds like any of a number of OG teen comedies from the 1990s.

At least fifty kids mill around the green below the house, the dock, the water. Pairs, trios, and groups pan out across the acreage, from hidden snatches of color among the sunflower garden to the shade under the deck to the water itself, where every canoe and stand-up paddleboard is either in use or at the ready.

There's a cornhole game going on with burly boys in Northland orange, girls curled up on lawn chairs set out in terraced rows on the shallowest part of the hill, and a couple of tables clustered with a smorgasbord of homemade goodies, sweating coolers shoved under them for relative shade. The sounds of laughter and Taylor Swift rising above the din, announcing that "You Belong with Me."

Over on the flattest part of the property, near the sunflower garden, is the Zavala-Mack family's volleyball net, woefully unused because Lily Jane forgot the ball.

After a few Where's Waldo attempts, I spot Nat and Artemis tossing horseshoes with Lily Jane and Topps, and Peregrine sticking her toes in the water with Ryan plus the current and former Balan's trio of Jada, Avalon, and Kashvi. Can't wait for Peregrine's debrief on how *that* went.

Birthday girl Sunny is mixed in on the cornhole game, standing next to Liv and her just-graduated Captain America stand-in boyfriend, Grey Worthington, laughing heartily with Nick Cleary, a really beautiful Black girl I've never seen, and some other football player I don't recognize, who totally just put an arm around Sunny. I mean, I assume he's a football player given the company and the fact that he looks like he could easily javelin Sunny into the lake. I'm going to have to interrogate her about that later...

"Where do we start?" Alex asks, clearly as overwhelmed as I am.

I nearly say, "By turning around," because this is our first official outing as a couple and these people are mostly much older and completely intimidating. But I'm no coward and it's Sunny's birthday, so I say, "Food?"

"Always an excellent decision."

We march over to the potluck spread and find a home for my offering among the other desserts already there, protected by thick trappings of cling wrap and toothpick tentpoles. Sunny's laid out little place cards and a Sharpie, and it's clear from her "example" desserts that each dish is to be labeled.

I set down the brownies and grab a notecard and pen...and pause.

I can't actually call them "black bean" brownies or no one will eat them. But I promised Alex I'd finally make some for him, and Sunny is a fan—I'm just not exactly sure how all that extra fiber will go over with this much cooler, much older crowd.

"Brain fart?" Alex is smirking at me as I hover over my obvious pan of brownies with an uncapped Sharpie and notecard.

My eyes snap to his. "Was that a bean joke?"

"Maybe." And by that he means definitely.

Alex unseals the clear lid. The distinctly thick smell of cocoa and sugar rises into the air between us as the cracked, fudgy top of the dessert is exposed. He pointedly takes a plastic knife from a utensil lineup of marked Solo cups and cuts himself off a little square of corner.

"They're chewy," I blurt out. "They're meant to be that way."

Alex swallows and cocks an eyebrow, giving no other indication of what he's thinking. Rather, he steals the Sharpie and the little card straight out of my grip and begins to write. When he's finished, there's not a shred of misunderstanding in what he thinks.

There, in his neat, squared-off handwriting is a single word, and it's not "brownies."

DELICIOUS.

He slices himself another piece that's at least half of the first row and says, "Come on, that volleyball net's looking pretty lonely."

Then, just like that day on the basketball court, he tosses the ball at me. This time, I don't dodge it, but I don't catch it either. Instead, I simply bump it overhead straight back at him, an all-out grin on my face.

"Good thing someone taught me how to play."

Epilogue

"Match point, Miss Kepler."

The words are mine—the athletes keep score in the annals of non-championship high school tennis. I let them pinball around the gray matter and viscera of my mind, cordoned off from my laser focus.

On the ball, on my opponent, on my serve.

The crowd is silent—all eyes on me as I dribble the ball three times.

Coach Brandt's voice cuts through it all, a reminder from practice just days ago as much as it is a mantra: *Coil, elbow up, loose arm on the release.*

I check my opponent across the court. A freshman from Central in head-to-toe red because apparently their uniforms are meant to be completely distracting.

I toss the ball straight up, coil back, twist up for more power on my release. My elbow is high for a fluid motion. And when the ball is at the right height, I smash it down with everything I have.

The ball skids straight off the far ad corner, and the girl from Central raises her racket to return. I bounce on the balls of my feet, ready to chase down whatever she's got. The girl manages a clean forehand, but the direction is listless, and it ends up coming straight back at me.

I wind up, new, stronger backhand at the ready, and plow a winner straight into the opposite corner. My opponent is running on fumes and doesn't make it, the ball skipping past the reach of her racket before drilling itself into the covered fence.

Holy shit. A winner for the win.

That focused dam in my mind bursts open, all my thoughts and fears and hopes and excitement pouring out as I do something that never would've been truly acceptable as a gymnast.

I scream. At the top of my lungs.

My first tennis victory. In straight sets, 6–3, 6–2. In my inaugural high school tournament.

I'm on the junior varsity, but who the heck cares.

I tried a new sport. I worked hard. I won.

I pump my racket and face the mini stands with a huge grin. Dad and Nat are on their feet—Dad jostling his phone and trying to clap, Nat being as loud and obnoxious as an off-duty cheerleader is expected to be. On the other side of the two-rung bleachers is Alex in full grass-stained soccer gear—straight from practice of his own, a late joiner sneaking into the corner.

I jog to the net to shake my opponent's hand. Next, I crash into the crowd, which is small because it's high school girls' tennis on a weeknight. Not, you know, the level ten state gymnastics meet. In rapid succession, I thank Coach Brandt, my teammates, and finally Dad and Nat. I wave at Alex, who is, in true Alex Zavala fashion, being polite—standing to the side to let the Central team skirt by to head back to the bus.

"Say something to the girls," Dad says, handing his phone to me.

I bobble my water bottle and racket to accept it, wondering if I'd misheard him and he actually meant Mom. But as soon as I view the screen, things suddenly make a little more sense—Olga, Sunny, and Peregrine crowd into a single FaceTime camera view.

"We saw the last two points. Incredible!" Olga shouts, so excited her accent makes an appearance. "That strong gymnastics core—it will take you places in life."

"Also hard work, dedication, good coaching—" Peregrine lists off all my advantages until Olga pats her head hard enough she ducks from view, the phone clearly Olga's. It would be super weird if Dad called my friends instead of his girlfriend.

"Really great work, Caro," Sunny says, gym mom tone proud. I thank them all before handing the phone back to Dad as he tries to get Olga to hang on for one second longer, saying something about their reservations for Saturday night.

Arms wrap around my waist and lift me off the bottom step of the bleachers. "Your first win!" Alex whisper-shouts in my ear, twirling me around and then setting me down gently on the court.

"I know! How much did you see?"

"The last three games. But Nat recorded the whole thing and already airdropped it to me."

Good use of school Wi-Fi, bro. Sheesh.

"I don't know that I ever want to watch that tape." I cringe even though, truly, I can't stop grinning.

Alex's dimples wink. "I hear video is the best way to learn about a new sport..."

I look up at him from under the brim of my orange Northland visor (yeah, I know—but it's not as distracting as the red-on-red monstrosities the other team wore). "How about I order us a pizza and we do a little crash course sometime?"

"What are you doing Friday night?" Alex asks, flipping our hands.

He leaves Saturday for the Winston-Salem tournament. If he keeps winning, it's possible he might miss an entire week of school next week and a soccer game, but it'll be a good test—of whether he can balance all the things, and if he *wants* to.

I grin. "Ordering a Mozza-Monster and hoping that video doesn't make me want to die?"

"It won't."

"How do you know?"

Alex drops a quick kiss on my lips but keeps his mouth low, his handsome face filling my vision. The night falls away. "Because I know you, Caroline Kepler, and you can do anything."

He's right. I can. And I have so much more to do. In tennis, in life, with him.

Watch this.

Acknowledgments

Caroline's story is one that kept me afloat during the first year of the COVID-19 pandemic. I spent the summer of 2020 with these characters, dreaming of a world without the virus, when we were safe, healthy, and stable. I sent my characters to restaurants, parties, and sporting events during a very tumultuous stretch for myself, my family, and everyone else. This story lived in my head as a bright spot during that summer even though it's about the struggle of walking away from big, lifelong dreams. And maybe that was why I was always eager to come back to it—knowing that I could create a happy ending during a time when everything was so uncertain.

I was a competitive gymnast like Caroline—though not nearly as talented!—and walking away from a dream that was in my life so long it was basically my identity was difficult. Finding myself again was difficult. Everything was difficult. And… so common. As a kid, a teenager, an adult, we all exchange stories of our dreams—successful, unsuccessful, satisfying, incomplete. Or, if we're lucky, ongoing. I feel extremely fortunate to have had a chance to tell stories in book form, which was a dream of mine back when I also spent a lot of time in a leotard. Actually, I feel luckiest of all that I got the chance to use one dream (writing) to tell the story of another (gymnastics) in this way. No matter what dreams live in your heart, I hope you found something relatable in the stories of Caroline and Alex, Sunny, Peregrine, Nat, et al.

Of course, none of my dreams for this story would be possible without the best crew in the business. First, thank you a million times over to my agent, Whitney Ross, who is a superstar on so many levels. She sold this book during the pandemic, all the while under lockdown and pregnant (!) half a world away. She is a cheerleader, a therapist, an expert gluten-free chef, a magician, and a friend. And she's probably even more organized than Alex, which is totally saying something.

Next, I'd like to thank my editing tag team of positivity, Hannah Milton and Hallie Tibbetts. Hannah, I miss you and I was so lucky to have you as my first editor and advocate for both this book and *Throw Like a Girl*. Hallie, you accepted this story with humor, grace, and a keen eye for storytelling, and I'm so glad Caroline and Alex became yours to love.

Thank you to Caroline Clouse, my extremely detailed copyeditor, for her thoughtful and erudite read. To the production team for shepherding this story safely through from manuscript to beautiful book. To the publicity team at The Novl, for your constant positivity and support in getting the word out to readers. To Ana Hard, who took my ex-gymnast feedback with aplomb in creating our adorable cover art, and to the design team that brought it all together into its sunny, sporty, romantic final form.

And last but not least, thank you to my support network—there is literally no way this book could've been done without you. Thank you to my fellow Kansas writers, who make the best collective sounding board in the whole wide world. To Jennifer Iacopelli, my forever sports romance writer buddy, who dropped everything to talk through Alex's tennis career arc with me. And, of course, to my family, who gave me the space (or at least tried) to work through this story during the year we couldn't go anywhere. Mom, Dad, Justin, Nate, Amalia, Emmie—you all are the best virtual cheering section I could ask for in the sport of writing, and I'm so grateful you're mine.

Fally Afani

Sarah Henning

is a recovering journalist who has worked for the *Palm Beach Post*, *Kansas City Star*, and Associated Press, among others. Sarah is the author of several books for young adults, including *It's All in How You Fall* and its companion, *Throw Like a Girl*. Other books from Sarah include the Indies Introduce/Indies Next selection *Sea Witch*, and its sequel, *Sea Witch Rising*, as well as *The Princess Will Save You*, *The Queen Will Betray You*, and the forthcoming finale to the trilogy, *The King Will Kill You*. When not writing, she runs ultramarathons, hits the playground with her two kids, and hangs out with her husband, Justin, who doubles as her long-suffering IT department. Sarah lives in Lawrence, Kansas, hometown of Langston Hughes, William S. Burroughs, and a really good basketball team.

GET INTO THE
THROW OF THINGS WITH
SARAH HENNING

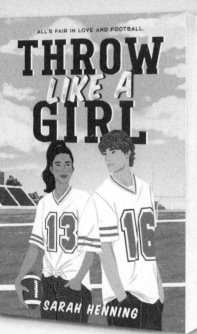

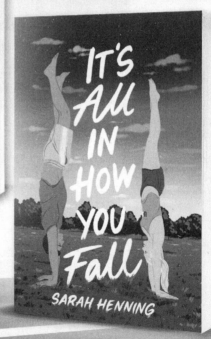

 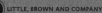

BOB1051